3 0132

D0231205

Worthless Men

Worthless Men

Andrew Cowan

SCEPTRE

First published in Great Britain in 2013 by Sceptre
An imprint of Hodder & Stoughton
An Hachette UK company

1

Copyright © Andrew Cowan 2013

The right of Andrew Cowan to be identified as the Author of the Work has been
asserted by him in accordance with the Copyright, Designs and Patents Act 1988.

All characters in this publication are fictitious and any resemblance
to real persons, living or dead is purely coincidental.

A CIP catalogue record for this title is available from the British Library

Hardback ISBN 978 1 444 75940 2
Trade Paperback ISBN 978 1 444 75941 9

Typeset by Hewer Text UK Ltd, Edinburgh
Printed and bound by Clays Ltd, St Ives plc

Hodder & Stoughton policy is to use papers that are natural, renewable
and recyclable products and made from wood grown in sustainable
forests. The logging and manufacturing processes are expected to
conform to the environmental regulations of the country of origin.

Hodder & Stoughton Ltd
338 Euston Road
London NW1 3BH

www.sceptrebooks.com

For my daughter, Rose

1
Gala Day

gala day

Market day is a gala day, even this far into the war, though it's no longer weekly but eked out to twice monthly and there are fewer fat cattle for sale, fewer pigs, barely half the pens holding sheep, less poultry per lot in the auctions, fewer men. Yet still the bunting will be out in the city, the flags unfurled, the candy-striped awnings shading the shop fronts, penny goods placed for sale on the pavements. The hurdy-gurdy man will perform by the Guildhall. The trams sashaying down Balmoral Road will be standing room only and the streets will be eagerly running with errand boys (they had better be eager) pushing handcarts, wearing white aprons. Every main thoroughfare into the city will clatter with traps and wagons and charabancs, dogcarts, drays, even motor-cars, despite the shortage of fuel. The smell of spent petrol will hang in the hot air. Frowning pedestrians will cover their noses.

Even now, in 1916, a certain class of countryman will arrive with his wife and pull into his customary stabling, one of the many inns round about, where the ostler – a boy, an old man – will be waiting to greet him and take care of his horse while he proceeds to the market – or to his land agent, his solicitor or stockbroker – having first installed his wife in the tea rooms where she will meet her companion for the day, another lady, with whom she will visit the shops and department stores over-looking the rickety stalls of the fruit and vegetable market, their purchases – of drapery, millinery, hosiery, even confectionery

– delivered as finely wrapped parcels to the respective ladies' rooms of their inns, ready to be loaded onto their carriages for departure at four thirty once they've been seen to take tea in Osgood's or the Grand Hotel and their husbands have concluded their business, which might include the sale and purchase of livestock but also the acquisition from Wragg's Engineering of essential tools and machines – or items for the repair or improvement of tools and machines – and from the veterinarian certain medicines, and from the seed merchants in the Corn Hall several hundredweight of cattle cake and poultry meal, all of this recorded on order, to be collected on notification by postcard a few days hence from the sidings of their nearest station.

Other farmers will leave their wives at home where they belong.

On a market day a few of the public houses in the vicinity will be tolerated to open at eight and remain serving till late, despite the change in the law, and it's in these rowdies that most of the countrymen will congregate, the farmers and farmhands, drovers and dealers mingling more or less peaceably (at least until evening) with the men who live locally, some of them known to be poachers and some of them soldiers on leave, who may be inclined to belligerence.

Trading in the sale rings will go on until four but a good deal of business will also be sealed in the pubs, the prices agreed with a slap of licked hands and toasted with pints of the pissy government ale brewed as per War Office orders by Callard's of Riverside Road, the poor condemned animals then left unattended until the close of proceedings, some plainly distressed and all of them naturally shitting on the hay-covered setts in their pens, so that in summer especially – on still, warm latesummer days such as today – the air on this side of the city will hum with fear and flies and the throat-gagging stench of the farmyard, even after the Corporation men have come on at five thirty to begin sweeping and hosing the wide sloping expanse of standings and stalls, sending down hundreds of gallons of water

2

to wash the excrement into the ditches and drains and swiftly out through the underground channels to the river, where the slick of effluent might briefly disturb the composure of the day-trippers returning from the coast on the pleasure steamer *Lord Nelson*, the deck packed with men in boaters and white Homburgs, some in white suits, the ladies sheltering beneath the escalloped canopy, and the uniformed soldiers beside them sporting clean dressings.

2
Walter

as small as any effigy

Not every casualty will be as conspicuous as the men on the pleasure boats, for instance Walter Barley, aged just eighteen on the day he was posted as missing (the letter still sits on the mantelpiece, awaiting confirmation of worse), who has spent this morning in his lice-ridden khaki upstairs and stands now by the half-open door to his family's small, crowded kitchen, his posture as stiff as any funerary statue, his arms crossed over his chest, hands flat to each shoulder, legs straight, his weight supported by his head on the wall (at five feet two, Walter is a bantam, and as small as any effigy in nearby St Cuthbert's), quietly watching his younger brothers and sisters as they go about their Saturday duties, presided over this past hour or so by Mabel, who has returned ahead of Mother from their Saturday half-shift in Beckwith's Engineering to prepare their dinner of bread and dripping and tea, and perhaps – if Mother can secure some from Joe Orford (their landlord and neighbour, a butcher, her fancy man) – a couple of rashers of bacon.

Mabel sets their miscellaneous cups and cracked plates on the table and Walter says, 'Not for me, Mabe, I'm not hungry,' but of course she pays him no attention, for she will not be able to hear him.

Walter sighs, and drops his arms. He shoves his hands into his pockets and turns his face to the door, to the sunshine and tattered washing outside, and from across the way he hears a clink of spoon on enamel, Mrs O'Brien stirring her tea, and closer, the constant trickle of water from the tap in the yard. He hears a baby crying, ceaselessly crying, and the jolting of the drays coming from the brewery, the heavy clop of those horses, and the thrum of machinery in the yards further down, the clank of metal on metal, men's voices, and – seeming somehow miles distant – the muffled cacophony of the cattle market, where his brothers Arthur and Harold have gone, hoping to earn a few pennies, as Walter once would.

Arthur is thirteen now, Harold eleven – the middle children of twelve, not all of them living – while here in the kitchen are James and Elsie and Ada, who are younger, and Walter's favourite, Doris – called Dot – who is fifteen and sitting straight-backed on the edge of the armchair, completing however many rows of knitting it is her task to run up every day, the needles pleasantly clacking, the ball of wool in her lap twitching as it unravels. Elsie and Ada, aged nine and ten, stand at the table, their faces flushed with the heat, methodically folding and pasting lengths of stiff card to make matchboxes, for which Mother will receive a ha'penny a dozen, while next to them sits James, who is seven and nestling a heavy black boot between his thin thighs, dreamily delivering a long thread of spittle from his puckered lips to the tin of blacking in his palm.

The sun spirals in his spit, and not for the first time Walter is struck by the sensation of spectating on a scene from his own childhood, a scene from which he has been removed, for this also used to be his job, and afterwards, the boots gleaming, his father might reward him with a farthing – if there was a farthing to be had; supposing his father was cheerful – to take along to Mr Aldrich's, where Walter would hold out his cap and watch as the grocer scooped a portion of pea scuds straight from the tray with the shovel of his hand.

Mr Aldrich who took his own life, and whose windows are now black-boarded.

A beetle crosses the floor of loose brick, and Walter tenses, his instinct to kill it. The Barleys are poor but not slatternly. Even now, with Father away at the fighting and herself in employment, Mother (when sober) will not tolerate idleness or insects or dirt. Yet theirs is the least healthful of places to live, so near to the end of the yard and the damp from the river, which seeps into everything. The ceilings and walls are discoloured with rot, bulging with wet, and the drains in the yard frequently clog and spill out. The stench is constant – of sewage and chemicals, rotting vegetables, the privies – and always in summer they will find themselves infested with creatures: tiny bugs in the closet, ants and cockroaches, beetles, snails, slugs, mice, sometimes rats. And, of course, flies: the flies are perpetual, caught in the twisting, gummed papers that hang in each room and drawn no doubt by the mortuary, which is next door, and by Joe Orford's abattoir, which is directly behind them, the sounds of the killing often audible through their shared wall.

Walter hears a scuffling now, hoofs skittering on the blocks and somebody cursing, which briefly attracts Mabel's attention. Bad language upsets her. 'Oh, that poor thing,' she says, and Walter grins.

'It's all right,' he murmurs, 'there's worse fucking holes,' for though Joe and the other slaughtermen will rough-handle an animal if it is stubborn – yanking and poking, kicking its rump to get it to move – Joe likes to be thought of as decent, a respectable man, humane in his treatment of the animals he slaughters and reliable in the quality of the produce he sells.

JOSEPH ORFORD, FAMILY BUTCHER, PURVEYOR OF HIGH-CLASS HOME-KILLED MEAT, reads the sign above his shop front, and Walter has several times seen him dispatch a cow on a market day, the killing swift and tidy, a single blow from his poleaxe and the animal's legs collapsing beneath it. In two, three easy strokes Joe will open its throat, the blood spurting out, gushing from the gape in its neck to a runnel in the floor and continuing to stream over its jowls as it's hoisted to the ceiling, a chain looped round one ankle and its legs reflexively pawing and stamping the air, its big old tongue flopping down. Seconds later he will have the head away – hurled into a corner – and begin the undressing, first slicing open the pelt, then parting the pale belly beneath, nicking and cutting until the rent is wide enough for another man (John Cherry usually, with the oddly slanting eyes) to reach inside and remove the mass of muddled parts, bluish, yellowish, white, which he will dump on a slab and begin to organise as Joe deftly strokes and slices the flesh, carefully detaching the forelimbs and disrobing the carcass, the skirts of skin flapping open, rippling like undergarments, then slipping away to reveal the purple bodice beneath, as shapely as a torso in a corset.

All of this in less than half an hour, and the animal's siblings still lowing in their pens on the market.

Later, at work behind his counter, Joe will be dressed in a suit and collar and tie, even when going about his butchery, and always from his belt – worn over his apron, under his paunch – there will dangle his 'steel', a metal stick with a deadly point to it, used for sharpening his knives. Smartly moustached, his hair slick with brilliantine, his manner forever courteous and friendly, he it was who offered to take Walter on as his errand boy, as a favour, he said, to Walter's mother, after the Beckwiths had sacked him, and though he revealed a much meaner temper in private than was ever evident in public, and frequently cuffed Walter for his sloppiness, Walter now remembers this as the best of his Saturday jobs, the position he was sorriest to lose.

Often Joe would send him down to the abattoir to collect whatever bits of carcass he could carry back up on his shoulder, or along to the ice house with the hand-barrow when the barge was due in, or out around the city on the bicycle, a rattling old Sunbeam, its basket loaded with packages marked in pencil with abbreviated names and addresses (*Bak 27 R'glen, Law 91 F'std*). These were the chores that Walter most hoped to be given, but on a Saturday morning he would present himself early and be glad of whatever there was. Already at breakfast-time the shop would be jostling with wives in their aprons and caps, and in the clamour – 'Half a pound of pig's fry, please, Joe!'; 'Have you got my husband's sausages, Joe?' – Walter would be forced against the bodies of beef and pork hanging from the hooks round the walls, and it would not bother him, then, to get a clot of blood on his shirt or the side of his face, even when it was still warm.

Aged thirteen, he found he had the stomach for butchery, and what he especially enjoyed was to watch as Joe packaged up a bit of pig's fry – the animal's liver, lights, sweetbread and kidneys all hanging in a fat clump from which Joe would take careful slices, neatly catching the flesh on a flat of paper in his left hand. Which was a treat he liked to give Walter at the end of the day, to take home to Winnie, his mother.

'That'll make a lovely gravy, Sunday,' he'd say. 'She'll appreciate that.'

payment in kind

Mabel empties the steaming kettle into the teapot and says, 'That sounds like Mother coming down now.'

She is yakking with someone in the yard, and Walter realises even before she comes in, flushed and jaunty, that his mother has taken a drink, which he cannot abide.

'Mr Orford's done us a turn, look,' she says, and slaps a soft, thin parcel on the table and pulls out a chair. The legs scrape against the brick. Elsie and Ada look at her cautiously, then smile.

'Mr Orford,' Walter repeats to himself, shaking his head.

'He's a good man,' his mother says, and ushers the girls to move along. 'You can't say he isn't a good man . . . Mabel?'

'What?'

Their mother frowns. 'He is a good man.'

'Yes,' sighs Mabel, and places the teapot on the table. She removes the bacon to the range. 'He is a good man.' She waits for the dripping to sizzle in the pan, then lays the two rashers over it and takes the breadknife to the loaf, tucks it under her arm and begins to saw through it.

'Well, you know what puzzles me?' says Walter, affecting to yawn, his gaze drifting to where the wall is coming away from the ceiling. 'What puzzles me is why such a good old boy would want to charge us rent on a rotten, stinking slum like this one. Why ever would good old Joe want to do that, I wonder.'

But even if his mother were able to hear him, she would not reply, for she hasn't the energy to argue; the spirit has already left her. Sighing, her face smeared from the factory, she pours herself a cup of tea and takes from somewhere beneath her blue Beckwith's gown a five-pack of Woodbines, a crushed box of matches. She tips out a cigarette.

Time was, before her husband and son went away, Winnie would never have accepted the need to sit in her own kitchen and wouldn't have submitted to being waited upon, but then she never was a drinker before, and hardly ever a smoker. With trembling hands she lights her cigarette and exhales lengthily from the side of her mouth and stares at the letter on the mantelpiece – which still claims that missing needn't mean killed, not necessarily; the words are there in plain English – and wearily tugs off her factory bonnet, her hair slumping out, and taps some ash on the edge of the table. She turns her gaze on her youngest, hunched over his boot.

'That's assuming,' Walter persists, 'he *does* still charge us. Cash, I mean.'

Elsie and Ada concentrate on tidying their boxes. Dot pushes her needles into her wool and gets to her feet, stretches her arms, while James – who is properly absorbed now in his task – rubs up a shine on the boot, unaware of his mother's attention. She is watching him sadly. With the backs of her fingers she strokes the side of his face, and this sentimentalism too is unlike her.

'Not that it needs to be cash,' Walter continues. 'It might be payment in kind. Would you call it payment in kind, what Joe is after?'

But Mother would not call it anything, since nothing, it seems, will get through to her; Walter is wasting his breath, and when she turns to Mabel and says, 'He reckons there's a train coming up tonight, with the first ones, the wounded,' he reaches for his cap on the coat peg beside him.

'Yes, I heard that,' says Mabel, and distributes slices of bread to the plates. 'There's a lot saying that.'

'Are you going?'

Mabel grimaces, uncertain, and turns back to the pan, the crackling bacon.

'He might be on it, Mabel. He might be one of them.'

'He might not be,' says Mabel, and flips the rashers with the tip of her breadknife.

Mother rubs the corner of one eye, her fingernails dark with grime from the factory. Then, 'Please,' she says, 'I would like you to go.'

The fat spits back from the pan. Mabel leans away from it, still gripping the handle.

'Mabel.'

'Yes!' she says. 'All right, I'll go. If that's what you want.'

Mother nods. 'It is,' she says, and sucks deeply on the cigarette, her face momentarily lost to the shape of her skull, her cheeks becoming dark shadows, and Walter is suddenly revolted by the sight of her, as revolted as he is sorry. He sighs. He fastens his tunic, presses the buttons into their holes, and straightens his cap. He waits. But he will not be acknowledged, and as his siblings take their places at the table – the youngest three standing – he says, 'Fuck this, I'm going out,' and turns abruptly and leaves them.

He steps into the yard and ducks under Mrs O'Brien's damp washing, thinking he will take a turn around the market, hoping he might spy Gertie Dobson, the pharmacist's daughter, but then sees a child, a small boy, crunching on a pair of copulating snails by the standpipe, cracking their shells with his heel, pressing down on their flesh, and the sliminess of that is too reminiscent, too sharply familiar. Giddy in the sunshine, Walter reaches a hand to the wall and steadies himself. He spits into a drainhole, inhales the wet stench of it. He retches. And when his brothers Harold and Arthur come haring down the yard, each concealing something under his jacket – a stolen egg, perhaps, some milk still warm from the udder – they don't acknowledge him either, but hurry on by, as if he isn't there.

3
Gertie

not one of them handsome

The broad slope of the market covers eight acres, and there are five separate sale rings (the largest of these being Studland's), with the sheep confined to the top, which is geographically the south, and the fowls in their coops to the east, the pigs to the west, the cattle in the centre and north, while here at the foot of the hill, with no sense of occupying the northernmost tip of this scene (but then she never has had much sense of direction, magnetic bearings, her place), stands Gertie Dobson, aged almost eighteen, who is loitering where she knows she must not at the parlour window above her father's pharmacy, veiled by lace curtains and scanning the afternoon haze for young men but finding only farmers and drovers and auctioneers, not one of them handsome.

She sighs, and hears herself sighing, and looks quickly behind her. The door to the landing is open and soon her mother will come through with a bowl to tend her wounds, the cuts she picked up in Beckwith's this morning.

Stealthily Gertie steps over and closes the door; less stealthily she returns to her station. She makes a gap in the curtains with one finger and surveys the market for Land Army Girls (they at least might be interesting) but finds no females at all, especially not females in breeches, and gazes instead at the auctioneers on their platforms, who are standing maybe three feet taller than anyone around them, and recognises Mr Studland himself, a fat old fellow with a growth on his neck so large and oddly shaped it might well be an additional head. He walks slightly slantwise, as though to make room for it, or as if being nudged from the side, prodded like one of the cattle.

But these countrymen are often ugly, and often they resemble the animals they tend, with their livid pink faces and white bristles, their snouts and buck teeth and slack mouths. She hears them braying and grunting and thinks of her country cousins, her mother's stocky nephews, with their ruddy complexions and suety smell, whom she hasn't seen in years and perhaps never will again. A letter arrived for her mother just yesterday: the last of them – Michael and Joseph – have finally been shipped overseas, where most of the others have perished.

she jounced along on his lap

Gertie can't quite recollect which of her cousins is which, and in truth she doesn't much care what becomes of them. Michael and Joseph were as alike as any two pigs in a litter, and she remembers the shambles they made of helping her home, aged ten or eleven, on the last occasion she was sent to stay with her aunt out at Raworth (her mother having been taken poorly, as she often was at that time). A carrier's cart dropped her there on a Wednesday; she can't think why it didn't come back to collect her, or why her aunt thought it best to return her by train.

Gertie, being dreamy, sometimes remembers things wrongly, but her memory of this is quite clear.

There was a bowl of tomatoes on the kitchen table, and her aunt Enid, her mother's sister-in-law – a tiny body with gnarled, blue-tinted fingers – first treated the nettle stings on Gertie's elbows and knees with a cloth dipped in vinegar, then handed her a tomato for her journey and tugged straight her pinafore, adjusted the tilt of her hat, and instructed Michael and Joseph – who were standing gawping in the doorway – to deliver their cousin to Raworth Mill station, a walk of just over a mile through fields of barley and maize.

Aunt Enid said this quite plainly: one of them was to carry her bag, and they were to escort her all the way onto the train, and to pay for her fare. She gave them the money; Gertie saw that. But within minutes, just a short distance out from the row of cottages where they lived, her cousins entrusted her to the care of a man they called Tom, who said he was heading for the city in any case, carrying pickles and jams in a van drawn by a grey speckled mare, and who required her to sit up on his knee, there being no room at his side, his arms loose around her and his beetrooty breath on her neck.

For a couple of miles then she jounced along on his lap, watching the horse's enormous behind and clutching her bag to her chest, the tomato warm in her fist and neither one of them speaking until they arrived at the next village along, where abruptly he stopped and said she had to get down; that was enough. She looked at him, but he would not look at her. And despite being so far from where she was sure she wanted to be, Gertie complied: Tom seemed so determined, his face so red with what she supposed was annoyance, and of course she had no other option. She couldn't comprehend it.

But she was fortunate – or so it seemed to her then – because a drayman she recognised from Callard's came by not long afterwards and asked her where she thought she was going.

'Cattle market,' she told him, squinting into the sunshine, her bonnet slipping back on its ribbons.

'Cattle market,' he confirmed, and offered his hand, which was enormous and calloused and held on to hers even after she was up there beside him. He stroked a rough thumb over her knuckles, wheezing a little, his breath yeasty with drink, seeming for a moment quite lost in his thoughts, and then he looked at her and asked, 'Claude Dobson's girl?' and she nodded. 'You'll be all right with me, old pretty,' he said, and finally let go of her hand, gave a lazy tug on the reins and set the drayhorse to clopping. 'You'll be all right with me,' he repeated, and said not another word though he looked at her frequently, just looked and looked at her.

He stank, and he was huge, every aspect of him filthy – his galoshes and apron, moleskins, cap, tobacco-stained beard – but he brought her home, conveyed her safely to the pharmacy, and perhaps if her father had been occupied, too busy serving to notice, all might have been well. But Father saw her getting down from the cart, the drayman holding her closely, his arms round her middle, and he was furious, incandescent: that Enid should have sent her home with one of those notorious men, and that Gertie should have agreed to the arrangement.

Which prompted the poor girl, aged just ten or eleven, to attempt an explanation for what had occurred, which only made the matter much worse.

'Remember those sheep!'

Claude Dobson isn't a harsh man, not really, not in Gertie's opinion, despite his short temper and buttoned-up manner, though of course he requires her obedience, but while Gertie has never been as articulate as her father would like, neither has she ever shied from speaking her mind, which can be provoking, she knows, her father being so rational and so unsympathetic of childish or female confusions.

And that day she provoked him. He took her over his knee and struck her several times through her skirts with the flat of his hand, and later, when he had calmed himself and she had stopped snivelling, he summoned her upstairs to the bedroom – where Mother, still somewhat poorly, was sitting propped against the pillows, her features taut with alarm – and paced back and forth in the space between the bed and the wardrobe, tugging repeatedly on his beard, and at his ears, his collar and cuffs, and delivered a long, frowning speech in which he conceded that while he was correct in believing that the best course for a child was to allow it the liberty of discovering its own limitations, free from parental interference and soft-heartedness, he recognised that he had a duty nonetheless to protect that child from the prospect of harm, in which regard he had been mistaken in allowing Gertie to travel unaccompanied to Raworth, which had only served to encourage Enid in the assumption that the girl could be returned home alone and unannounced and by the first conveyance that chanced to come along.

And so, he had decided, Gertie would not, for her own safety, be permitted to make any more unchaperoned journeys, and – he coughed, he tugged at his beard – neither did he think it appropriate for either of them, Gertie or his wife, to maintain their association with the family in Raworth, about whom he had long held misgivings, as his wife was well aware.

Thus, there were to be no further visits; did they understand?

'But we may at least write?' asked his wife.

'Yes,' he said irritably, 'you may at least write,' and then added one other decree, that Gertie was not to venture from the house on a market day, not for the foreseeable future, since clearly she hadn't the sense to look out for her own safety.

'Oh, good,' sighed his wife. Then to Gertie, 'Remember those sheep!'

'Dorothea!' cried Dobson, quite angry. 'It isn't the livestock that concern me.' Then, exasperated, he turned and went from the room.

All of which was a long time ago, and though his prohibitions no longer apply – and couldn't, since Gertie is now engaged in important war work and obliged to give her Saturday mornings to Beckwith's as well as her Mondays to Fridays – she remains content to spend her Saturday afternoons indoors, helping Father in the pharmacy if required, and her mother with the housework if she's allowed to (they have no servant; Father is particular about that), though twice lately she has been dispatched to Beckwith House on her bicycle with a delivery of medicinal ointment for Montague Beckwith, who is recuperating from his ordeals in France, and would gladly be sent there again.

Certainly she does not mind to be out, for crowds have never intimidated her, and neither have the market-day animals – especially not the sheep – though her earliest memory is of standing on the front step with a palmful of shelled nuts in her hand, watching mesmerised as a streak of mud-spattered pigs came grunting down Riverside Road, the men shouting, thrashing at the beasts with their sticks, and then, after they'd gone (and perhaps she fell into some reverie, perhaps many minutes elapsed, though it seemed a mere matter of seconds), a sheep appeared from nowhere and barged her full in the chest, her monkey nuts scattering, so that she fell in the shop doorway with the animal, as she remembers it, standing calmly above her, apparently intending no harm. Untroubled, assuming her mother to be somewhere nearby (she wasn't), Gertie lay and gazed up at the sheep's claggy white wool and black face, its wide twitching ears, until abruptly a man appeared and yanked it away by its pelt and hurled it back into the flock, then stooped to claim Gertie too, which was when she began screaming, frightened not by the sheep, as her mother supposed, but by the man, his suddenness and size.

Not that men much worry her either. Gertie is appreciative of men, especially now that she is older and so many of them are at war (or invalided and sent home, like poor Captain Beckwith). A man will be careful of you, she's sure, if he can see that you are decent and deserve to be cared for.

4
Walter

cow whacking

In Walter's neighbourhood the dwellings are often quite tiny, dark-painted to the height of the first window, whitewashed above, and the white is filthy with mould and moss and the dirt that lifts off the river in summer and falls from the chimneys all year.

Kitchen, chamber and garret, the smallest of them are called, and they are poky, low-ceilinged (but then the people too are small, though not to each other), and so closely packed a man need only lean out of a window to shake hands with his neighbour. The roofs and guttering let in the wet, the drainpipes are leaky, and in some of the yards a runnel of water snakes down the slope to the river, whatever the weather, though lately even these streams have begun to slow to a trickle, leaving lines of brown sediment, food peelings, rubble. The heat has been constant for days, inside and out, and while most of the windows and doors are wide open, many of the curtains and blinds remain drawn, for decency's sake, as if these places were not dark enough as it is.

And some are very dark. The entries to Mortuary Yard and Slaughterhouse Lane are as broad as a coal-cart, but others are so narrow that even the sun cannot slip down them, for instance Upper Pig Lane, where John Cherry now lives, or the arched opening to Shott's Alley, which requires a grown man to duck as he goes in, then descend several steps, but is deceiving because the passage curves round to a broad courtyard where formerly the men would gather at weekends to bet on cards, dice, pitch and toss, Walter's own father among them (which meant he might earn a few coppers keeping watch for old Beaver, the constable, or running errands for the men to the tobacconist's and pub, though rarely enough to make up for what his father would lose).

That courtyard is concealed behind the red-brick building in which the Friends' First Day School is now housed, after which comes the turn for Flower-in-Hand Lane and the workshop of Solomon Postle, then Mrs Rymer's the draper and Sheldrake's the rag merchants, and the entry for Wylie's Wharf, where Walter hears a commotion, a clamour of children calling out to a steamboat – some of the boys flapping their caps, others excitedly waving – and pauses a moment to watch them, for always the pleasure boats on this stretch of the river will be pestered by children like these, yelling for money, which it's customary for the day-trippers to toss to them and then laughingly watch as the children scramble about in the mud and gravel and fight like pups over just a few farthings.

Girls as well as boys will ply for coins in this way, many of them barefoot, his own sisters included, while their older brothers are pilfering food on the market, or helping to drive the animals in and out of the city ('cow whacking', they call it), which is the main opportunity for a boy of Harold's or Arthur's age to earn a penny or two on a market day, and something that Walter himself used to do, before his brother William was killed by a bullock and his mother warned him against going again.

Poor William, who was just two years and three months when he died.

Walter walks on, and as he passes the gates of St Cuthbert's he almost collides with a couple of boys hurrying away from the market, and swings a heavy boot at their arses, and shouts, 'Mind where you're fucking going!' But they will be hungry and racing to get home for their dinner, since they'll have been out since six in the morning, when it's customary for any number of boys to troop along to the pens at the railway station, or else a mile or two into the countryside because quite a few farmers, and not only those nearest the city, will be looking to save themselves the cost of freighting their stock by rail and will drive the animals directly in from the farm: cattle and sheep in the main, but also pigs and occasionally geese.

The farmer himself, as often as not, will follow up at the rear of the herd and might have a couple of lieutenants to assist him, one policing the left flank, the other the right, but additional drovers will always be needed, especially in controlling the cattle delivered by rail – which are fresher and more desperate to kick out from their confinement – though it hardly matters how far they've been driven: once the animals meet the city and the distractions of gardens and side-streets and alleys, the pace will quicken and the drovers be put on their mettle.

Herds of twenty, thirty and more will come hell-for-leather up Riverside Road and there will be four, five or six boys hired at a penny-ha'penny a time to run alongside them, whacking their haunches with sticks to keep them on course, yelling and trilling. They will make a racket that can be heard half a mile away, and if all proceeds without mishap then the clattering, mooing, shrieking mass of energy and bodies will come and go in a matter of moments, leaving behind nothing but dust and silence and long splats of manure in the road – for which a use will always be found: the younger boys and girls will be sent out with shovels and buckets to collect it, and the rate-payers of London Road will usually be happy to buy some.

On a good run the herd will hit its stride and pass thunderously by, and of course it's a thrill for the boys to make so much noise (and to be so important) but for the poor animals, accustomed to the quiet of the fields, or the confines of their sheds, the clamour and pace of the town will be terrifying and the bullocks especially will want to run amok. They will want to go everywhere but in a straight line, and should one of them slip down a side-alley and panic to find itself loosed from the herd, it will be truly menacing, a danger to every-one, because it won't know how to stop or where to turn, in which case the happiest outcome will be for its momentum to carry it straight to the bottom and into the river, except that certain of the alleys become exceptionally narrow towards the end – Mortuary Yard being one, where the Barleys have their home – in which case an animal might easily find itself wedged or unable to turn about, and that is the trickiest, most aggravating thing, to reverse a beast fattened for market or stupid with fear and inclined to unpredictability or sheer stubbornness.

The farmer will need to assign someone to retrieve it, and a small nimble boy then will be an asset, if he is able to climb around by the next yard along, risking a dip in the stinking river, to harry the animal from the front – flapping his cap at it, perhaps threatening to whack it – while the occupants of the yard keep their distance behind it. The cows will shit themselves of course, which can be messy, while some of the livelier ones will also kick out, which can be deadly, as it was for young William.

The scene was confusing

On that occasion Walter was helping to drive some cattle down Riverside Road, and though he had done this many times previously he hadn't been aware before then of his father Eddie looking on, as he happened to be that morning, standing in the doorway of the Crown with his arms crossed over his chest, seemingly smiling beneath his moustache. He turned and said something to another man, something approving: that was what Walter supposed, and perhaps he lost concentration, or became too casual, showing off, acting more in control of the animals than he actually was, because one of them veered suddenly into Mortuary Yard, its hoofs skittering on the cobbles, its horns catching on the washing, and found itself not only blinkered but cornered at the foot of the yard, with too little room to turn about and too narrow a gap to escape through.

It panicked, and the commotion brought out the neighbours, more than a dozen of them, including William, who wandered across from the kitchen, quite naked.

The scene was confusing, and Walter – distracted by Mrs O'Brien, who was attempting to shoo the beast by beating on a saucepan with a spoon – yelled not at his brother, which he ought to have done, but to his mother indoors (he assumed she was indoors), and felt the displacement of air as the bullock kicked out, the first time at nothing, and the second, by chance, at William. One of its hoofs connected with the little boy's skull, and the impact knocked him clear off his feet. He landed badly too, his head whipping back and cracking on the cobbles. The crack was audible. The blood was everywhere, and his face was crushed on one side, his eye socket opened.

Walter saw of all this quite clearly, in the instant before his mother began beating him, the first furious blow to the side of his head making him stagger, half deafened. She dropped the parcel of meat she was carrying. She had been to Joe Orford's. She was hysterical. And her husband, arriving flush-faced from the pub, had to drag her away. He yanked her by her hair. He came for Walter later.

some are sickly from birth

But children do die. Families are large and so too are the losses, the little ones taken by measles, meningitis, whooping cough, typhus, influenza, diphtheria, scarlet fever, tuberculosis; all of these. Some are sickly from birth, some slip away in their sleep. Accidents are common, and while Walter has seven siblings alive, he knows of three others – three more besides William – who failed to survive, the oldest of those being Beattie, who lived and passed on before Walter was born, her age still measured in weeks and nothing to remember her by but the precious few details her mother can recall of her. There isn't a headstone, a keepsake, a photograph, and Father, it seems, has lately even forgotten her name: 'Beattie' was his suggestion when the most recent baby was born.

'Same as my old mum,' he said.

'Same as your first daughter,' said Mother.

That child they named Alice. Four years younger than James, fifteen younger than Walter, she was poorly and tetchy through-out her short life, constantly crying or coughing, and eventually she died in her sleep. Walter remembers looking down on her pale, pinched face – her mouth agape, snot crusting her nose, the blue tint of her lips – and feeling no pity or sorrow, not even regret for her. Soon she would be disposed of. Certainly she was too small for a coffin, too young to be worth the expense. Of the dead ones, only Percy was allowed the palaver of that, because he was older: a plain deal box, no handles or trimmings, but a coffin nonetheless and his corpse laid out for inspection on the table in the kitchen until the time came to seal and bury him in the grave-yard of St Cuthbert's or up at the municipal cemetery.

Percy was five when he died, taken by typhoid, and possibly there were others, babies who died in the womb or at birth – whether by chance or design, by miscarriage or the effects of a purgative, such as those sold by Claude Dobson, the pharmacist – but neither Walter nor his siblings would have known about that; such matters were never discussed. Alice was a 'surprise' – that was the expression he heard – yet to the children these babies were always a bit of a puzzle, where they came from, where they concealed themselves. Something would be the matter with Mother, that would be plain, and then it would happen, another baby to feed and make room for.

Walter knows better now, of course; he believes he knows the full facts. And possibly Mabel does too.

So there were twelve children – twelve who lived long enough to be named – though Walter does also remember seeing one other, a stillbirth, its face wrinkled and ancient, its body curiously twisted. 'A girl,' his father whispered, standing over the crate, and then draped her beneath some sacking and placed her – whoever she was – on a shelf in their closet for the rest of that morning, a piece of business to be attended to later, once he'd done whatever else he had to do on a Saturday and could take her to the municipal cemetery and pay a few pennies to have her laid in a hole and covered over, forgotten like Beattie, like a lot of them were.

Whether or not she was theirs, Walter has no idea; he never did ask. His father disposed of several babies during his childhood, fetched a wooden crate from Aldrich the grocer and a certificate from the doctor and took the body to the cemetery as a favour for a neighbour, who would pay him the price of the burial, and perhaps a bit extra, and sometimes Walter would be allowed to accompany him – when he got older and stronger and could take a turn at carrying the crate, which became so much heavier towards the end of its journey.

They did three such favours for Mrs Palmer, he remembers, who still lives at the top of Mortuary Yard and has had no luck at all with her babies, eight of them dying in infancy and the only surviving girl an imbecile, her two grown-up sons meanwhile in khaki in France.

But the Barleys are not too badly off. Others in the vicinity are burdened by much larger families – for example the Cockeys, who live beside the slaughterhouse in the next yard along, the cries of Ma Cockey's babies as clearly audible as any sounds that come from Joe Orford's abattoir. She has another every year, doesn't know any better, and while some are stillborn and others don't last very long, it amounts to twenty-four children in total

24

– two dozen live births – though eleven of those were already dead by the start of the war, including Jack Cockey, Walter's best friend in school.

Walter remembers being taken round by his father at the age of thirteen to pay his respects to Jack's corpse – after his mother had said that he mustn't – and being greeted by a bulbous-eyed Mr Cockey, drunk as he usually was, who hung a heavy arm across his shoulders and guided him through to the coffin, which was propped on two orange crates in the downstairs back bedroom. 'Look at that,' he said. 'They've done a lovely job for the boy, a lovely job on him.'

Walter looked. He supposed 'they' were Jack's mother and aunts, though why 'lovely' he couldn't quite see.

Jack was still Jack – sleeping, perhaps, or resting his eyes – and after a few moments Walter's attention drifted to a photograph hooked over the mantelpiece. Properly framed, it was the only picture in the room and showed a pretty young woman with moist eyes and dark eyebrows, a tiny plump mouth and rose-tinted complexion. She too appeared to be gazing down on poor Jack, about to shed a tear for him, and though Walter had seen the picture many times previously he had never before noticed the young woman's comeliness, how very lovely she was, or how much she resembled Gertie Dobson, the pharmacist's daughter, whose own comeliness he had noticed years earlier and still secretly cherished.

'That's Pearlie,' said Mr Cockey, gripping him tighter. 'She was another one. She died. She's gone.'

Which was when Mr Cockey started to cry, the first time Walter had seen such a thing, the spectacle of a man in tears more terrible to him then than the sight of his friend's body laid out in its box.

Embarrassed, a little frightened, he eased himself free and slipped quietly away – his father standing outside with some other men, all of them smoking, none talking – and immediately turned in the direction of the cattle market and the pharmacy, his arm aching where the dead boy's father had squeezed him and his mind teeming with things he would tell Gertie Dobson, if only he should bump into her; if only he could be sure of evading her father, and she should remember him.

5

Gertie

a comely girl, plump and attractive

Her mother coughs twice, three times, as she climbs the steep stairs and Gertie takes a last quick look round the market and notices Mr Studland with his goitre and peculiar gait, apparently coming this way, crossing the road to the pharmacy. She follows the top of his bowler, angles for a better perspective, and sees him sidle up to the end of a queue in which there are four or five other men. Standing slightly on tiptoe, she presses her face to the window and looks precipitously down through the lace. An ice-cream vendor has pitched his fancy barrow on the pavement below. Close to her own age, and dark-skinned, with slicked shiny black hair, he is dressed in a crisp white jacket and white apron. His nose is convex. Gertie assumes this must be a Roman nose, and decides that she likes it. He would be Italian, of course. All the makers of ice cream come here from Italy.

'Gertie,' gasps her mother. 'Get away from there!'

Reluctantly Gertie drops back on her heels and turns from the window and quietly waits while her mother unfolds an old towel and lays it over the card-table and positions a porcelain bowl on top of it. The antiseptic liquid is milky. 'You were gone for a long time,' says Gertie.

'Father required me,' says Mother, and produces a wad of cotton wool from the pouch in her apron. She dips it into the bowl. 'But you mustn't make yourself so conspicuous, Gertie,' she says. 'Imagine if he were to see you.' Her voice is breathy and small, and she is tiny, her eyes as bright and quick as a sparrow's.

'Who?'

'Father.'

'But he's indoors. How could he see me?'

'Someone might mention you – a customer might.'

'No one is looking,' says Gertie, and gestures outside. 'You can see for yourself.'

'I will certainly not,' says her mother, and holds herself stiffly, her head oddly cocked as though listening for something, a noise on the stairs perhaps, men laughing outside. She twitches.

But Mother is often this nervy, inclined to be fretful, and cautious, and when she repeats, 'I will not,' Gertie sighs and comes forward, lazily offering the first of her cuts, a snick in the pad of her thumb. Frowning, her mother examines it closely, searching out splinters of metal, any other contaminants. Despite the tremor in her hands she dabs at it firmly and Gertie winces. 'It will sting,' murmurs her mother, 'you know that it will,' and scrutinises the cuts that Gertie picked up in the week, which are now healing, then takes her other hand and gives a small sigh. 'Goodness, Gertie,' she breathes, and squeezes the cotton wool over the bowl, dunks it again. 'How clumsy you are!'

Gertie's hand is grazed raw on each knuckle and the grazes are gritted with dirt. 'It isn't only me,' she objects, and would try to explain that cuts and grazes like these are quite common in Beckwith's – among the old men as well as the girls – and that she is far from careless in her work, but her eyes are beginning to water. She bites her lower lip and turns her face to the window and wishes she could still see the Italian – he would be distracting – but the angle was already against her and so too now is the weave in the lace. Even from this short distance she cannot see through it, and as she gazes blearily into the white fabric, the sun glowing brightly behind it, she hears the cries of the animals outside and is visited by another scene from her childhood: a snowy white cloud of geese cresting the hill at the top of the market, honking and flightless, in the days before the tramlines were laid, when it was customary to drive the birds out to Crag's Meadow to be fattened for Christmas.

They were shipped over from France, she remembers, where the fighting now is, and several of the women in Beckwith's were once employed in the plucking sheds and paid not by the hour but tuppence for every bird that they fleeced. Mabel Barley's mother was among them; Mabel who works the machine next to hers. The money in Beckwith's is much better, she's been told, and the work is less bloody, since the women in the sheds were required to pluck out the birds' tongues as well as the feathers so the tally man could count them and determine their wages.

'The poor geese!' Gertie exclaimed at the time.

The poor men in France, she thinks now, and pictures the tongues, those dripping pieces of flesh, and the clouds of snowy white feathers, and then she remembers Walter Barley, who delivered the ice to Beckwith House, and whose name she was sure she'd forgotten – though not his face, his face out of so many, which keeps coming back to her, and the white feather she once gave to him. They had been children in the same school, and she ought not to have been so unkind to him.

'Oh,' she says, startled by the thought of it. He would be Mabel's brother, she now realises, the one who is missing.

Her mother looks up. She has finished. 'You'll live,' she says, and drops the cotton wool into the bowl.

Gertie watches a fine red thread of her blood slowly dissolving into the liquid. Her knuckles are stinging. 'Yes,' she murmurs, and thinks of poor Mabel, who is lately so quiet. Then, 'Sorry,' she says.

'Sorry?'

'For making a nuisance.'

'Never mind,' says her mother, and gently pats Gertie dry with one edge of the towel. She dries herself. 'But I do wish you wouldn't slump like you do.' She sighs, for something is awry with Gertie's posture, it seems, and with the line of her dress.

Her mother pinches the fabric, tugs it this way and that. She presses back on Gertie's shoulders, then pulls on her wrists to straighten her arms and attempts to adjust the hang of her sleeves. 'You would have such a smart figure,' she says, 'if only you would hold yourself correctly.'

'Father prefers it,' says Gertie.

'Prefers what?'

'That I don't have a figure.'

'Nonsense.'

'He does,' says Gertie, for she is a comely girl, she knows, plump and attractive, with ringlets and a sweet round apple-cheeked face. 'He finds my figure provoking – my bosom and bottom.'

'Gertie!' Her mother instantly flushes. Briskly she begins tidying up. 'That wasn't my meaning. That wasn't at all what I meant. Oh, whatever makes you say such things?'

Gertie stares and is silent, for she is conscious that certain topics are not to be touched upon, even between a mother and daughter, and here it appears is another one, as disturbing to her mother as the subject of childbirth – or, worse even than that, a woman's monthly cycle, which Gertie is forbidden ever to mention.

'That wasn't my meaning,' her mother repeats, laying her towel over her forearm and taking up the bowl of disinfectant. 'It wasn't at all what I meant, and you mustn't refer to yourself by those particulars, Gertie. Do you understand me?'

'Those particulars,' repeats Gertie. 'My bosom and bottom, no, I shan't.' And then she smiles – she can't help it – and is surprised by the suddenness of her mother's reaction, the sharpness of the slap she receives. 'Oh,' Gertie says, and lifts a hand to her cheek. Outside there is shouting, men's urgent voices, heels clacking on the cobbles. A cow must have got loose from its pen. 'I'm sorry,' says Gertie, 'I didn't mean to,' and attempts to touch Mother's face too, but Mother flinches, and thrusts the towel at her.

A splash of pink water has spilled onto the linoleum.

'Would you wipe that up, please,' says her mother, and hesitates, uncertain what to do with the bowl. She places it on the table, then decides that she should take it, despite leaving the towel, and hurriedly goes from the room, downstairs again to help Father.

her poor body

Sighing, Gertie lowers herself to her knees and dabs at the spillage, her face smarting as much as her grazes, and recalls the only other occasion on which her mother had cause to strike her, which was the day she first found blood in her underwear, a discovery that was quite dumbfounding since no one had told Gertie to expect such a thing, just as no one had warned her five or six years earlier that playing hatless in the midsummer sun would cause the world to spin and her nose to begin dripping such fat crimson splats onto her pinafore. Despite her giddiness then, aged eight or nine, and her horror, she had also been curious, oddly detached from herself, and when at the age of fourteen she found she was bleeding from her private parts she was similarly intrigued, as much drawn by this new phenomenon as she was startled. The stain was darker, less pure than the blood that had dripped from her nose, and bending her head to it she recognised the ammonia smell of her water, but something thicker, less familiar besides, and immediately took the garment down to her mother, who hit her.

'Oh, you rude girl, take it away!'

'Where?'

'To the wash, to the laundry!'

Her mother was tensed as though ready to fly, and Gertie could not help but feel a little sorry for her, though sick to her stomach as well. No doubt her father would have a cure for it, but she could not possibly go down to the pharmacy to ask him, and neither could her mother, it seemed. Gertie nodded, and apologised, and it was then – as she turned to leave Mother's bedroom – that the real flow began, a sudden streak along her inner thigh. She hitched up her nightgown and stood and gawped at it. She thought perhaps she was dying, felt for an instant quite faint, and steadied herself with a hand on the bedstead.

'Oh, don't let him see you!' her mother exclaimed, and closed her tiny hand around Gertie's wrist, seeming to want to drag her away, to find somewhere to hide her. 'Use your things, your drawers – mop yourself, quickly. I'll get you a towel.'

Gertie gripped the fat ball of her drawers and patted the blood from her leg. It had dripped onto the linoleum, too, and panic-stricken she pressed her drawers to her crotch and stared at the floor. She didn't know what to do, and didn't know how to explain her dilemma when her mother returned, though of course Mother saw it at once, and as she stooped to wipe the floor with a rag she pressed another on Gertie and irritably said, 'I told you about this, Gertie. You can't have forgotten already.'

But she had forgotten; she must have done, because she had no recollection at all of her mother having broached the subject. None whatsoever. And surely she ought to have remembered; surely that wasn't something she could have let slip from her memory. 'I'm sorry,' she said then, and felt more betrayed by her feebleness of mind – which so irritated her father, she knew – than by her poor body.

her head in his lap

Gertie folds the towel neatly. She places it on the card-table and takes up her station by the window, and as she watches Mr Studland sidling back to the market, gripping an ice cream, she notices Silly Jack Edwards, the youngest son of the stonemason next door, giving piggy-back rides to a jostle of boys outside the Turf Tavern, and thinks of the day she was demoted to sit with the dunces and clowns in Riverside School on account of her want of intelligence, her troubles with letters and numbers. One of the dunces was a dribbler with mongoloid features, and another was Silly Jack Edwards, who couldn't speak more than a few words but was already as tall as most men. And Gertie didn't much mind, for she was joined by another boy – it was Walter Barley – who wasn't a defective but sent to sit with them as a punishment for his insolence, or possibly lateness.

They occupied a long wooden settle at the back of the room, while just in front of them sat a perpetually phlegmy boy called Cameron Campbell, whose accent was no different from theirs but whose features were as Scottish as his name – a pale freckled face and gingery eyebrows and a fright of red hair. His neck was crawling with lice, and when Walter leaned over and attempted to flick them with his pencil, Cameron looked around at him and smiled. His teeth were green. Carefully he pincered one of the lice between his grubby fingernails and audibly cracked it, then sucked clean the ends of his fingers. And it was this that Gertie described to her mother when she arrived home that day from school – because it was so unhygienic – but found Mother less concerned with where the insect had gone than where it had come from.

'He has lots of them,' Gertie said, displaying her neck, 'all around here.'

'Come and kneel down,' sighed her mother, sitting in a chair by the fire, and motioned Gertie to lay her head on her lap so that she could search through her hair – her scalp, her neck, the backs of her ears – the examination so soothing that Gertie's breath lengthened and slowed and she felt herself on the warm, heavy cusp of falling asleep. Such gentleness in her mother was rare, and might not come again, and so at school the next day Gertie persuaded Walter Barley to pet her in just the same way, first demonstrating the procedure on him, then pillowing her head in his lap and closing her eyes, and discovered that his touch was equally gentle and calming, and again she might have drifted to sleep but that their teacher spotted what they were doing and shouted at them to stop, after which – a mere week or so later, once the headmaster had mentioned the matter in passing to Father – Gertie was enrolled at Jeremiah Beckwith's Academy of Housecraft and Manners for Girls, and did not encounter poor Walter again until the day he called at the home of the Beckwiths, making his delivery of ice.

a charity girl

Not that Gertie much missed him; she forgot about Riverside School and everyone in it almost the instant she left there, and never once had cause to connect Walter with Mabel, his sister, who was a charity girl at Beckwith's Academy, and is a good sort, not often smiling now but a decent companion, amiable and pretty, and a favourite like Gertie of all the old boys in the factory, despite the elasticated caps the girls must wear, and the blue voluminous gowns, which make them appear so shapeless and comical. At work behind their machines, Gertie and Mabel will sign to each other, and make faces, since the noise is so loud, but when the hooter sounds they will clean their hands in the same tin of paraffin, and share the same strip of old rag to wipe themselves, and then they might natter as they amble along to the canteen, where mince and mash is tuppence and milk pudding a penny more, and where Mrs Beenie, their forewoman, will come and sit with them sometimes, because they are good girls, hardworking, and without airs and graces, despite their having come over from Beckwith House, where Mabel was a maid and Gertie a companion of Edwina and Emma, the Misses Beckwith, who are now serving their country in France, helping the wounded.

Which places Gertie a cut above the other girls, of course, including Mabel Barley, including Mrs Beenie, though she knows better than to mention this, or the standing of her father, and does whatever is required of her, and smiles at the other girls' banter, and while Mrs Beenie is adamant that Gertie ought to have been assigned to one of the offices, with her nicely spoken ways, Gertie knows better on that account, too, since she would have been ill-suited for any work involving spellings or sums, and indeed, it occurs to her now, were it not for her feebleness of mind she would never have been placed among the dunces, and if she hadn't been placed among the dunces she would never have been caressed by Walter Barley, and so wouldn't have been withdrawn from the school on Riverside Road and placed in Beckwith's Academy, which means she would not have been able to graduate to her apprenticeship in Osgood's drapery department, and would not then have attracted the attention of the Misses Beckwith, and so would not have been invited into their home.

Which is a train of thought she would like to share with her father, to demonstrate that good things may often come of bad, but knows she must not, since it will only antagonise him: her nonsense, he calls it.

6
Walter

other unfortunates he's seen

At one time in his life Walter kept many lists in his head – football matches he'd been to, courting couples he'd spied upon, motor-cars he had followed down Balmoral Road. And of course corpses. He used to keep a tally, used to know the number precisely, and as he makes his way through the crowds around the pubs and cafés on the way to the market he begins to count them off on his fingers, whispering to himself as he goes, and arrives at fourteen before he reaches the end of Riverside Road, all of them children – including his siblings and cousins and neighbours – to which he adds the six little bundles he once saw on the back of a coal-cart on Kilmarnock Road, the dead babies of paupers all wrapped in grey hessian and tied up like parcels with string.

Whatever contagion had killed them, they were being transported that damp afternoon from the Workhouse to the municipal cemetery, where they would share the same unmarked hole in the ground, and Walter followed at a short distance, freewheeling Joe Orford's bicycle, in the hope of seeing the bundles unravel as they were tipped into the grave. But they were bound up too well; they didn't unravel, nor were they 'tipped', and disappointed he returned late to the butcher, who boxed his ear for taking so long.

Which brings his tally to twenty, and as he climbs the narrow steps of Saracen's Lane – a less populous route to the top of the market – Walter wipes his clammy hands on his trousers, flexes his fingers, and begins a tentative count of the several other unfortunates he's seen, the strangers who came down Mortuary Yard on the heavy deal handcart pushed by Constable Beaver, their faces hidden beneath a rough-woven blanket, the unsprung wheels clattering over the cobbles and drawing a crowd of jostling children, the boldest of the boys fighting to tug at the blanket in the hope of revealing a complexion turned blue by gas poisoning, or drained bloodlessly white, or hideously bloated and pecked at by fishes.

Most of these dead were drownings or suicides, and while Walter's mother might pause a moment in her chores at the knell of the wheels, straighten her back and murmur, 'There goes another one, poor soul,' she never would come to her doorstep and gawp like the neighbours, or allow her children to join the scrimmage around the set-upon constable, who would brandish his truncheon, affronted and flustered, and poke at the boys' bellies to get them to stand clear, and even threaten to cosh one or two. (The girls would flummox him utterly.)

Beaver wasn't a bright man – everyone said that – but he was good with the dead and would sit with them sometimes in the mortuary if Orford's abattoir happened to be busy when they came in, if it seemed their first moments of peace might be disturbed by the squeals of the animals just the other side of the wall – which of course was to credit the dead with some awareness of the world they had just left behind, and Walter for one never used to believe that; he didn't want to give any credence to stories of hauntings.

He has seen perhaps a dozen such bodies, and a dozen more who died in old age – close neighbours and relatives – the most memorable of those being Mrs Ball, a tiny black-clad widow who sold toffee apples and paraffin from a pantry of a shop in Thompson's Yard and who scowled or glowered at everyone, never smiled, frightened the children, and was said to have been sealed in her coffin once before, twenty years previously, when she had spent all of three days laid out in her living room, seemingly dead, mourned over by her family and friends, only to wake and irritably knock on the lid of her box as soon as it was screwed down and the bearers about to lift her away. This at least was the story; it explained her bad temper.

Walter used to see her more or less daily, a dark wizened creature in her shop, or hobbling down the road, bent-backed over her stick – a kind of pantomime figure, a character out of a storybook – and when she really did die there were queues to look at her, just to make sure, Walter and his mother among them. Mrs Ball was less scary then, no longer so angry.

But certain of the deceased would always attract more interest than others: for instance his grandmother – also a widow, though kindlier, more neighbourly – who was ill for almost a year and nursed to the end by her daughters, the six still alive who lived locally, including Winnie, his mother.

Several times daily one or other of those daughters would take a turn at her bedside, and sometimes Walter would accompany his mother and do what he could to be useful, since he was a good boy; all his aunts said so.

They would sweep for her, sit and talk to her, and perform some other more intimate duties that required Walter to make himself scarce. She had no appetite, refused everything but liquids, and as the flesh began to crawl from her it was Walter's job sometimes to beat the egg that his mother would mix with brandy and feed to the old lady through a funnel and tube. The egg was to keep her strength up, the brandy to ease her discomfort, and both were supplied by the benevolence of her dead husband's former employers, the Beckwiths.

Always her room would be dark and somewhat sour-smelling, and it was uncommonly quiet, too, since Walter's uncles had put down a layer of peat on the cobbles to deaden the noise of the horses and carts passing in and out of the brewery nearby. Not that she seemed particularly troubled by that: long before the end she disappeared into herself, her eyes unable to focus, rolling

38

up and showing the whites, then snapping back, as if she were repeatedly waking from a dream she wasn't prepared for, after which she would smile, sheepishly, toothlessly, a little distant, and it would all begin again, the slow retreat into herself and her eyes rolling up, until at last she didn't return.

Walter regrets not being there when she went, and remembers his hesitation before he looked into her coffin, fearful her eyes might still be open, showing the whites. But they weren't; they'd been closed, for she too was 'sleeping'. Her hair was tidily pinned, and she'd been dressed by her daughters in her Sunday-best bombazine, but she was by then all skull and bones, barely much more than a skeleton. The gaslight flickered in the waxiness of her skin, and that was the worst thing – the animation in the light, the suggestion that she might still be breathing. Walter glanced to his mother, who frowned and came forward and encouraged him to touch his lips to his grandmother's cold forehead – for luck, she said, and so that he wouldn't have any bad memories of her.

Which had seemed to work. Walter hadn't been haunted, and his dreams had never been spoiled, not by this or any of the other corpses he had seen in his childhood.

a looker

Where Saracen's Lane emerges at the top of the market – the egress so narrow Walter must turn himself sideways – the sky is criss-crossed by tram wires and a number ten service is stalled in the sunshine, its passage impeded by a flock of sheep on the rise past the Corn Hall.

The sheep are Suffolks and the tram-driver is female, small and buxom in a brass-buttoned uniform and determinedly facing directly ahead, her gloved hand on the crank, her cheeks flushed in the heat, while no more than two paces away stands a gent in a bowler – his legs crossed at the ankle, his weight supported by his cane – who is staring straight at her as if she were the illustration of an idea, a proposition requiring some thought. He strokes his moustache, purses his lips, and appears almost to smile when Walter nudges against him and says, 'She's a looker, this one,' then straightens his posture, coughs into his fist.

A metal gate clatters open nearby, and as the sheep begin to pour into their pen the tram jolts to life. Blue sparks spit from the wires. The young woman rattles her bell, glances quickly around, and the gentleman adjusts his stiff collar, the tilt of his boater, and moves briskly on. Advertisements for Epp's Cocoa and Belcran's Pills pass before Walter as the tram pulls away. He glimpses a full load of passengers, submerged in sunshine in the saloon, and whistling to himself, he crosses the road to the market.

Here on the eastern perimeter the aisles are covered with canvas and Walter heads down a long tented passage of fowls, dozily clucking and burbling in their coops, and takes off his cap, wipes the sweat from his brow with the cuff of his tunic. He breathes the sourness of droppings and hay. Many of these birds will be left here for hours, and some will be certain to lay, their eggs sought after by the boys from the neighbourhood, who will bide their time, loiter all afternoon if they must, and when at last the coast is clear – the farmhands finally succumbing to boredom or thirst – they will nip in and slip the latch on the likeliest cages, just as Walter once did.

It was rare that he ever had his hand pecked, and as a boy, too, he would get among the cows and fill a bottle with milk taken fresh from the udder, despite the risk of being spotted and whacked with a droving stick, for then as now the drovers could be cruel men, harsh in their treatment of the boys and very much harsher in their handling of the animals, such that even Walter's father – who isn't remotely soft-hearted – once took umbrage and went after a farmhand for whacking a calf repeatedly on the backside with a stick made wicked by the addition of a nail through its tip.

'You lousy sod!' he shouted, and grabbed for the stick, broke it over his knee. The nailed end he threw aside, the other he hurled at the farmhand, and then he squared up to box him. But there was never any danger of it coming to blows: the drover had no choice but to hurry after the animal, whacking its rump with his open palm and yelling as he ran alongside it – here on the left, quickly then with a halt and a side-step to its right – though he did manage briefly to look back and shout something so low and disgusting that another man, passing by with his wife, also barracked him.

They can be brutal, but then it's their job to frighten the animals, and as Walter comes towards the cattle pens, stepping from shade to bright sunlight, he hears the clank of a gate being slammed, the squeal of another swinging open, and watches from a distance as eight or nine bullocks are harried down a channel of fences to Studland's sale ring, the hard ground made slippy with excrement and the animals skating, almost falling, in their panic to escape the old drovers behind them, who are barking and yelping, lashing out with their sticks. Which is a spectacle Walter might once have enjoyed, but now doesn't. He lifts his gaze to the great elms in the west, and the cathedral beyond them, and fills his lungs with the smell of the animals, their distress, and hawks up a fat gob of phlegm and spits as far as he is able. He wipes his mouth on his sleeve and turns towards the foot of the hill, where most of the dairy Shorthorns are penned and where Gertie's father has his pharmacy.

She will, he feels certain, be standing at the parlour window.

a genuine boner

The crowds down this way are thinner, the pens more often empty than occupied, and he passes a couple of drovers, breathing heavily from having noosed a runaway heifer, and then a

41

group of young scholars sitting up on the railings in their mortar boards, sketching a gargantuan black bull, which is tethered and eyeing them dolefully, its mouth a froth of saliva. It blares at the sky, releases a stream of piss into the straw, and Walter realises that one of its horns has been broken, the stump a red mess, still bleeding.

But there is damage wherever he looks; the scene is very sad. On the haunches of the bullocks there are many fresh lesions, and he notices a cow without a tail, the high cup of bones round its anus brimming with excrement. An emaciated calf is lying on its side, its coat caked with dirt. A Shorthorn in a neighbouring stall bellows as he approaches, its udder heavy with milk, and when he reaches a steadying hand to its shoulder it shies as though spooked, the other cows shying with it. Alarmed, they turn a half-circle, and momentarily he is able to see into the next stall along, where he glimpses a scrawny-looking lad on his knees in his breeches, his forehead pressed to the bars of the pen and his arms tucked beneath a great fat-bellied cow, squirting her milk into a beer bottle.

This too could be a scene from his earlier life and, curious, Walter steps into the adjoining enclosure, the gate already open, and edges around for a better perspective. A few yards distant, he crouches.

From this angle, the boy might well be a Barley; he might well be Walter, aged no more than fourteen, perhaps a year or so younger. The boy's boots are loose and in need of repair, and his hair is cut crudely, uncombed, his neck shadowed with dirt and his fingers quite filthy. Hunched over, he gives a quick spit on one hand then gently, firmly, he tugs at the udder, his action practised, familiar. It is not unlike wanking. There is a knack to it, a kink in the wrist, a right way to apply the pressure, a right way to grip, the fingers squeezing not all at once but in sequence, the outer sheath pulling over the shaft underneath, and as Walter looks on he slips a hand inside his breeches and imagines how it might feel to experience again the first stirrings of an erection, such as used to surprise him at the oddest of moments, prompted not by the sight of a pretty face or a young woman's shapeliness, not always, but the ease perhaps of his stride on a warm afternoon, or the rhythmical jolt of a carrier's cart, or even the chill he once felt when left alone in Joe Orford's abattoir, with only a pig's bloodless carcass for company and its corpse freshly shaven, seemingly human.

But nothing occurs; he cannot be roused.

The cow shuffles, her hoofs clacking on the cobbles. She turns her soft gaze on Walter, her lashes girlish and white, and lets go a tumble of shit, which spatters at her heels. The boy shifts his position but keeps on milking, conscious no doubt of the urgency, the likelihood of being discovered, dragged out and thrashed if he dawdles. Away off, other cattle are lowing, pigs squealing. There are shouts, auctions and negotiations occurring. But down here, sheltered by the animals and the distance from the sale rings, there is a hush of sorts. Walter listens to the milk squirting into the bottle – a Callard's Imperial Label – and it recalls to him the sound of his father pissing into the pot at bedtime: two, three swift squirts, then the full flow, sometimes for minutes it seemed. After which their bed would shimmy and creak as his father attempted to settle, the warm musty smell of his piss lacing the darkness.

All night then he would snore. For many years Walter shared a bed with him and many times woke beneath the weight of his father's arm or pressed by his bulk to the wall, revolted by the stench of him and fearing – as he got older – that either one of them might betray himself with a genuine boner. It hadn't happened, or not so that Walter had noticed, and he doesn't now remember how long it has been since he last enjoyed one, even when waking in the morning.

The boy has finished milking. He stoppers the bottle with the pad of his thumb and tucks it under his arm, inside his jacket. Hunched over, head down, he scurries quickly away – through the bars of one pen and into the next, then out into an aisle and off in the direction of Dobson's – and as he flees he gives several quick glances behind him, as though conscious of being watched or pursued, but fails to identify Walter, and then he is gone. He disappears into the traffic outside the pharmacy, the Saturday bustle of Riverside Road, and as Walter stands and searches among the carts and pedestrians for this boy just like himself he remembers how he too would keep his bottle hidden under his jacket, not only as he hurried down the street but also after he had turned into Mortuary Yard and then as he made for his door and the safety of his mother's kitchen, for he would not have wanted even their closest neighbours to see him with the bottle and guess that he had been stealing; or worse, perhaps, suppose that he had been sent to fetch a pint of ale for his mother, who was otherwise thought to be temperate, a respectable woman, abstemious and moral. Back then, Walter would not have wanted anyone to be given cause to think wrong of her. The shame would also be his. But Winnie Barley isn't the person she was, and neither does Walter possess the same scruples.

That boy is gone, that life, and with a sigh Walter steps into the open. He clambers over the top of one pen and traverses the next and positions himself in the dead centre of the last empty enclosure, facing across to the pharmacy, to where a queue is waiting for ice cream and where Gertie will be gazing down on the market.

With one hand tucked inside his breeches and the other unfastening his flies, Walter scrutinises the upstairs windows. He searches for her silhouette behind the lace curtains, the familiar form of her, and lifts out his limp penis and balls. They are warm. He cups them in the cradle of his hands and stands at the ready as a wagon goes by, its bed loaded with hay and the driver up on his feet, bow-legged. The horse is an old one. It sneezes; it is on its way out. And as Walter waits to see if Gertie at least will

44

acknowledge him, he seems to hear the chanting of children; he seems to hear his own childish voice – *load of hay, on your way, bring me some luck today* – and feels his eyes losing their focus, rolling upwards, showing the whites.

He snaps them back, concentrates.

7
Montague

his baffling affliction

In the grounds of Beckwith House, summer's waitingness hangs over everything and Montague Beckwith looks out on a capsule of cleanliness and order and silence in which two dozen hospital tents stand taut and white in the sunshine, each of them numbered, the guy-ropes seeming to hum with anticipation, the entrance flaps folded identically open. The first line of twelve canvas wards descends from the rear of the house to the wide slope of the lawn, where formerly the tennis and badminton courts were marked out, and where Montague's old archery target still stands in the distance, a bank of dark trees behind it. The second line is arrayed at an angle of ninety degrees to the first and terminates in a Union flag, the white lance of the flag-pole piercing an indigo sky, the flag barely stirring. A couple of orderlies stand smoking beneath it. The bustle of preparation is over, and Montague watches as a solitary sister confirms the tents' readiness – pausing, peering in, moving briskly on – her tunic gripped at the thighs, the hem of her skirt hoicked as high as her calves. He hears the report of her heels on the duckboards. There is no other sound.

Naked, he retreats from the balcony before she should notice him.

The last of Dobson's ointment has gone, used up in the night, and he had hoped the air would be similarly soothing, slightly cooling, but the heat today is oppressive, as much an irritant to his condition as any clothing might be. He cannot sit

46

in these chairs, and would rather not lie down again, or take another bath, and so stands irresolute in the shade beside his bed, confronting himself in the mirror, his baffling affliction, which is peculiarly selective, leaving unaffected his softer, fleshier parts – his abdomen, buttocks and calves, his thighs and upper arms, his genitals – yet forming a tough, reptilian carapace on his ribs and shoulder blades and the bonier parts of his limbs, while in the darker, moister areas of his underarms and groin, as well as at the backs of his knees (he twists round to see), it persists as a rash, the inflammation more purple than red, and with a whitish, weblike sheen to it: observed close to, it resembles a kind of crazing on his skin, like the crackle effect on certain of the household ceramics, or the patterning in his riding boots. These manifestations he assumes to be the advanced and primitive forms of the disease, with an interim stage to be found in the tightness of his fingers or the waxy, flaking aspect of much of his face, where again the affliction is oddly partial: he has in places been spared, for instance at the nape of his neck and all around his left cheek, from his temple down to his jaw-line.

But while the waxiness causes him very little discomfort, the rash can be maddeningly itchy – especially on warm, cloying days such as today – and the scaling too readily irritated by his clothes, which tend to chafe him, both of which symptoms can make him appear even more stiffly upright than usual. He walks like an automaton, he suspects, or as if constrained by a frame of some kind, an exoskeleton or a suit of scaly armour, and plainly, given all this, it would be absurd for the Medical Board to declare him fit for duty and a return to the trenches, as seems to be their intention.

The summons was delivered this morning – brought up to him by Eileen, the only housemaid they've retained – and lies now beside the door, where he tossed it after she had withdrawn. He has an interview in ten days, a mere month and three weeks since he was required to abandon what remained of his bolt-hole and the letters he was determined to write to the next of kin of his men – every one of them having been lost – and while the members of the Board may be aware that the swiftness of his evacuation was facilitated by the absence of any wound requiring surgery, or even a dressing, and are doubtless right to suppose that a man of his calibre ought by now to have regathered his wits, they would not have reckoned on the peculiarity of his condition, for which there is no recognised term, and which has developed only since his arrival in Blighty.

He ought to consult again with his doctor, before he submits to any examination, or even agrees to the interview. And certainly he ought to order more ointment, and pull on some clothes, since neither Eileen nor the cook will be amused by his nakedness, any more than will the nurses and orderlies, or the men who will soon be everywhere about the grounds, or indeed the pharmacist's daughter, Miss Dobson, whom he hopes will make the delivery.

Indeed, he will ask for her expressly; he may even invite her to stay and take tea with him. 'I am,' he will say, 'rather starved of civilised company.'

a source of raw and enduring embarrassment

In this part of the house, which has not yet been turned over to the authorities, Montague is very often alone – the cook and the housemaid excepted – since his sisters are themselves now serving in France, driving motor ambulances for the VADs, and Father is away at the Works, forever industrious, and Mother once again absent from her marriage and household – on this occasion, it seems, for the duration of the war, and certainly for as long as her home should be a hospital (which may or may not have been Father's intention).

But such is the nature of his parents' relations, and always has been, for as long as Montague can remember.

No matter the season, J. A. C. Beckwith & Son will be ever-demanding of Father's time and attention, and no matter the external cause, or how often it has happened before, his mother will have commenced her next slow decline, becoming increasingly listless, indecisive, distracted; and then she will be gone – to visit her sister in London, a cousin in Yorkshire, other relatives elsewhere (or so she will say) – usually to return several days, weeks or even months later, without ceremony or notice or explanation, but always appearing in some way rejuvenated, and even affectionate, if only temporarily.

As infants the children were raised in the main by their nurse and it was rare if ever that their mother should interrupt their routine in order to see them. They were to be presented to her for an hour each afternoon, and were to take their meals in the nursery until they were old enough to eat in the kitchen with the younger of the servants, and it wasn't until they'd achieved adolescence that they were permitted – which is to say required, against their private wishes – to dine with their parents, who barely conversed with each other, and certainly not with their children, though Father would sometimes subject them to a fusillade of questions – a test of their knowledge – as if he were a schoolmaster and their dining room a classroom.

They were expected to address him as 'sir', and accept his authority if he told them their answers were wrong, however much they might think they knew otherwise.

The girls were schooled by a succession of governesses, whereas Montague was dispatched first of all to a preparatory school in the next county from which he could return at the weekends, then enrolled in a more distant establishment, a highly reputable school for young gentlemen from which it was much less convenient to return – a situation that suited him perfectly – yet even after he had gone up to Cambridge and supposed himself a man, his father remained somewhat remote to him (as to them all) and should Montague ever have cause to visit him in the Works he had first to present himself to his father's secretary,

Mr Davey, a supercilious fellow in a swallowtail coat and stiff collar who smelt of cologne and had been with the firm since before the children were born and was apt to make Montague aware of this seniority by requiring the younger man to wait in a reception room while he enquired as to 'Mr Beckwith's present availability'.

Nevertheless, despite his prosperity and his standing in society, Montague's father is properly conscious of his humble antecedents and the company's modest beginnings and is inclined towards a Christian or democratic view of his workforce and servants – more so than is held by his wife, to be sure – and is content to believe that most of them are honest, diligent and loyal, possessed of their own share of dignity and entitled to some additional consideration besides the provision of stable employment, which is in itself of definite benefit not only to his employees, but to their dependants, the people in the immediate vicinity and, he will argue, the municipality more generally.

None of which his son would dispute.

Entire families across four generations have been employed in the Beckwiths' factories, many of them beginning straight from school as boy labourers and graduating to the men's list at eighteen and remaining then with the firm until they retire – all being well – when they will be provided with a pension and continuing access to the benefits of the company's sickness insurance scheme.

For this and other reasons, Montague remains proud of his future inheritance, since J. A. C. Beckwith & Son is in every respect a model employer, a first-rate firm, and the family no less considerate of its servants, who are obliged to work hard and to know their place and show every respect to their benefactors, but are rewarded twice in every year with a beano of some sort: a party on the lawn in the summer, providing the weather is suitable, and a dinner in the Guest Hall at Christmas, when there will be goose in addition to beef and pork and venison, as well as cakes, trifles and jellies, fruit punch, ale and even champagne, all of this served to them by Montague and his sisters as their parents circulate and make conversation, after which Mr Beckwith gives a speech of thanks and says a solemn prayer, then calls the servants forward one by one in order of seniority to accept a small gift from him while Mrs Beckwith and the children stand to one side and politely applaud them.

Such is one of several customs that Montague grew up with, and although he did come to understand some of his mother's distaste for it – which his sisters, who have the common touch, certainly did not – and always sensed that certain of the servants shared in her discomfort, he never presumed to question his father's judgement or show any sign of reluctance, but performed his duties as they were assigned to him and circulated with bottles and trays and replenished the drinks of gardeners and scullery-maids, until the summer at the start of the war, when every tradition and quirk of old England seemed more than ever worth cherishing, and he allowed the heat and his youth and a sharpened sense of life's urgency – as well as the informality of the occasion – to lead him to behave in a way that continues to smart in his memory, a source of raw and enduring embarrassment.

a soft, warm bundle beneath him

Always in the organisation of the Beckwith household there will be an under-housemaid assigned to sweep and dust in Montague's room when he is at home, and replenish his ewer and carafe, remake his bed, and clean the grate and lay the fire, if the season requires it, and typically this (and much more) will be done in his absence, mid-morning, some time after he has dressed, taken breakfast and greeted the day, so that he will have no idea as a rule which of the servants to thank for the tidier, more fragrant room he comes back to (and nor would he want to, or suppose that he should).

But that summer two years ago, when he was newly commissioned and still so flush with pride in himself – and having heard such tales in the officers' mess – he contrived to linger one morning upstairs, as he had promised his friend Wortley he would, and found that his maid was not only a young one, but nicely made too (though uncommonly small), and when she gave a yelp at finding him in the wicker chair behind the door, one booted foot resting on his knee and an Ordnance Survey map opened out on his lap, he couldn't help himself laughing, and smilingly apologised, then insisted she mustn't mind him – she must get on with her work – and was more than half surprised when she curtsied and did as she was told.

Montague folded the map and placed it neatly on the table beside him. He cracked his knuckles, hooked his hands behind his head, and managed for a few minutes to watch her, relishing a little her evident awkwardness, even enjoying the fact that he was able to cause such discomfort and provoke such pretty colouring simply by being there, but soon began to feel a little guilty too, a little small in his soul, and attempted to engage her in conversation, which didn't suit her, the replies to his questions being so very formal and stilted and unnatural. Nor did it suit him.

Her name, he learned, was Mabel, and she was happy in her work, and yes, she lived locally.

'Good,' declared Montague, slapping himself on each knee as he got to his feet, 'then I'm very pleased to have met you, Mabel. Don't let me disturb you a moment longer,' and picked up his map as he departed the room.

More than a fortnight went by before he saw her again, though on that occasion Montague's presence upstairs wasn't due to any contrivance on his part but the result of his drunkenness the evening before – which had lasted through most of the night – and Mabel happened to find him slumped in the armchair in his dressing room, apparently asleep and still wearing his braces, breeches and boots. The connecting door to his bedroom was open. His money was scattered all over the floor – shillings, sixpences, pennies, the paltry remainder of his latest attempt to prove himself a gambler – and Montague watched through half-open eyelids as she perfected the folds in his bedclothes, rear-ranged the flowers that his mother insisted they should have in every room in the summer, then knelt to gather his money – accentuating her shapeliness, the curve of her rump – and placed it in tidy piles on his chest of drawers, after which she appeared not to know what to do next, whether she ought to wake him, and how she might manage that. Tentatively she approached and gave a small cough, and was perhaps about to flee when he reached out and took hold of her arm.

She didn't resist him, but stood and looked obliquely across to the door – perhaps across to his bed – and in her docility he thought he detected something like acceptance, or even encouragement. He stroked around the bone of her wrist with his thumb, gazing at her slim, work-reddened hand, and found himself dreamily unable to distinguish between his own desires and hers and could not discern whether in her passivity there was a great yearning – a hope that he would draw her towards him, perhaps onto his lap – or merely a tolerance of his misuse of her, possibly even a fear of him. Then in a surge of self-disgust or self-reproach he let go and said, 'Thank you, Mabel,' with such finality that she departed at once, her head bowed, her heels curtly clicking on the boards.

She was angry; he didn't propose to ask himself why, since she was, after all, no more than a maid. He resolved to avoid the possibility of any further encounter, no matter how persistent she might be in his thoughts, and possibly he would have succeeded in this, given the imminence of his departure for France, but that the servants' summer party on the lawn came only a week or so later, to which a great number of local worthies were also invited, in addition to numerous of his fellow officers and a band recruited from his regimental barracks in town, and however much he hoped not to have to acknowledge her presence as he circulated with his bottles and tray, Montague found himself repeatedly looking in her direction, repeatedly found her looking back at him, until the awkwardness of this became intolerable and he attempted to slip away from the gathering but was intercepted by Edwina, the older of his two sisters, who placed him in charge of the drinks trestle, where he allowed himself several glasses of wine as he served and achieved such a state of pleasant inebriation that his scruples came to seem unnecessarily restrictive, even unpatriotic. The moment the band struck up a tune that he recognised he stepped smartly across to her – blind to any other possibility, or to what might be thought of him – and asked if she would care to dance.

Mabel blushed, most uncomfortable, and said nothing, quite passive, but he took her firmly by the hand and immediately she fell in with him.

She had a pretty smile. Montague noticed the soundness of her teeth, and the clarity of her eyes, and although she was sweating a little and her hand was quite moist she had no noticeable odour: she was healthy, and strong, despite her diminutiveness, and gradually as they turned in the sunshine, the grass spinning beneath them, she lost some of her shyness and complimented him on his uniform, asked about his forthcoming departure, and said several other things besides, none of which he would later remember, only that they had found a connection, an easy though breathless exchange of friendly remarks. When the music ended – two, perhaps three tunes later – he suggested she might want to recover from her exertions by resting a while in the cool of the Guest Hall, which would be empty, the french windows open to the terrace for air, and she said that she might, if that was allowed.

'Everything is allowed today, Mabel. This afternoon is entirely for your amusement and recreation. And the Guest Hall is as much at your disposal as the grounds.'

He made an extravagant gesture, and she nodded, her smile somewhat less certain.

'I suggest you make your way along there in minute or so, why not?' he added. Then, as casually as he was able, he strolled alone across the lawn, looking this way up to the sky – as if wondering at the prospect of rain – and that way across to the trees – as if noticing for the first time the peacocks that were nesting there – and tapped his thigh with one hand as his other hand sought out a pocket in his military breeches, then clasped both hands behind his back and strode briskly up to the house, relieved to be walking away from the party rather than towards it, since he was not only blushing but displaying the start of an erection.

Mabel came into the Guest Hall soon after him, and gave a loud gasp, seemingly flustered to find that he too was there, and made an effort to laugh off her surprise, pressing one hand flat to her chest and making a flapping motion in front of her face with the other, and perhaps it was the possibility that she had come there on a misunderstanding that hastened his behaviour, for he lost all sense of composure and attempted at once to embrace her, unprepared for her sudden cry, her evident fright.

Alarmed, Montague placed a firm hand over her mouth and gently shushed her, and as he eased her down onto a settee he realised his erection was pressing into her hip and hoped she would not recognise what it was, but feared too that she might. He braced himself on one knee and tried to lift himself away from her.

She was a soft, warm bundle beneath him – her eyes wide and startled, apparently uncomprehending – and breathing heavily, he took his hand from her mouth and pressed his lips against hers. Their teeth clicked together and she groaned, a rebuke, full of distaste. But he persisted, sinking heavily onto her, his erection now pressing into her belly, and still she resisted: she was furious. Very soon they were wrestling in earnest, his ears becoming hot where she was boxing him, and when at last he accepted that she would never willingly concede to him, he gripped her tightly by the wrists and forced her hands back against her shoulders and pressed himself hard into her groin through her skirts, arching his back as she contorted beneath him – her face twisted, determined – and was conscious in that moment only of wishing to cause her some pain since she had brought him to this and deserved to be punished.

But she wasn't going to scream, he realised; she wasn't going to bring that shame upon him, for which he ought to have been grateful. He should have apologised. Instead he pushed himself fiercely away from her, stumbling backwards, and shouted, 'Fine! Very well! You're afraid of me, a coward! I understand.' His shirt had come loose and he turned his back on her, tucked in his tails, and marched from the room. He went swiftly upstairs. Later, still angry, he masturbated into the lavatory.

8
Gertie

superior to most of their neighbours

The Dobsons, of course, are respectable, superior to most of their neighbours, and they are fortunate especially in having their own wash-house, their own copper and tap in a brick lean-to outside, where Dorothea is able to wash their undergarments in privacy and pass them through a mangle and hang them to dry in the yard, which thankfully they no longer need to share with Mr Edwards, the stonemason next door, who has latterly extended his premises as far down as the river and had a new water closet constructed behind one of his workshops, out of sight of the grieving sensibilities of most of his customers, and of the pharmacy, so that the Dobsons are now able to enjoy sole access to the existing privy, which formerly they shared not only with Mr Edwards and his family but with the men he employed.

They are fortunate in these amenities, but while Gertie's mother is hardly a drudge in the manner of most of the wives of Riverside Road – who age so quickly in marriage, and neglect their health and appearance and lose all pride in themselves, lose whatever sweetness of temper they might once have possessed, and sacrifice themselves to the burdens of childcare – still her domestic round appears to Gertie unending, a daily tax on her nerves and health and her energies, which nevertheless she refuses to share with her daughter, who is accustomed to drudgery from Beckwith's Academy, where household chores were part of the curriculum (and set, in addition, as punishments).

The Dobsons' coal-hole is situated at the end of the yard, and they have a ton at a time tipped into it, every hundredweight of which must be hauled up the stairs by Mother, two or three scuttles a day in the winter, and this in addition to the water she collects from the tap in the lean-to, a pail or two daily but much more at the weekends when she will take down the galvanised tub from the wall in the wash-house and carry it upstairs on her back, as if it were a turtle's shell, and place it by the hearth in the parlour, then fill it slowly with kettles, which is one chore at least that Gertie is allowed to assist in: her mother's hands shake so much when she is tired.

Father bathes on a Saturday, at the end of the week just concluded, while Gertie and her mother share some water on a Sunday, anticipating the week still to come, and afterwards, in either case, the water must be emptied into the sink in the kitchen, and the tub returned to its hook in the lean-to. All of which may be healthy – the physical exercise and the exposure to the fresher, cooler air of outdoors – but there is so much else that Mother must also attend to: coal grates to clean in every room; fire surrounds to blacklead; surfaces in need of scrubbing and polishing; meals to prepare; her husband to serve, his temper to manage.

From Gertie's perspective her mother is never at rest, always appears to be busy, even on their excursions to the pictures at the Alhambra (whose Wednesday variety bill always begins with a comedy, *the SPICE of the Programme*, and concludes with a serial, every episode ending with the heroine in a state of dire jeopardy) when she will bring along some mending for the intermission and some knitting to do in the dark for the troops, or else in the evenings at home when she will not only occupy her hands with her needles but somehow contrive to balance a book on her knees from which she will read aloud to her husband, who suffers from headaches and whose eyes by the end of the day cannot endure the strain of focusing on the printed word, or even on his wife. He will gaze into the grate, or up at the ceiling, or else lower his eyelids, but he will not look at Mother.

A kiss, perhaps?

Left alone now in the parlour, her parents downstairs in the pharmacy, Gertie pictures them as they will be this evening – as they will be most evenings – seated to either side of the hearth in their old armchairs, the coals unlit if the evening is fine but the wall mantles burning, the gas gently hissing and popping, which is often sufficient in summer to warm up this room and by whose light her mother is able to read the books of history and science that so interest her father (his particular concerns: the improvement of the race and the decline of past civilisations).

Gertie herself will not read, and if she attempts to listen her attention will wander. But though she is blind to the shape of letters and the spelling of words – as she is to the nature of numbers – she is gifted in many more practical ways and will occupy herself most evenings with some sewing or embroidery, often quite intricate, sitting on the settee facing the window and dreaming of a day when she might be allowed to bring a young man into their home, someone such as the Italian boy, for example, who will sit neatly beside her, his back straight and his hands on his knees, which will oblige Father, since they have a guest (a rare occurrence), to make conversation, assuming he is satisfied that the boy is decent, intelligent and physically able.

Gertie looks down on the Italian boy's head, his centre parting, the width of his shoulders, and decides he is all of these things, and that there can be no harm in joining his queue for an ice cream. The glass bowl on the mantelpiece will usually contain a few coins, small change for the hawkers who come by now and then, and hurriedly Gertie scoops out a clutch of pennies and checks herself in the mirror and even as she goes from the room she begins to anticipate the development of their courtship, for soon the boy will be old enough to enlist, and once the war has been won they will surely be allowed a measure of privacy – perhaps assuming the fireside chairs – and the boy will read to her in his Italian accent from books of poetry, she supposes, or from novels, though she can't think of any titles, and her imagination cannot extend far beyond the rudiments of this companionable scene.

A kiss, perhaps? Gertie is not sure, for she is nervous of the consequences, ignorant of what might follow it, where it might lead.

In Riverside Road, it is well known, there are girls of her age and younger who are already mothers, and this is one among many things that distinguishes them from people of her own class, their lack of decency and restraint, though restraint (it is her father's word) from what, precisely, she isn't quite clear. She has a notion, but the full facts are not known to her, and certainly she could never enquire of her mother, who would be flustered, embarrassed, or of her father, whose temper is sometimes thunderous and who would be scandalised even by her wishing to know.

A pregnant woman is easily distinguished by her belly, she understands, though how the baby gets out of the belly is another question that troubles her, and while she suspects that the mechanics of making the baby might be the same for people as for animals – the livestock on the market are an example – in that the private parts are involved, a certain physical intimacy, she wonders if love might also be a prerequisite in humans, and if kissing might be the expression of that, though here too she harbours some doubts for she cannot imagine there to be much love in the rougher homes on Riverside Road; she doesn't suppose there to be much in the way of fine feelings at all, and yet somehow they manage to multiply. They have very large families, much to the annoyance of Father.

At the foot of the stairs she steps into his storeroom and office, a slew of papers and books on the table, a strongly camphorous smell, and hears him conversing with Mother, the low sound of their voices. Glancing through the partition she finds the pharmacy for the moment quite empty – Father smoking a cigarette, Mother dusting a counter – and slips out by the back door, then

60

the side gate, and enters the high, wide passage to the side of their building, which gives access to the stonemason's yard for the carts that come up from the station.

Dank-smelling and dark, the passage resembles the underside of a bridge – the walls slick with wet; mice (she is sure) in the shadows – and lifting her skirt she hurries to the great double doors at the end, a fine shimmer of light outlining the smaller gate into the street. The latch is heavy, the hinges rusty, and as she steps through to the heat and clamour of Riverside Road a farmhand looks around and grins at her, touching the peak of his cap, his teeth a row of black stubs.

He too is waiting for ice cream, and despite the stench of him, Gertie behaves as though unaware he is there.

Here at the edge of the shop the display shelves are backed by stained glass, the interior hidden, and she turns to her reflection in the pharmacy window and confirms that her hair is in order, and her collar and buttons, then surreptitiously slides her gaze along the glass to the vendor, but momentarily she fails to find him: for an instant his face appears overlaid by another, the fleeting image of poor Walter Barley, his startling grey eyes, and Gertie lets out a gasp; she lifts her hand to her throat, for he must after all have returned.

A shiver runs through her, and she looks sharply around, but there is no one, just the usual scene of men passing left and right on the road, carts and horses and bicycles, and as she searches the various faces she decides this can't have been him, however close the resemblance, though why anyone else should have been staring at her in quite that way, and why he should then disappear, Gertie cannot imagine.

Tightly she clutches her coins and concentrates on the Italian boy and his marvellous barrow, which is painted up like a fairground ride, its wheels and panels glossed in red, white and green – the livery, she knows, of most things Italian. The rings on the barrel from which he scoops the ice cream are polished to a coppery sheen and the sun is sparkling from a glass cabinet in which are displayed several columns of upturned cornets and waffle cups and a pair of silver shakers for toppings – chocolate powder, perhaps, and hundreds-and-thousands, though they are bound to be empty: sweet things are now so expensive.

He doesn't seem aware of her, and as the queue edges forward she stares at him and confirms to herself that she prefers a large nose on a man, a boy – an Italian boy with just this one's dark eyes and smooth olive skin, his lean forearms and rolled-back sleeves and his way of presenting a cone with the merest of flourishes: a slight rotation of his wrist, his fingers delicately poised. And they are delicate fingers, refined, agile, slim. She is gazing at them when the farmhand departs and she finds herself at the front of the line with the boy regarding her as he might do any other customer – alert, at work, even a little impatient. She takes a breath before speaking, inflating her bosom and tilting her head, her lips moistened, but the boy speaks before she is ready.

'Cornet, is it?' he says, and his accent is exactly like hers, no Italian about him.

She nods, attempts to smile, and he takes a cone from the column.

'All right sort of day,' he says briskly.

'Yes,' she says.

'Close, though.'

'Yes.'

'Just the one scoop?' he asks, and digs into the barrel.

'Please,' she murmurs, and as she waits she realises she will be visible from this spot to her parents. She peers through the pharmacy window, preparing to wave, but finds that her father is occupied, her mother now gone back upstairs. 'No,' she says then, 'give me two cones.'

'Two cones?'

'Please. One scoop in each.'

A shadow of annoyance crosses his face, and he takes a second cone from his cabinet and delves again into the barrel, a glint of sweat on his forehead, a small frown. He mounds the ice cream onto the cone and turns to face her. 'That'll be two pennies, then,' he says, and accepts her moist coins in exchange for the cones, the same practised twist of the wrist – first one cone, then the other – but his eyes are already leaving her, looking to the next person in line.

Gertie hesitates, then mumbles her thanks and walks casually past him, as casually as her disappointment will let her, licking her soft ice cream and hoping, as she approaches the door to the pharmacy, preparing a smile for her father, that the boy gets his wheel stuck in a tramline, just like that other one she saw, two summers before, the tram bearing down on him, sounding its bell, and the vendor flushed in the face and unable to shift his handcart in time. She hopes this befalls the boy with the big nose, his fancy barrow smashed to smithereens – if he isn't conscripted, as he ought to be, if Fritz doesn't get to him first.

9

Dobson

a chemist of great experience

Even now, in 1916, and no matter that he has been trading from
these premises since the start of the century – his reputation
established, his clientele fixed and dependable, his income steady
in spite of the war – the pharmacist Dobson has put himself to
the expense of a full-page advertisement in Kelly's local *Directory*
and in the *County Almanack*, and has reproduced this as a hand-
bill for dissemination by the distributors of the *Advertiser*, and
has placed a framed copy in his shop window, and while the
details have been amended from previous announcements to
take account of some additions to his veterinary and general
lines, the wording remains much as he composed it in his fourth
year of business and is, he is satisfied, an exemplary text of its
kind:

> *Invention and Science have long been conjoined in the task
> of devising new means of alleviating human suffering,
> whether by Medicinal Remedy or Mechanical Appliance.
> For those with an interest in the subject a visit to Mr Claude
> Dobson's Family, Veterinary & Dispensing Chemist will be
> most instructive. Situated at the junction of Riverside Road
> and Cattle Market Street, this is a business-like Establishment
> in direct proximity to the Cattle Market and Corn Hall. The
> interior is well fitted up, and a large stock of proprietary
> articles is kept, including vigorous and effective Tonic
> Stimulants, Patent Medicines, and Pure Drugs and Chemical*

Extracts in both liquid and powdered form. Among the **noted preparations** *are several compounded on the premises, such as 'Dobson's Medicated Lozenges', 'Dobson's Quinine and Bark Pills', and 'Dobson's Ointment for Rectal Disorders'. Most conspicuous among Mr Dobson's specialities ranks the preparation of remedies for* **female ailments,** *such as those for the treatment of neurasthenic conditions accompanied by sleep loss, headache, indigestion and general fatigue. Mr Dobson prepares his own highly effective specific for vomiting in pregnancy, and his pills to maintain* **monthly regularity** *are supposed by many to be the equal of any more celebrated brand. The dispensing department receives Mr Dobson's particular attention, and all physicians' prescriptions and family recipes are promptly and accurately compounded of the* **purest ingredients.** *In the provision of appliances for almost every form of weakness or defect, Mr Dobson also does a significant business. Notable here is a large stock of Trusses and Supportive Bandages, Ladies' and Gentlemen's Abdominal Belts, Elastic Stockings for Varicose Veins, &c., besides Appliances for the Nursery and Sickroom, such as Inhalers, Bed Pans, Urinals, Enema Apparatus, Waterproof Sheeting, &c. In its proximity to the Cattle Market, Mr Dobson's Establishment is a centre of great activity on market days, and a significant* **veterinary** *trade is conducted in the supply of Ointments, Condiments, Draughts, Powders and Dips for pigs, sheep, horses and cattle. Recently added items to the stock include Elastrator Rubber Rings for Castration and Gostling's Veterinary Embrocation for All Livestock. The business is an important one, with farmers and others availing themselves of the opportunity to lay in supplies, and among sundry additional articles to be found here are Tooth Powders and Pastes, Hair Dressings, Stain Removers, Pest Killers, Straw Hat Revivers, Deodorants and Disinfectants, Bath Crystals and Soaps, Turkey Sponges, Colognes and Perfumes, &c. Mr Dobson is* *a chemist of **great experience**, whose Establishment has gained a wide popularity, and he merits the **confidence** and **respect** of all social classes.*

But while there is no doubt that he deserves the esteem of all social classes, in truth it is rare that Claude Dobson attracts the custom of any ladies or gentlemen with the leisure to be curious about science and invention, and despite his private correspondence with Montague Beckwith on matters of eugenical science, and his recent fulfilment of two personal orders from Captain Beckwith for Dobson's Soothing Lotion (Antiseptic & Healing), and the apparent adoption of his daughter as a favoured companion by the Misses Beckwith, the contract to supply dressings and medicines to the workforce dispensary at Beckwith's Engineering, for instance, went not to Mr Claude Dobson's Family, Veterinary & Dispensing Chemist, but to Wm. Scotland & Sons of City Parade, a less proximate though far grander establishment with branches in Osgood's and Rossiter's and well-advertised connections to all the leading families of the city and county, including the Beckwiths.

Which still rankles, four years since it was settled, and while the establishment of an auxiliary hospital in the grounds of Beckwith House has already resulted in one substantial order for gauzes, plasters and bandages, and may yet result in more, the popularity of his pharmacy remains highly circumscribed socially, barely extending beyond the likes of his market-day visitors and the many inhabitants of Riverside Road and its crowded environs, among whom he is more trusted and more readily consulted – and more affordable, his consultations being free – than any general practitioner.

Claude Dobson dispenses the medicines, and sells the appliances; he also diagnoses the ailments that require them.

every trouble imaginable

The environment alongside the river is hardly a healthy one, and the people do suffer a great many ailments, for they are most of them poor and eat badly and drink to excess and live – to his mind – insanitary, incontinent lives. They procreate without thought, without sense or restraint, and condemn their unwelcome and unfortunate offspring to years of malnourishment, and sometimes mistreatment, dressed often in rags and prone to coughs and colds in every season – their noses invariably crusted, their sleeves used as handkerchiefs – and not only colds but any number of other afflictions, for they are prone, in fact, to every trouble imaginable.

They come to him with ringworm and head lice, laryngitis, bronchitis, eczema and asthma, diarrhoea, constipation, biliousness and jaundice, carbuncles and boils, broken bones; all of these, but also much graver conditions, including measles, meningitis, whooping cough, typhus, influenza, diphtheria, scarlet fever, tuberculosis, the rest.

He has nostrums for most of these things; he does what he can for them, and does what he can for the mothers, whose notion of their own good health is so often no more than the gap between illnesses, or merely the illness that is supportable – that doesn't obstruct them from getting through the chores that must be got through in a day – and among his particular skills, he believes, is never to allow a female customer to feel she is making a fuss about nothing, and if she appears shy of referring to certain parts of her body, then he is able to supply the words for her, often euphemistically, often going some way around the houses, but in the end arriving at an understanding.

He is most adept at disguising his impatience, and sometimes distaste, even disgust, and has as a consequence become especially well known for his sympathetic understanding (or so he hopes it must appear to them) of female infirmities, the list of which is unending: the discharges and vague, unspecified discomforts, the backaches and headaches so frequent they are accepted almost as normal, the constipation and haemorrhoids, flatulence and heartburn, the missed, heavy or irregular menses, the kidney and bladder infections, cystitis, nephritis, rheumatism, arthritis, weight gain and weight loss, gallstones and gout, mastitis, tonsillitis, eye strain and toothache, palpitations, phlebitis, ulcerative legs, hot flushes, water retention, and the general weariness and depression of the spirits that are so common among them (and no wonder).

In pregnancy especially the women will come to him, anaemic and listless, undernourished and unable to discharge their bowels, plagued by aches and pains of every description, their legs ropy with varicose veins, ankles puffy with fluid, and some of them so poor – or so self-neglectful, or so lacking in the maternal instinct, or so bone-tired of maternity – that they will suffer a diet of bread and tea throughout their pregnancies and thus give birth to weak and underweight babies with no chance in life but to die young (or to live, which is worse, as burdensome invalids).

After which many of the mothers will present the ailments that are consequent upon childbirth, the prolapses and tears and persisting anaemia, the constipation that cannot be remedied so long as they haven't the time to establish the habit, and above all the insomnia and related physical and nervous exhaustion, their beds being shared not merely with husbands (who are frequently drunk, if they haven't yet enlisted or been conscripted) but with various of their other children, including the nursing, colicky infants who were so recently born there, all of them huddled beneath inadequate coverings in damp, unaired rooms that are rarely quiet, the walls being so thin and the neighbourhoods so very noisy.

No wonder, then, that the women (and sometimes their husbands) should also come to him in the hope of relief from the burden of childbearing, whether before or after the fact of conception.

a short, scruffy fellow

The time is now approaching a quarter past two. The minute hand on the clock in the corner gives a click as it jerks forward and Dobson notices that certain drawers in the drug run are open and pushes them properly closed with a fingertip, and places a pestle back in its mortar, and corrects the hang of a display card of nail-files and the orientation of a case of colognes, and when he is satisfied that all is in order he takes a long drag on his cigarette and considers the letter he has been writing to Montague Beckwith and wonders if he might now slip out to review it, since trade has become so uncommonly slow, but then the brass bell above the door rocks on its spring as Gertie comes into the shop, its clatter discordantly chiming with the quarter-strike of the clock, and Dobson accepts without comment the ice cream she presents to him; he permits her to place it between his forefinger and thumb and holds it as though temporarily, as if expecting her to take it away again, and when he sees that she's uncertain, concerned she may have done wrong, he allows her something close to a smile and quietly says, 'Thank you,' as he picks up the end of his smouldering cigarette and stubs it out in an ashtray around whose rim runs an advertisement for Kay's Linseed Compound for Coughs, Colds and Bronchial Affections. The ashtray is an old one, and full. He clears his throat. 'Have you eaten?' he asks, for on a Saturday their meals tend to be makeshift.

'I've had some soup,' she offers, and lowers her ice cream as though thinking she ought to conceal it. 'What was left over from yesterday. When I got in . . .'

'*Which* was left over,' he says.

'*Which* was, yes.'

'I didn't see you,' he says.

Her eyes cloud; she frowns.

'I didn't see you come in,' he clarifies. 'Earlier. I must have been busy.'

69

'Oh, yes, you were,' she says. 'There were people all the way out to the street.' Gertie gestures behind her, a vague wave of her hand. 'Mother saw me, though. She came up and cleaned my *war wounds*.' Gertie smiles and shows him the raw skin on her knuckles.

'As long as you've eaten,' says Dobson, and tastes his ice cream as he walks across to the door, his boots creaking on the boards. He releases the catch on the blind and looks to his left down Riverside Road – beyond the Eyetie and his painted-up barrow – then right into Cattle Market Street, where he sees a number four tram approaching a group of idling farmhands, the top deck crammed with young matrons in boaters, their infants in frilly white bonnets.

The tram's bell must be sounding, though from here he can't hear it: startled, apparently laughing, the farmhands abruptly disperse and Dobson's gaze drifts up the hill to the acre of sheep by the Corn Hall, then down past the sale rings, the pig pens and cattle enclosures, and alights for a while upon a scholar and his mother, who are descending the central aisle of the market, the boy wearing a mortar board and his mother a hat resembling a pith helmet, her gloved hand in the hook of his arm, a furled umbrella slanted over her shoulder.

It would seem they are sightseeing, enjoying the spectacle, and as he follows their progress Dobson notices brawny Jack Edwards playing with some much younger boys outside the Turf Tavern, a couple of them wielding long sticks from the cow whacking, experimentally whipping him while the drinkers by the tavern cheer them on.

The same age as Gertie, and built for hard labour, Silly Jack Edwards has the mentality of a small child, his speech worse than a deaf-mute's, though he can certainly hear, and respond to instructions: given a task to perform, he will set to at once and become like a pantomime of a man, all self-importance and cack-handed show, though what he likes best, it would seem, is thoughtless rough-and-tumble, to play the donkey for three smaller, sharper boys, and doubtless it would have been better if he hadn't been born, though his genes at least are unlikely to survive him: so far as girls are concerned, he appears oblivious.

'Where's Mother?' asks Gertie.

Dobson lowers his blind. 'Hmm?'

'Mother.'

'Upstairs, I should think.'

Gertie licks her ice cream; Dobson licks his. The minute hand clicks forward a notch. 'Isn't it *quiet* now, though?' says Gertie. 'When is it ever this quiet on a Saturday?'

'It shan't last,' says Dobson. The time is now twenty-two minutes past two. 'Though yes, it is unusually quiet.'

'Perhaps they've all gone up to the station.'

Dobson confirms the accuracy of his pocket watch against the clock and resumes his place at the counter. 'And why would they do that?' he asks.

'To see the soldiers coming back.'

'No,' says Dobson, 'I doubt that,' and feels a sudden pique of irritation at Gertie, her loitering presence and the appetite with which she's consuming her ice cream: it has melted onto the side of her hand and around the inside of her wrist. 'No,' he confirms, 'the train isn't due in until this evening, and they won't be coming *back*, Gertie, not necessarily. They may not be local men, and they may not be in the best of condition.'

She nods; she licks her ice cream. 'But some of them may be? Local, I mean.'

'Perhaps.'

'Some of the ones who are supposed to be missing?'

'Missing?' he says, and flinches a little as she licks herself clean, then notices that there are drips of ice cream on her dress, too, and on the floorboards, and testily says, 'Gertie, be careful.' He reaches under the counter for a piece of old flannel and flaps it towards her.

But something has snagged her attention. Wide-eyed, alarmed, she is looking across to the window, to where a short, scruffy fellow has cupped his hands to the glass and is peering in through a gap between the carboys and specie jars, seemingly staring straight at them. 'Upstairs now, please, Gertie,' says Dobson, and dunks the last of his ice cream in the ashtray, then tips the ashtray into a rubbish pail and wipes his hands on the rag. 'I suggest you change out of that dress.'

His daughter hesitates.

'At once,' he says, and she appears almost to curtsy as she hurries past him, though she can't resist pausing on the threshold to the back room and looking over her shoulder as the shop door opens and the bell begins jangling. The smells of the market rush in with the sunshine. 'Upstairs and change,' repeats Dobson, and she goes.

Electricity has yet to arrive at the pharmacy. The interior is illuminated by gas mantles and a single naked flame, which is always alight, softly combusting at the blackened end of a narrow-gauge pipe behind the dispensary counter, and as the short fellow shuts the door after him he blinks exaggeratedly, makes a show of scanning the cabinets and shelves, as though looking to remind himself of what it was that he came for, and when he has completed his survey of the displays and has no excuse but to present himself at the counter, Dobson quietly says, 'Good afternoon.'

The man swallows, and glances towards the back room. His face is flushed, though Gertie has now disappeared: Dobson heard her heavy tread on the stairs.

'How may I help you?'

The man's gaze shifts to the counter, and flits to a card of infant comforters, then lifts to Dobson's beard – though only as far as his beard. 'A packet of preventives, please,' he says.

'A dozen?'

'Eh?'

'Twelve at two and six?'

'Yes.'

Dobson nods and takes a key from his waistcoat pocket, with which he unlocks the drawer nearest his right hand, and takes out a box of prophylactics, then lifts with his left hand a brown-paper bag from the stack on the counter and slips the box into the bag and performs a swift, complex fold of the opening to make it secure. The man has prepared the exact money. He drops the warm coins into the pharmacist's palm and delays for a moment, as Dobson confirms that the sum is correct, then turns without a word and promptly makes for the door, shoving the package into his pocket, but seems for a second uncertain whether to push or pull to get out, and is obliged to step aside to allow someone else to come in, and ducks and is gone.

Which is just as he behaved, Dobson remembers, on each of the three previous occasions that he came into the shop. He has never visited on any other business.

10
Walter

their famous humanity

Walter knows the Beckwiths quite well, though they do not appear to know him and would never condescend to acknowledge him, for all their famous humanity. Which is anyway a sham, in Walter's experience, and it galls him that locally they might almost be taken for royalty, such is the esteem in which they are held, including the daughters, Edwina and Emma, who would come along Riverside Road most Sabbath-day mornings, heading for the Congregationalist chapel in town, and minutely incline their heads to the doffed caps, and even curtsies, of the respectable men and women in their Sunday-best clothing, who lined the pavements and stood on their doorsteps in anticipation of the trap trotting by, the children waving, the Misses Beckwith indulgently smiling.

Latterly they even invited Gertie Dobson to sit up alongside them, one of many conspicuous kindnesses they extended towards her.

But then the Beckwiths are known to take seriously their obligations to those less fortunate than themselves, which includes not only this daughter of a pharmacist, and those scores of families whose well-being depends upon a father's continuing employment in the Works across the river, but also the deserving elderly, widowed or abandoned, and the needy and distressed, all of whom benefit from the Beckwiths' generosity, as do so many other noteworthy causes, such as the school for young ladies and orphans that Gertie attended until the age of fourteen and from which

Beckwith House is supplied with most of its servants – Mabel Barley included – or the annual outing for the crippled and poor children of St Cuthbert's Sunday School, which at one time would have meant Walter himself.

And the great sadness of it – or so it appears to him now – is that such a mean jamboree did work its trick on him, and while he didn't go, as some others did, to two, three, and even four different Sunday Schools in order to qualify for the additional outings that were the children's incentive and reward for regular attendance, he nevertheless looked forward to that annual excursion as the highlight of his year, it being the greatest excitement in his young life to be given the opportunity to stand on the scrubbed flat-bed of a coal-cart and set off down Riverside Road with as many as half a dozen other carts, each one bedecked in bluebells and gorse and the children as clean as they would be all year, in clothes as smart as could be mustered – newly patched, mended and washed – the girls with ribbons in their hair, the boys with flowers pinned to their jackets, and every one of them chorusing hymns as the heavy old horses plodded along, their harnesses also prettified with ribbons and flowers, stoical in their humiliation at the hands of these children, to a field in the grounds of the Beckwith estate where the peacocks would be strutting about and some flags and bunting would have been put out to denote the festive import of the occasion. There the children would be jollied to participate in many a clean, competitive pursuit in the fresh air – racing, leapfrogging, jumping, tagging – after which, all breathless and aglow, they would sit down to a feast of bread and butter, gooseberries and lemonade, the refreshments provided by the Beckwiths, who also paid for the hire of the coal-carts and the horses, before finally the children would gather on the forecourt of the great house, some of them clutching pretty peacock feathers to take home to their mothers and all of them facing the vicar, Reverend Brown, who would conduct them as they sang through their repertoire of hymns, Mr Beckwith himself coming out to the steps, smiling in his morning suit and tie, to join his wife and daughters and several of their servants while Montague looked down, expressionless, from some upper window.

But they did not know Walter. However enthusiastically he beamed at the Beckwiths – chin up, chest out – they gave no indication that they recognised his face among those other choristers. And yet from the age of eleven until he was almost thirteen Walter Barley was in their employ, beginning work at six thirty each morning, when he would present himself at a side door to their home, knock lightly – for he'd been advised that he was expected and wasn't to make a disturbance – then be required to wait, whatever the weather, until the door opened just wide enough for one of the maids to hand out the pair of heavy iron keys that allowed him access to the higgledy-piggledy rear of the house, first passing the shuttered french windows of the drawing room, then skirting the white-framed conservatory with its ferns as tall as trees, and entering the kitchen courtyard through a tiny gate half hidden in the dark of a yew hedge.

The first key opened the gate and the second the door to the scullery where he would find the boots and shoes he was required to take away and polish, presented in neat pairs along the perimeter of that cool, green-painted room, which smelt always of flour and scouring powder, and if the cook, kitchen-maid or any other servant should happen to be about they would barely acknowledge him, and certainly would not allow him to linger. He was to gather up the shoes and carry them across the courtyard, around past the Beckwiths' ice house and under the stone arch that led to their garage and stables, where he would find Mr Smith, the chauffeur-cum-groom, polishing, mending or smoking, but no more willing to speak to him than the servants in the house.

Smith wasn't a talker. He might greet Walter with a nod, but that would be all. He would finish his cigarette and get on with his work, and Walter would be expected to get on with his.

There was a stool for him, and a polishing kit that included a bone-handled knife, and what he liked best was to tackle a pair of Montague's mud-encrusted rugby boots, scraping away at the dry, fibrous dirt, knocking out clumps of it, though this was only ever an occasional treat since Montague spent so much of the year at his college, he wasn't often at home, and most of the other shoes hardly required Walter's attention. His task was merely to polish the polish, or increase the shine on a shine, which was, he came to understand, the privilege of the well-to-do, to demand such superfluous labour from the needy in return for their charity. Which in Walter's case amounted to a shilling a week, plus breakfast, such as it was.

Walter wasn't a big boy, and never would be big, since none of his family was capable of stature, but he did have an appetite, and every morning that he spent at the Beckwiths' he would find himself disappointed when he returned to the scullery and was presented by the kitchen-maid with a pewter pot – old and battered – of sweet weak tea and a single slice of bread and scrape: margarine, never butter. Often he woke hungry, and arrived hungry to work, and despite this breakfast he would have to leave hungry too, running the half-mile to his school on a near-empty stomach and frequently receiving two strokes of the cane for his lateness.

But then he had so many other chores to complete in addition to shining the family's footwear; he was to do whatever the cook or the gardener required of him, whether that meant scouring the burned base of a saucepan, picking snails from the lettuce bed, sweeping the courtyard, or cleaning peacock droppings from the lawn, and when Montague was at home he would be kept busier still, collecting the debris from beneath the cherry trees, for instance, after the young master, so-called, had spent an afternoon taking pot-shots with a pistol at the birds who came to feed on the fruit, or worse – the most unpleasant of all the jobs he was given – scrubbing out the dovecote in the summer of 1911 when Montague was seized by an enthusiasm for

77

breeding pigeons and recording the variations in their colouring and size.

On a Saturday Walter would ordinarily work from eight until noon and all through that summer his last task of the week was to carry down a pail of disinfectant and begin with the perches where the birds roosted, scraping their mess to the boards and sweeping the mess from the boards to a dustpan, then emptying out the nesting boxes and feed-trays and washing down everything, the birds cooing and skittering and giving him the creeps. He would clean that stinking loft, and work up not only an appetite but a temper and perhaps reward himself with a small addition to his wage – an egg or two to sell on to a neighbour at a ha'penny each – then go along to the scullery and find his shilling lying on the window ledge with the key to the gate, and after he had locked up and returned the key to the maid at the side door he would take his hunger directly to Gaudio's fish and chip shop on Riverside Road to buy a penn'orth of chips before heading home to present his mother with the change. She didn't complain about the missing penny.

Walter often found he was peckish, and that in the end was his undoing, for at the rear of the house the upper windows had white slatted blinds and while he couldn't see in, he was doubt-less visible to his employers, who got up at a regular hour, and if he could hear them – the running water, the drawers and cupboard doors, the voices – they would surely be able to hear him too and might perhaps look out as he was stealing an apple or some cherries from the trees, or picking peapods from the vegetable garden, or reaching into the gardener's greenhouse, where there were tomatoes and ripening bunches of grapes. Possibly Montague also kept a tally of the eggs he expected to find in the dovecote. Walter had no idea what they had seen, or which of them had seen it, but one particular Saturday when he went to pick up his wages the cook was waiting for him, her fat arms folded beneath her big bosom, over which she stared down at him with a face as pink as a salmon, holding in one tightly clenched fist the shilling she would drop into his hand after telling him he need not come back because the family were most distressed by his pilfering and he should think himself fortunate that the matter would not be reported to the police.

And really he didn't much mind. He had done enough for them, and taken more than enough strokes of the headmaster's cane as a consequence, and was glad at last to be out of it. He began work as Orford's errand boy the following week, and didn't need to present himself again at Beckwith House for almost four years, by which time he was working for Cyril Greenland, delivering ice that day to the gentry, and it was Gertie Dobson, not some maid, who answered the door to his tentative knock, and stepped out as smartly as if she had been waiting all that while for him.

11
Gertie

she once almost drowned

Up in her bedroom beneath the steep pitch of the roof Gertie sits on the edge of her bed and placidly watches a fly, black and iridescent green, repeatedly butting the lower pane of the window, sounding increasingly impatient and cross, and idly wonders why it doesn't realise the top sash is wide open, and supposes it must be because the air is so still, so stiflingly warm: there isn't a breeze to carry the scent of outdoors, nothing to entice the fly upwards and over.

The noise of it makes her feel weary, and hot, and she puffs out her cheeks and loosens the top of her dress, then flaps her collar a little in the hope of fanning her face but catches a faint whiff of the factory, a sour male industrial smell of metal and grease, and decides she really ought to change into something else, as her father suggested; she has been wearing this dress now for a week and besides being smelly it is noticeably dirty, blotched with oil and paraffin and all the things she's been eating, including her ice cream.

Slowly she unfastens her buttons, gazing beyond the fly to the darkening blue of the horizon – which suggests a storm may be coming – and when she reaches her waistband she stands and wriggles her shoulders, pulls her arms free, and allows the dress to fall to her ankles. She steps out of the bundle and draws her petticoat over her head, lets that drop too, and then in her under-wear, her all-in-one combinations, she takes from her wardrobe the first of several frocks that she saves for the weekend, all of them given to her by Edwina and Emma – the Misses Beckwith – this one a pretty afternoon dress in white cotton with an over-bodice of white voile, to which she once added (at Emma's request) a trim of embroidered white lace. She lays it delicately down on the bed, fearful that her hands, which are so sweaty, might leave a mark on the fabric, then selects from her top drawer a pair of white cashmere stockings – another gift from the sisters – and places these over the dress, precisely where her legs would be, and sits back on the edge of the bed to take off her boots and roll down the dark woollen stockings she's been wearing since Wednesday, which are crusty with dirt and dried sweat at the toes – and in need of some darning, she sees – and uses these to wipe the dust from her boots before bundling them into a ball and dropping them onto the pile on the floor.

She scratches herself. Her garters have left pink indentations around the mottled white of her thighs, and as she stands she tugs straight the legs of her combinations to cover them. Barefoot and bare-armed, she feels a little cooler, somewhat carefree, and skips along the side of her bed to the window and tugs up the top sash, then the lower one, so that the bluebottle may make its escape. Still furiously buzzing, it jinks and dips and is gone.

Gertie smiles through a yawn. She wipes a pearl of sweat from under her eyebrow and rests her forearms on the windowsill and leans out to look at the river. The sun is sparkling on the silky green surface and she notices two men in a boat, bent over, just drifting along, presumably at the end of a sprint or a race, though they don't appear to have any competitors. They are kitted out in the maroon and white stripes of the rowing club, and shading her eyes she tries to determine the age of them but they are too far away, beginning to dissolve in the glitter of the sun on the water.

She once almost drowned; the shimmer on the river reminds her.

It is different now, but in previous years she and her mother would spend a few days at the seaside – escorted there by her father, who wouldn't remain – which was one more of those things that set the Dobsons apart from their neighbours, for whom a half-day excursion in a rowing boat hired at sixpence an hour might be as much as they could afford, the poor father heaving his family perhaps a mile or so into the countryside, the children waving to the yachts and lighters, steamboats and barges that would have to navigate round them, a picnic or a pub at the end of it. Gertie herself would wave to the rowing boats. The train that conveyed them to their resort ran alongside the river.

Every year they lodged in the same establishment, a boarding house at the top of the strand called the Madeira, where their landlady was respectable and would oblige them with meals if they supplied the provisions, and run a bath on Thursday evenings if they paid sixpence extra. With Dorothea and Gertie securely installed, Dobson would leave on the evening train and come back to collect them at the end of the week, by which time the air and the exercise and sometimes the sunshine would have begun to show in their faces, Gertie's especially, though her mother always complained it was the carbolic in the soap that was burning their complexions (at home they used Sunlight, since it was stocked by the pharmacy and advertised on a tin hoarding beneath their parlour window: *Used all over the Civilised World*, it said – everywhere except the Madeira).

Their room was clean and spacious at least, and opened onto a balcony that looked down on the beach and a cluster of creosoted shacks from which ice creams and teas could be bought and bathing huts hired, including some machines that could be wheeled into the sea, and most mornings Gertie would be sent to amuse herself on the sands while her mother retired to the balcony to 'recuperate' or 'convalesce' – though from what, she never specified – after which they might attend a free concert on the pier, or take a tour in a charabanc, or wander through the Winter Gardens, admiring the tropical plants and the skaters. Such was their routine for most of those summers, until at last

Gertie persuaded her mother to buy her a costume and hire one of the machines so that she too could go into the water.

Gertie wasn't a swimmer, of course, and didn't intend to wade any further than the depth of her knees, and though she recalls much of what happened, the interval between the first cold lick of the waves and the sight of the crab-boat that came to her rescue is now lost to her, entirely gone from her memory.

She remembers the mangy backside of the mule that drew her machine down to the shore, and the coarseness of the rope that she gripped at the top of the steps, then the glint of the sun on the sea, which was mesmeric and blinding, and the warmth of the afternoon breeze on her face and bared shins. But the hush of the waves was like the native sound of her thoughts, and perhaps she lost her place then, forgot where she was, since the next thing she recalls is her panic in the water, and the belly of the boat looming over her, then the faces of the two white-bearded fishermen who were reaching to grab her.

She remembers the weight of the blanket they draped her in, and the creak of their oars, then the sight of her mother's fraught face as they came up to the shore. But most persistent of all is her memory of the small crowd of onlookers who gathered on the tideline to applaud her rescuers, and the interested expression of one particular gentleman – dressed in a boater, stiff collar and spats – who quipped something to the fishermen as they lifted her onto the sand, then threw back his head and laughed at whatever they replied to him, and how mysterious this seemed to her, the evident difference in the men and yet the understanding between them, which she supposed would always elude her.

a sombre, murmurous gathering

From below in the stonemason's yard comes the sound of men's voices and Gertie leans a fraction further out to look down – as

83

far as she dares in her underwear – but the slope of the roof is against her and she draws back inside.

Her view from this window is limited to the lower end of the stonemason's premises and the mossy glass panes of his carving shop, which appears now to be empty of workmen – though not of their statues, submerged in the green-tinted shade – and the various pantiled shelters where Mr Edwards stores the great blocks of stone that come down from the station and require two, sometimes three heavy horses to transport them and must be offloaded using grips and chains and a movable gantry, besides a great deal of sweating and swearing, after which they will need to be sawed into smaller, more workable blocks, a dusty, back-breaking task that requires the stonemason's men to strip to their vests, and sometimes even their waists.

Gertie has watched them, her interest drawn most of all by the presence of Sammy and Fred, the stonemason's two eldest sons, who were at one time apprenticed to the business but are now fighting in France.

She sits on her bed and crosses her legs to pull on her clean stockings and supposes they will be the crack shots of their regiment, cheerfully picking off the Germans in their spiked helmets as though at a funfair – which is how Sammy, smartly attired in his newly issued khaki, described the shooting range they had set up in their attic, just the other side of the wall from her fireplace, a space as long as a school hall or a gymnasium, he said, in which there were drawing boards, easels, all the paraphernalia of the draughtsman's workshop, and where he and his brother practised their marksmanship by hunkering down at the far end of the room with an air-rifle and a packet of pellets and taking pot-shots at a candle they had placed on the mantelpiece. They aimed to put out the flame, he said, and they succeeded, more often than not. 'Good enough to win the coconut,' he smiled.

Gertie said she had heard them from her bedroom, a sharp *clack* followed by a soft thud, a noise she'd found startling at first, but was by then getting used to.

'Well, don't worry,' said Sammy, tugging on his nose, speaking confidentially into his hand, 'they'll be shipping us out soon – you won't be hearing it much longer.'

This was also a Saturday, almost exactly one year ago, and they were attending a function to mark the installation of a telephone in Mr Edwards's display room, the first extension in their locality. 'Shipping you where?' asked Gertie.

'To France,' he said.

'To fight?'

'I shouldn't wonder. I can't think why else, can you?'

Gertie clasped her hands together and brought them up to her face and pressed her mouth to her knuckles. She lifted herself onto her toes, then dropped back on her heels.

Her excitement seemed to amuse him. Several inches taller than she was, he stooped and made a quizzical show of observing her face, his interest teasingly exaggerated, and she almost laughed then, but swallowed, and when at last she had calmed herself he privately smiled and straightened and looked across the room to where his brother was standing, also in uniform, conspicuously polished and upright in the company of their neighbours, most of them tradesmen. Surrounded by headstones and effigies, gargoyles and bits of fancy ecclesiastical carving, it was a sombre, murmurous gathering, in which only Mr Edwards, with his usual funereal air, and Gertie's father, with his perpetually dour expression, seemed remotely as comfortable as the two soldiers.

The stonemason was standing a few paces distant, and Gertie marvelled at his ugliness, especially compared to his sons – his elongated jaw and slack mouth, the stumps of his lower teeth always on show, and the heavy-lidded slant of his eyes, as if the bones in his cheeks had collapsed and everything else had subsided. Gertie's mother, she knew, could not abide him and sometimes shuddered when he went by. He made her think too much of the grave, she said.

Sammy touched Gertie's elbow and she gave a small start. 'I'm wondering,' he said, 'have you seen our workshops, Gertie?'

She blushed, and shook her head, though she had tried many times to see into them, and not only from her bedroom window but from her parents' room too, as well as the kitchen, which required her to stand on a chair.

'Would you like me to show you?'

'Show me?' she said.

'Yes,' he said blandly, 'you might find it interesting.'

'I'm not sure,' she said, since she knew a young woman ought to appear reticent, however much she might want to go with him – at least to begin with – and as she thinks back to it now Gertie finds she is blushing again, her hands and underarms clammy, sweat streaking her spine.

Sammy crooked an arm for her. 'Shall I give you a tour of the lettering shop, Miss Dobson?'

'Why?' she asked. 'What's there?'

'Lettering,' he said; then softly pressed her: 'We might not have another opportunity, you know.'

Gertie frowned – comprehension came slowly – then realised she could not refuse him, since soon he would be gone, perhaps never to return, and was about to accept his invitation when she heard her father pronouncing her name.

'Gertie.'

And that was all, no particular inflection, no hint of a warning or rebuke, and nothing in his expression, which remained flatly inscrutable behind his grey beard, but she understood – with some relief – that she was to let go of Sammy's arm; she was to come back and stand instead with her father. Which Sammy understood, too, for after a few moments he worked his way across the display room towards Fred, and surreptitiously she watched them conferring, heads bowed and grinning, until their younger brother Jack, the imbecile, appeared behind them and reached his arms round their uniformed shoulders, puffed up with the occasion, which was when her father thanked Mr Edwards for the interesting demonstration, and guided Gertie back to the pharmacy, seemingly satisfied, even quite cheerful.

Gertie pats her flushed cheeks. She stands to examine herself in her mirror and makes a face like Mr Edwards's, her lower jaw jutting forwards, and blows forcefully upwards, but her breath, too, is warm, as well as stale-smelling, despite the ice cream she ate earlier, and even when she picks up the dress from her bed and cautiously whips out the creases she does no more than disturb the air without cooling it. Softly she bunches the fabric, finds the armholes and slips the dress over her head, and once she has managed to fasten the buttons she attempts to comport herself as her mother advised her – her posture upright, her bosom and bottom pushed out – and decides that she is prettier in this frock than even Emma Beckwith, for whom it was measured exactly. Standing back to admire herself in full profile, she imagines how it might be if either of the stonemason's sons were to come into the pharmacy this afternoon and once again offer an arm to her and perhaps suggest a tour of the lettering shop, or a turn about the town; she wonders if her father might now look more favourably upon them, brave Tommies on leave from the war – whether Sammy or Fred, she hasn't a preference; decorated or wounded would be equally fine – and whether in her white Beckwith frock they might find her figure even more agreeable than one year ago, her particulars no less provoking.

12
Montague

the appalling thick of it

In Belgium and France Montague determined to forget the under-housemaid Mabel and enjoyed the company of several other pretty young things – some of them very young – their lips rouged, clothes loosened, falling half off them, their manner indulgent, compliant, and all of them happy to strip and lie naked the moment he had finished his brandy and was ready to take them into the bedchamber to complete their transaction, which was always recuperative. In his paybook he took with him everywhere the letter issued by Lord Kitchener to all the troops sent overseas – to the officers as well as the men – enjoining them to show themselves in the true character of the British soldier and warning against the temptations of women and wine, the former to be treated as ladies, with perfect courtesy, but not to be engaged with on intimate terms, and though he paid little heed to this, he wasn't a fool and wouldn't contract a disease for, as Lord Kitchener's letter reminded him, his duty to his country could not be done unless his health remained sound.

Montague used prophylactics. Through his friend Wortley he had located a reliable supply and was content to let the girls help him on with them, and even encouraged one or two of the prettier ones to take his penis into their mouths first, to help it to harden, and though a few of the women were clearly intent on satisfying his requirements in double quick time, he didn't altogether mind this since they employed certain techniques to hurry him along, and with practice he got to prolong the pleasure whatever their strategems; he got his few francs' worth.

And it was more than satisfactory, given the debasement of the front and the filthy, inhuman conditions that prevailed there. Montague felt no darkness on his conscience, then or now, and he considers it no more of a stain on a man's immortal soul to copulate with a French prostitute than to impale a German soldier, or to shoot a deserter. He was properly courteous to the women, and while he is aware that certain of his fellow officers adopted a quite different attitude and guarded against their own base appetites in deference not to Lord Kitchener but because of some rectitude or religious influence in their upbringing, it remains his conviction that the sexual act is as much a physical necessity for a soldier as rest and a regular diet, and equally as sustaining to a man's morale as the letters and food hampers he receives from his loved ones at home.

Montague's self-certainty on this point is buoyed by his confidence in the rectitude of his own moral upbringing, but while he isn't in any sense profligate or unprincipled, neither would he describe himself as priggish, or pious, which is how he is so often perceived by others, he realises, no doubt on account of his habitual stiffness of manner and bearing. Athletic he may have been at one time – as a boy playing rugger and cricket, as an undergraduate runner and rower – but Montague has also always been noted for his upright posture and the peculiar inflexibility of his facial expressions, which have resulted in certain compliments – that he has the natural physique of a Guardsman, for one – but also a fair number of taunts – that he has a fucking poker up his arse, to quote his sergeant major – and he is conscious that many people, whether friends or associates, have found him haughty, somewhat lacking in humour or vitality, and even – according to his sisters – a stick in the mud, all of which criticisms may well be justified since he is inclined towards judgementalism, and finds extroverted or theatrical types tiresome, a little perturbing in their lack of reserve, and has never much esteemed expressive, emotionally demonstrative people, with the exception perhaps of his sisters, who continue to write to him regularly, almost daily, and sometimes attempt in their letters to ape his own sardonic style, though this isn't an attitude that either of them wears particularly well, since they are enthusiasts, Edwina and Emma; their customary outlook is one of optimism, even now, in the midst of a war, and themselves in the appalling thick of it.

the residuum

Dressed in his pyjamas, slippers and dressing-gown, Montague pauses at the head of the blue staircase, absently caressing the bald crown of a bust on a plinth, and gazes down into the vestibule they call the small hall, where the clock is chiming a quarter to three and a young nurse – who ought not to be there – has just wandered in from the gardens, apparently lost. Tentatively she tests one door, then another, and when she locates the main corridor Montague delays a moment longer to be sure she is gone, then begins his descent, holding on to the handrail.

The stairs wind down in five flights from his room, with four interim landings, and although they aren't steep – which has been a great boon, given his condition, the stiffness of his limbs and the chafing of his skin – he goes slowly, passing a procession of crude portraits of his antecedents and an absurd abundance of potted plants and ornaments, some on pedestals and tables, others placed on the stairs, and most of them brought here from the larger part of the house to accommodate the requirements of the hospital. They are a nuisance, and dusty, but there is nowhere else for them to go, and not enough servants to attend to them.

The clutter continues into the conservatory – it continues everywhere – and as he enters the bright light of the glasshouse he notices that the gardener, Logan, has been in to crank open the windows, though it remains no less warm than is usual, and no less unkempt. The hanging baskets contain as many weeds as flowers, the tips of the leaves on the ferns are beginning to crinkle, and sighing – there is nothing to be done – Montague negotiates a passage around a plethora of cane chairs and tables and rugs on the floor to a cushioned Bath chair in a nook at the end, which is shaded by screens of honeysuckle and guarded by two mossy goddesses, amputated at the shoulders, and blind.

Most days he will come here with a letter from his sisters, just as most days in the trenches he would occupy his time alone by retiring to the bunk in his foxhole, where he would read and reread the news they had sent to him, and experience a certain irritation at their lack of awareness, as well as fondness, exasperation, amusement, all the banished emotions of safety and home, and be struck as well by the uncanny sensation of hearing in his inner ear the teasing, affectionate tone of them, a strange and precious commodity in that environment, where he was surrounded always by men's voices and the brutal battering that came from the guns.

Cautiously, in case it should tip, Montague kneels on the Bath chair and carefully brings himself down, lying first on his side before easing slowly onto his back, then crosses his arms at his chest – his hands flat to each shoulder, his legs straight – and gazes up to the floral motif in the topmost panes, but this posture is rather too reminiscent of the grave and he places his hands instead in his lap, and gently raises his knees, shifting a little to make himself comfortable.

The wicker creaks; there is no other sound but his own breath, and for fear of the sounds he might start to remember – the bombs, the cries of his men, Private Barley's distress – he hums to himself and thinks of the cakes his sisters would also post to him, and the soap and socks and cigarettes, and occasionally, too, the reading matter – the books that he would pass on, but also the journals he continued to subscribe to, and the letters he continued to receive from his correspondents, which soon came to cause him nothing but annoyance, those from the pharmacist

Dobson most of all, which he soon began to discard, ripped up, unread.

Of course, at the start, his sisters were far from unique in their optimism, and while most of England, it seemed, took the view that the Hun would be mopped up in no time and the war concluded by Christmas, the hope among these others of Montague's correspondents was for a war that was longer and might act as a purgative, sweeping away what was rotten, reducing the number of fertile males among the residuum. The good would come through, tempered and strengthened; the virile would prosper and promulgate. This was the lesson of history, it seemed, that the strongest and fittest in each generation should be drawn to the military, their manhood tested in the rigours of battle, their efficiency for improving the species established by their deeds in the field.

Yet that war of mud and barbed wire and cowering in trenches hardly allowed the individual to assert himself and was, in Montague's view, almost certainly dysgenic in the degree to which it sacrificed the cream of the race, even as it effected a cull of the worthless. Among the first to be eliminated were so many of the brightest and best, the initial wave of enlistment having recruited the most vigorous and healthy, the most patriotic and courageous, fellows categorised A1 for physique, who then died in their thousands while innumerable others of similar calibre were returned as invalids, disfigured and beaten, a waste that necessitated such a lowering of standards that men who might previously have been turned away – those rated B and even C, some of them degenerates, some of them criminals – are now also encouraged to take the King's shilling.

Only the absolute dross will be refused, the scrapings from the very pit of the barrel, and Montague doubts whether the men who prevail will have survived because they are the fittest, or merely the most fortunate.

But then the chaps in his command were a mixed crowd – although they all came to share the same fate and while it was true that some who responded to Kitchener's call in the second year of the war were poor specimens, morally and physically, and might never have been accepted into the ranks but that so many better men had already stepped up and fallen, others possessed substance and fibre and were plucky and steadfast and retained a bantering sort of good humour even under the most testing of circumstances. Despite being no less desperately tired than himself, and having endured no less terrible conditions, many revealed a stoicism in the face of affliction that was, he suspected, the very key to the national character.

Even so, their unfortunate want of physique and sometimes mental development were a continual disturbance to him, and often he wondered whom they would marry but females who were equally worthless, equally lacking in positive attributes, resulting inevitably in the birth of still more of their kind.

Few among them, he supposed, would ever demonstrate the volition to raise themselves out of their situation in life – if only they were to hold on to that life – and each time they assembled before him, their faces pinched and expectant, grizzled, stubbled, somewhat bug-eyed from strain and fatigue, he performed as was expected of him, whether that meant leading them over the parapet, pistol in hand, or ensuring that they changed their socks regularly and kept their feet greased in the wet. He was properly solicitous of their welfare, and felt sure they respected him and his superiority over them, but in truth he had no love for his men, none whatsoever. Exhausted by combat, spiritually on the verge of defeat, he accepted his responsibility towards them much as one might towards a servant or even a hound, whose loyalty is no more touching than it is a drag on one's nerves, and because they were trained as British soldiers, his men did as they were bidden – most of them – but still, he would rather they had not been his responsibility, those specimens who would in the normal run of things have been employed in his father's factories, because in the end he let them down; he rather failed in his duty to set them an example.

Long before those final shells landed, Montague's nerves had started to weaken. Even at ease in his foxhole or secure in the support line, he would feel the vibration of a bombardment communicating itself through acres perhaps of blasted land, and notice the flickering of his candles, and the trembling of his personal effects, and no matter how remote he might be from the shells – and regardless of whether they were falling on British or enemy lines – he too would start to tremble, and his face to twitch, just above his lip, just beneath his left eye, a symptom of nervous strain that has persisted, maddeningly, to this day, despite the fact that he is at home now, and safe.

The conditions were extreme and unnatural, and a great many other men of proven and respectable character were unmanned in battle, or succumbed to the funk, the terrors induced by those guns, and frequently since his return Montague has wondered if the education and independence of mind that distinguish the officer are the qualities that make him so ill-suited to a war conducted on such an industrial scale. Unused to thinking or acting as one of a herd, his moral and aesthetic disposition will be appalled, his sensibilities revolted.

Certainly, Montague was revolted, but then so many other chaps of his class did not weaken, or require to be withdrawn from the line, and if he has proven unworthy it cannot be ascribed to the genetic inheritance he has received from his father since his forebears on that side were modest, industrious men, hard-working but enterprising, who overcame the inadequacies of their class and far exceeded the expectations of their social position by ascending to their current standing in a mere four generations, such that Montague must remind himself sometimes of the great distance they have come, and the great good his family has done and continues to do for the people of the immediate vicinity, and for the municipality.

It was no ordinary ascent. And while he has been proven unmanly, the fault, he feels sure, is to be found on his mother's side, where considerably more than four generations of fine breeding and refinement have culminated in her example, high-strung and neurotic and lacking the temperament for setbacks or strain of any kind, and no doubt it is by attending to the female line – by choosing a mate for himself who is robust in physique, and steady in character, irrespective of her own social origin – that the reparation or readjustment may be made, and if that means selecting the likes of a housemaid, or the daughter of a shop-keeper, or some other girl of that kind, so long as she is respectable, then so be it.

So be it, he concludes, and laboriously manoeuvres himself to a sitting position on the edge of the Bath chair, and inhales the fragrant air, breathes deeply, and pushes himself upright with a groan, pressing his hands to his knees, then takes a short tour around the confines of the glasshouse to loosen his limbs, and another in the reverse direction, and finally, having nothing better to do with his time, ascends once more to his room, where he will await the arrival of Miss Dobson and his consignment of ointment.

13

Dobson

bone-headed and dangerous

Elsewhere in the county, no doubt, there will be pharmacists as obliging as Dobson in the matter of contra-conceptives, and possibly some among them will be guided by their intellectual convictions, but most to his certain knowledge are reluctant to stock such devices, or else place so many conditions upon their availability that few potential customers will have the courage to submit to the interrogation that must accompany their sale (or will be forced to approach the subject so tangentially that the pharmacist will have the excuse he requires to misunderstand them), while others among his rivals are steadfastly opposed to their provision whatever the circumstance, refusing to countenance the supply of any aid to the avoidance of unwanted children – or, indeed, of venereal disease – on the grounds that availability can serve only to encourage immorality and sexual incontinence; in other words, there remain those who believe that restraint is not only laudable but possible, even now, in 1916, and Britain in the midst of a war, and even here, among the poor, in a neighbourhood such as Riverside Road.

Which is a view that Dobson considers quite whimsical, or worse: bone-headed and dangerous.

At one time he thought differently, when he was not so wise as to the nature of his neighbours, and when it was also his policy to ration the provision of contra-conceptives, confining their sale to married women above a certain age who had already borne children, in the belief that women lacked a sexual appetite and possessed a greater natural modesty than men, and so would never come to him out of any low motive but only because they were subject to the dominating desires of their husbands and required some protection from the perpetual burden of carrying and caring for babies.

But his years of proximity to the poor of Riverside Road have persuaded him that most are the product of a genetic inheritance that guarantees their moral debility – their susceptibility not only to idleness and criminality but to promiscuity – and while he accepts that there may be some possibility of probity and decency among the best of them, the fact is that most have been raised in an atmosphere lacking in moral oxygen, the offspring of successive generations of intemperate parents, and there is no hope for them.

There is nothing to work on, and if their kind is not to be promulgated then the only strategy is to concede to the urgency and inevitability of their appetites, to allow them to satisfy their hungers, but meanwhile to prevent there being any addition to their numbers through the ready supply of prophylactics.

Certainly, it now appears to him, the old ideals of sexual chastity and self-control cannot possibly hold when there are so many more opportunities for fraternisation between the sexes, and such a fever among young women in particular for the passions of the moment – life seeming so cheap and the lives of soldiers so readily wasted – and all of this allied to such a persistence of ignorance as to the mechanics of the thing, for despite their upbringing in overpopulated homes, surrounded by babies and mothers about to give birth, it seems that most young people still know little or nothing of how these babies are made, or of how they are got out (the belly-button being the commonest surmise), let alone of how to prevent their conception.

The situation is a sorry one. And while the absence of so many men has resulted in there being less drunkenness on the streets, and fewer assaults, fewer accidents, and has meant that their children are better fed, better clothed and in better health as a

97

consequence of their mothers' additional earnings and the curtailment of their fathers' profligacy, the lifting of the controlling hand of the father has allowed the children an excess of liberty, the younger ones running to mischief, and even to hooliganism, while the older ones seek opportunities to answer the appeals of their appetites, and Dobson fears for the daughters especially; he fears, indeed, for his own, despite her many advantages, since Gertie is too often now in the company of her social inferiors, and is impulsive, suggestible, and overly given to foolishness.

'telephone call for you'

At three o'clock as a rule the pharmacist will take a cup of coffee or tea, and now as the mechanism winds up to the chimes he sees a burly, bowler-hatted farmer approaching the shop and hears Dorothea descending the stairs, her familiar tentative tread at the turn and the chink of his cup in its saucer. Her hands are unsteady. Increasingly he has noticed this, and there is no remedy for it, certainly not the Invalid Port Wine she has become so attached to, or the Wincarnis he would prefer that she drank, if she must have a tipple, since his pharmacy stocks and promotes it and would secure better terms if sales should improve: *The World's Greatest Wine Tonic and Nerve Restorative*, reads the mirrored sign surmounting the drug run. *Makes you a picture of Health!* claims the card in the window.

The bell rings as the door opens. 'Good afternoon, Mr Buttle,' he says.

'Pharmacist.'

'How may I help you?'

'I have a boil,' says the farmer, 'just here,' and points to the back of his neck.

The clock chimes the hour; Dobson stifles a yawn. 'If you'd care to take a seat near the window,' he says, 'I'll inspect it for

98

you,' and lifts the flap in the counter as Dorothea comes through with his cup. She places it next to the cash drawer, then stands with her hands at her sides and her head oddly tilted, as though for a moment quite lost, uncertain what she ought to do next. The farmer is sweating. He sits with a groan, his knees creaking, and Dobson stands directly behind him. 'Then if you could loosen your collar, Mr Buttle. And bow your head.'

'Can you see it?'

'Hold still if you will,' says Dobson.

The door bell jangles. An elderly woman looks at them sternly as she comes in, says nothing, and shuffles across to a chair by the veterinary products, behind a display case of sponges. She is wearing a black hat, a black shawl and black coat, despite the warm weather, and immediately closes her eyes, her hands clasped in her lap. Her mouth falls open. She may merely have come in for this rest; sometimes they do.

Dorothea clears her throat. 'Mrs Baxter? Can I help you?'

'Sorry, dear. What?'

'Can I help you, Mrs Baxter?'

'I'd like a purgative, dear, something pleasant-tasting, but not for a moment, if you don't mind.'

'No,' says Dorothea. 'No, of course not.'

Dobson concludes his inspection. The boil is as large as a greengage and beginning to suppurate. He corrects the man's collar and tells him, 'You have a sizeable carbuncle, Mr Buttle. You'll need to apply a poultice, a fomentation to draw it out,' and immediately Dorothea pulls open a drawer and looks for some scissors. 'My wife will cut you some lint, which you must soak in boric acid. We have some prepared. It isn't expensive, or harmful.' He walks around to his sink and begins rinsing his hands. 'It's a mild antiseptic. Wring the lint almost dry, then press it to the boil. The heat might make you jump but it will draw out the core. It shouldn't take long – a couple of days, if you do it regularly, at decent intervals. But you mustn't molest it.'

The farmer's stubby hands rest on his knees, a black crescent of dirt under each fingernail. 'I've heard that cabbage leaves are quite good,' he says, 'if you heat them over a fire.' The chair creaks as he pushes himself up. He is grinning. 'What do you think of that, Mr Dobson?'

The pharmacist dries himself. He has recorded a great many home remedies, some of them plausible, others not – fried mice to treat whooping cough; an infusion of ha'pennies to bring on a miscarriage – and perhaps in this case a towel soaked in hot water might do just as well, or a dry cloth heated over the fire, or indeed some hot cabbage leaves. But he says with finality, 'Lint and boric acid will do it, Mr Buttle. My wife will be happy to help you.' He lights a cigarette as the shop door swings clatteringly open and Edwards the stonemason leans in, his long face, waistcoat and trousers ghostly with dust, his brow caked where he's been sweating.

'That's a telephone call for you,' he says, his voice a lugubrious drawl, and Dobson hastily puts down the cigarette. The receiver is mounted within a glass-panelled cubicle on the wall of the stonemason's display room, and the connection is very frequently lost. But Edwards raises a hand. 'No,' he says. 'No need to hurry. He's rung off, nearly an hour since.'

'An hour ago?' asks Dobson.

'The wife took it,' says Edwards. 'Forgot to tell me.'

'Was it urgent?'

'Couldn't say. It was Montague Beckwith anyway. He asks would you make up that same order. This afternoon if convenient.'

Dobson is surprised, though doubtless the heat and humidity is aggravating to Beckwith's condition, which is a nervous disorder, as he understands it, not unlike eczema, brought on by his experience of the fighting in France that is everywhere rumoured to be nothing but shellfire and slaughter. 'Yes, of course,' he says sombrely, and picks up his cigarette. 'I'll send Gertie along. And perhaps you might ring him back to confirm? Or I could, if you'd prefer . . .'

'There's no need,' says Edwards, making way so that a couple of children may enter, a girl and a much smaller boy, both of them barefoot. 'It's Gertie he's expecting. The wife says he'd be obliged if Miss Dobson herself would deliver the item.'

'I see,' says Dobson, and draws on his cigarette, sips from his tea. Unaccountably his heart rate has quickened and the pharmacy seems suddenly airless, soured by the smell of Mrs Baxter and the two children, whose clothes are tattered, quite filthy. Edwards, he realises, is smirking, though he cannot think why. 'Very good then,' he says. 'I shall inform her. Thank you, Mr Edwards.'

'My pleasure, Mr Dobson,' says Edwards, his tone somewhat satirical, and steps to one side as Mr Buttle exits the premises, touching the rim of his bowler to the pharmacist, then quietly pulls shut the door and follows the farmer over the road, both of them heading towards the Turf Tavern.

a fine, impressive young man

In the minutes that follow, Dobson methodically reorientates the chairs that furnish his pharmacy and corrects the alignment of his counter displays and the position of his test tubes and measuring jugs, his beamscale and pill-machine, sealing wax and dispensing twine, and eventually lights another cigarette and stands to observe his wife as she attends to Mrs Baxter, who has finally shuffled across to the counter and demanded to be served before the two urchins, since she has been waiting the longest.

The time is twenty-three minutes past three, and he waits as the old woman's laxatives are sealed and passed over, then hastens to hold open the door for her and says to his wife, 'I think I may take a turn outside, Dorothea.'

'Will you be long?'

'No, not long,' he says. 'You'll be able to manage?' He gestures with his cigarette to the stairs. 'You can always use Gertie.' He is irritated to be questioned and possibly she senses this for she does not reply but thanks Mrs Baxter, who clutches her package in both hands and glowers at Dobson as she approaches the door. He is obstructing her way. 'I beg your pardon,' he says and steps to one side, but it seems she expects a further courtesy and lightly he touches her arm and guides her into the sunshine.

'Good day,' she says curtly.

'Good day,' murmurs Dobson, and watches until she has progressed as far as Flogdell the fruiterer's, then leans on the ledge of the pharmacy window, a few yards from the Eyetie and facing across to the market, but the afternoon, he realises, is no less oppressive outdoors than in, and the air no less foul-smelling.

The heat reflects back from the glass and radiates up from the pavement, and after a few moments he sighs and makes his way between the animals, carts and pedestrians on the road to stand in the shade of a sycamore, where he leans against an empty cattle enclosure, one foot braced on the gate, and attempts to listen to Alfie Atherton, a familiar firebrand, who is haranguing a small gathering outside the Red Lion, the traditional spot on which to pitch a soapbox on a market day, but he can hear nothing distinctly, and when Alfie steps down – the applause briefly audible, quickly tumbling away – Dobson drops the butt of his cigarette under his boot, then lights another, and recalls the first time he heard Montague Beckwith speaking in public, soon after he had come down from Cambridge, a fine, impressive young man with little need for the crate he was standing on, yet there he stood in his chequered tweed jacket, breeches and cap – his notion perhaps of rural attire – elevated above the assembled farmers and farmhands, drovers and dealers, his cheeks hotly flushed, his gestures so stiff, and while most in his audience were clearly inebriated from the pubs round about, and many were stupidly smiling, even leering, their expressions all a bit mocking, none of them heckled or spoke out against him (though neither did they give him much in the way of encouragement)

Dobson alone paid close attention, standing near to the rear of the gathering, where he was exposed to the sunshine and bothered by flies and obliged to listen with one hand cupped to his ear.

Montague, he remembers, was discoursing on the theme of eugenical science in terms he must have hoped would appeal to the agricultural mind, in which vein he acknowledged that a crop's prospects for growth would be stunted if it were planted in poor-quality soil, or in the wrong climate, just as livestock would fail to thrive if fed on inferior food, or housed inadequately, or treated unkindly.

Environment mattered, he said, and not only for crops and for livestock, but for people as well. And while improvements in educational provision and public-health legislation might help secure the conditions in which a man could grow to realise his full potential, it had also to be granted that not every man was fit to benefit from such reforms, and nor could any environment, however favourable, bring forth qualities that were not innately there.

As every countryman knew, declared Montague, not all the piglets in the farrowing crate would be equally robust, for there would always be runts, and some would die naturally, and some be so inferior that they would need to be culled, because no amount of nurturing could improve them.

So it was among men: the imbecile would not benefit by a scholarship; nor would the diseased at birth – the deaf, blind, crippled or deformed – acquire health and vitality in later life, however unsparing their parents' attentions and however solicitous the efforts of the institutions in which they were housed. In fact, there was every danger that too kind an environment would encourage the degenerate to multiply and lead to an increase in the birth-rate of the worthless or sub-standard.

There was that, and the fact that whatever the benefits enjoyed by one generation, and whatever the qualities drawn out of them, there could be no guarantee that those qualities would be passed on to their offspring, for while a person, plant or animal might be improved or abused in its own lifetime, the benefits and deficits would not be inherited since the effects of environment were only temporary.

Inheritance was key, as every good farmer would appreciate, for what keeper of livestock did not breed selectively? Who among his audience did not match the best with the best in order to improve the species, whether that be cattle or sheep, poultry or pigs, horses, pigeons or bees? The sensible farmer, acting rationally, controlled the fertility of the worst stock while allowing the best to multiply, thereby guaranteeing the continuation of the best characteristics of the breed, and not only that, but their steady improvement.

And it was this, proclaimed Montague, that was required in England's hour of national reckoning, when the urban population was being raised in conditions of such unnatural squalor and unhealthy overcrowding, and had become so out of tune with nature's rhythms and the natural requirements of the race, and when England's rivals overseas were becoming belligerent and there were enemies at every gate of the Empire.

Now more than ever before it was the example of the best farmer that would show the way, for the urgencies of the age demanded that every responsible parent should adopt the methods of the successful agriculturist and be extra-attentive to the signs of health and vitality in the young woman his son proposed to marry, or in the young man who sought his daughter's hand, and should not only encourage the best to cross-fertilise with the best, but should look to the bloodline, seeking thereby to improve the national stock by introducing genetic reinforcements from the open countryside into the towns and cities of England.

And no doubt Montague would have gone on to suggest some exemplary pairings for such cross-fertilisation, but that the farmers and farmhands around him were not, in truth, among the best of their kind, and this turn in the argument served only to provoke the worst in them, a volley of humorous and disruptive remarks, which despite his exasperated efforts to regain the situation soon brought a raucous end to his first speech outside the Red Lion.

There could be no hope of continuing. Montague nodded and adjusted his cap and stepped down from his crate, then waited for the crowd to disperse – the men returning to the pubs and the market – until Dobson alone remained and there was nothing but cobbles and litter and the upturned grocery box lying between them.

Seemingly unaware of the pharmacist, Montague contemplated the marketplace, and momentarily Dobson thought to introduce himself but was discouraged by the young man's demeanour, his nettled expression and stiffness of bearing, and resolved to return to the pharmacy so that he might marshal his thoughts in the form of a letter, except that Montague began walking directly towards him. Surprised, Dobson stood still, and found he was making an obstruction.

'Excuse me,' said Montague. He indicated a motorcycle propped on the railings outside Collingwood's seed shop.

'Ah,' said Dobson, and stepped aside. He cleared his throat. 'An interesting argument, I thought.'

Montague looked at him blankly.

'But an unfortunate audience.'

Montague's gaze remained steady.

'Pardon me. I'm Claude Dobson. The pharmacist.'

'I see.'

'I was wondering if I might commit some of my own thoughts to paper?'

'Your thoughts?'

'Regarding your speech? In a letter perhaps.'

'If you would like to,' said Montague, distracted.

'I would be grateful of the opportunity.'

'Then do, of course do,' said Montague, and pulled his bike clear of the pharmacist and hurriedly mounted it, facing away from him. 'I'll expect it,' he said, and with a single sharp kick on the pedal he set the engine to clattering before Dobson could say any more. He released the throttle, and pulled off in the direction of the Corn Hall, emitting a crack like a rifle shot and a scud of black smoke, then turned and was gone.

14
Walter

a promise

Always he was industrious. All through his boyhood, Walter earned money for his mother wherever he could: pennies and ha'pennies, farthings, shillings, even half-crowns. Aged eight or nine, he scavenged for manure to sell on, and coals that had fallen in the road, and any timber that could be salvaged or stolen, because that was how they heated their water, and their stove, and themselves. A little older, he knocked together a barrow from junk and went touting for business, moving small loads, conveying parcels for the gentry, assisting with flits, portering baggage at the station. And if Mother should require him to run an errand, he wouldn't dawdle; he'd run.

He was a good boy, and she trusted him to fetch her medicines, too, the tinctures, syrups and pills that she used to rely on, in the days before she became such a drinker. Many a time Walter would stand in the queue in the pharmacy, a few coins clutched in his palm, quietly whispering to himself the name of what he must ask for while Mr Dobson went about his business with such briskness and seriousness, rarely uttering a word he didn't need to, and if the shop was especially busy then Walter would be happy to gaze around at the green and blue glass of the vases, the curious inscriptions on the drawers, and the great variety of items in the cases above and below the counter – nowhere else would you see such variety – and be startled sometimes when at last it was his turn to speak, whether to Mr Dobson himself, who regarded him so sternly, or to his wife, who seemed kinder.

He was a dependable boy, and always asked for the right thing, except for one September market day in his fifteenth year when the rain was incessant and the shop so crowded with such a clamour of farmers that he could not see to the counter, could barely see past the foul-smelling drover before him, and when at last he squeezed through to the front he found that Gertie herself had been conscripted to assist Mr Dobson – not taking orders or handling the money, but bagging up goods. She was looking straight at him, and he blushed and pointed to a packet of Black Brompton Lozenges, the first thing he saw. 'I'll have some of those, please,' he said.

The pharmacist took Walter's money and gave him his change while Gertie sealed his package, and as she handed it over Walter noticed her eyes, which were brown, and the tuck of her cheeks because she was smiling, and how white was her tunic. He noticed these things, and remembered them afterwards, but he could not be sure if she had recognised him, nor could he explain to his mother why he had brought home some cough sweets rather than the medicine that she had asked for.

Mother looked at him strangely – he was talking such rubbish – then pulled her shawl over her head and went herself in the rain to the pharmacy, taking the lozenges with her, and said when she returned, 'Don't be such a bloody fool,' nothing more, and Walter hardly minded, but remained oddly agitated for the rest of that day and the next. He held on to the thought of the pharmacist's daughter as though a promise had been made to him, though of what, he couldn't quite say.

your mother's whatsitsname

Soon after his next birthday, in the autumn of that year, Walter acquired a bowler hat – his first – from Boothe's Clothier, Hatter and Juvenile Outfitter on Prince of Wales Avenue for three and ninepence (his savings) with a view to acquiring a sweetheart as soon as he could.

The proudest of his meagre possessions, the hat came in a stiff box, the vendor's name and crest printed not only inside the lid but inside the bowl of the hat too, and while his bill of sale guaranteed him a polish-up free of charge on any Saturday morning that he might care to call by, Walter found he never could get along there since he was by then in the employ of Samuel Meek's Steam Navigation Company and rarely released before knocking-off time, midday on a Saturday (sometimes much later).

Like most others who shopped at Reginald Boothe's, Walter worked a five-and-a-half-day week and, like most others of his age and station, as well as many who were older, or a social cut above, he looked forward all week to joining the Chicken Run of a Saturday evening, the long-established procession of young men and women – the local press called them *beaux* and *belles* (sometimes *cocks* and *hens*) – who paraded up and down the tree-lined pavements of the city's broadest thoroughfare, Balmoral Road, the honey-coloured edifices of the county's grandest hotels, ballrooms and emporia on either side of them, well-wishers and revellers whistling from their passing cabs and trams, a few errand boys smirking, gangs of smaller boys jeering.

It might take Walter an hour or more to complete the promenade, or a mere fraction of that, depending on whom there was to see and whom to talk to, but though one side of the road continues to be known as the Shilling and the other the Guinea, supposedly to denominate the class of person who walks there, in truth there never was much of a distinction, and where previously a few constables would be standing sentry in the doorways, now the parade is overseen by the far sterner matrons of the Women's Police Service and neither boisterous behaviour nor any impropriety will be tolerated.

Not that Walter ever witnessed any rough stuff. The worst he can recall was the ordeal of making his way down there from Mortuary Yard, since he would need to pass among the children of Riverside Road – filthy urchins – whose favourite sport was to try to knock flying his fancy headgear, first creeping along in his wake, then charging and leaping and taking a swipe at the hat, all ready to scarper the moment they landed back on the pavement – though by far the bigger prize (and a much safer bet) would be the hat of a young man who was courting a young lady since he would be too absorbed in his sweetheart to notice them, or at least too tied to her side to give chase. And what Walter wanted more than anything in the world was to be tied to a sweetheart. He wanted to be tied to Gertie Dobson.

In his imagination they would meet on the Guinea side of the street and she would be twirling a sunshade and be dressed all in white, her dark eyes finding his as they passed – a glint of recognition, a smile – and then on the next turn they would pause and converse and soon he would be escorting her along to the Hippodrome in the centre of town, her hand gently cupped in the crook of his arm, to take their place in a queue that stretched all the way back down to Woolworth's, where they would stand and enjoy the show that came before the show: the buskers who were as good as anyone you ever saw on the stage, the fiddlers and accordion players, crooners and comics, jugglers, magicians, and that fellow whose dog performed pirouettes to silent commands.

Usually Walter would invest in a haircut before going out, then redeem his Sunday-best jacket and trousers from Lincoln's pawnshop, and fasten his neck inside a stiff collar and polish up his boots, but then have to settle for the company of his usual chums in the absence of a sweetheart, and while he did still manage to enjoy some of the best of nights out for little more than a tanner, since a penny was all it would cost for a pack of five Woodbines, another penny for a cone of roast nuts or a pint of beer at the bar, then thruppence for a seat in the gods, second house, after which there might be a trip to the pie shop in Caldwell Lane, where it would cost a penny for a mince pastie, steaming hot and half a foot long and good to crunch on as you made your way across the market in the crisp, cold dark of a

December evening, nothing of that sort ever featured in his thoughts about Gertie, who would expect a bit better, and receive it: a seat in the circle; an ice cream in the parlour beforehand; a circuit on the number four tram to prolong the short journey home.

Always this was how he would imagine it, but in fact he never once met Gertie on Balmoral Road, not among the pedestrians, their nearest encounter being the time he saw her sitting in a carriage with the Misses Beckwith, stalled at the turn as he waited to cross back over from the Guinea to the Shilling, the horse's haunches rippling with impatience, its nostrils pluming in the early October evening.

She looked directly at him and smiled, her pretty white face pinked in the cold, and he had to look away from her. Blushing beneath his bowler hat, he fixed his gaze instead upon the Misses Beckwith, all snug in their furs, their narrow faces fringed about with soft sable, and remembered once asking John Cherry, who worked in Orford's abattoir, how it was that babies were got out of their mothers – his youngest brother James having only just arrived – to which John Cherry replied, 'Well, let's put it this way, your mother's whatsitsname was the first fur collar you ever had around your neck!'

Which made no more sense to Walter then than John Cherry's later advice that he mustn't throw his trousers on his bed if any young female should happen to be lying there – 'Not in these parts, Walter, not around this way. It don't take much more than that to make a baby!' – since the only young females he was ever likely to see in a bed were his own sisters, and it would be indecent to drop his trousers anywhere near them. Such was his innocence at that time, in his previous life, before he and his pals were overcome by the fever to find a young woman, and even get her into a bed ('try before you buy, sort of style'), the fever becoming so much worse in the weeks and months after war was declared and one by one they took the King's shilling, went into khaki, and prepared to kill the Hun, and while of course there were women around the back of the Railway Inn who would give themselves to any man for little more than the price of a bottle of stout or a glass of gin – so it was said – these were old women mostly, as old as your mother, all painted and gaudy and a little bit desperate as well as coarse and ill-bred, and when Walter went round there one evening with a group of pals to take a look at them, he found himself more wary of the women than the women seemed troubled by the sight of a gang of young men, most of them inebriated. 'Come along, my lovely,' said one of the tarts, and cupped her hand under Walter's arm and promised in a whisper to look after him – he needn't worry, she would show him what to do – but he was more revolted than tempted, and more afraid than revolted. He touched the brim of his bowler as he mumbled his apologies and tugged himself free, quite certain he did not wish to be looked after, since it was Gertie who glowed in his mind, and Gertie alone whom he hoped might one day call him her lovely.

15
Dobson

an innocent still

Dobson treads on the butt of his cigarette, the fourth he has smoked since he came from the pharmacy, and as he makes his way haltingly back over the road he recalls the ease with which he was able to argue against Beckwith's view of the agriculturist in the first of the letters he wrote to him, since there were several others among his correspondents at that time – in the Malthusian League, for example, as among the contributors to *Eugenics Review* and the *Journal of Heredity* – who held to a similarly misplaced faith in the countryman; which is to say, there were far too many self-declared eugenists whose view of the rustic was plainly, to his mind, idealised – romantic, imagined, unsullied by actual acquaintance – and with whom he had engaged in similar exchanges, for while clearly there were benefits to working the land and breathing its air, it seemed obvious to Claude Dobson that too close a proximity to brute animals and a tendency to breed within a confined gene pool must inevitably incline the country-dweller to physical and moral corruption.

Such at least (though he could not confide this to Montague Beckwith) would explain his wife's congenital failings, her infertility and nervous instability, as well as the moral obtuseness that gives the explanation for Gertie, who is not in fact their natural daughter but the illegitimate child of Dorothea's youngest sister, Ada, who died in childbirth at the age of fifteen and whose pregnancy was caused by a farmworker, a first cousin considerably older than she was.

The child was delivered into their care just a few days after its mother's burial since Dorothea's relations were only too glad to be relieved of the burden, while Dorothea was already resigned to her own barrenness and perhaps a little too eager to be consoled by the gift of this living connection to Ada.

The Dobsons' home at that time was a tiny, less favourably situated pharmacy in the north of the city, but Dobson had already begun negotiating the terms of their occupancy in Riverside Road and the child appeared to him then as yet more cause for optimism, an innocent to raise to respectability, possibly even in opposition to its own nature, the inheritance of his wife's country cousins with their coarseness of thought and speech and behaviour.

He sees their like every market day: a ragged procession of farmhands trailing into his pharmacy, and in each of their faces a kind of slow wit or low cunning, a beady air of anticipation, for it seems they come mainly in the hope of finding Gertie helping out at the counter, and – if they are twice lucky – a queue of old dears waiting before them, allowing plenty of time simply to stand and admire her. Claude Dobson is an outstanding agricultural chemist – he has heard it said many times – but his daughter would give you a hard-on (a genuine boner) just to look at her. He has heard that said, too.

And indeed as he re-enters his pharmacy, the clock showing six minutes to four, he finds a couple of drovers lingering near the display of scent bottles and diffusers, as though considering their potential application in the farmyard, while his daughter busies herself at the counter, folding and tying a small parcel of fancy soaps, a task for which she has a surprising facility, her corners sharp, every topknot neatly bowed.

She is overdressed for shop work, of course – wearing one of the garments given to her by Montague's sisters – and she is blushing, he sees, for her customer is a young man in uniform, and while Dobson would much rather she stayed upstairs, his wife will have had no choice but to call for her assistance in his absence the pharmacy has become somewhat crowded, his wife clearly fretful, and he notices that each of his chairs is now occupied, the furthest of them by Winnie Barley, the mother of one of Gertie's companions at work, whose air of anxious introspection (and inebriation) suggests the likely cause of her coming to see him.

He has helped her before.

'Gentlemen?' he says to the drovers, and the nearest of them grins as he empties a fistful of coins onto the counter and demands something for treating white scour.

'That's scour in calves,' adds his companion, who is much shorter and as dark as any Romany. Dobson calculates how much they have given him and crosses to the other side of the shop, passing Dorothea – whose own air of agitation will remain until the evening, he supposes, whatever restorative she might take for it – and comes back with a small box of Colistol. He slides out three pennies in change and draws the rest of the money to the lip of the counter and gathers it into his palm.

'Thank you, veterinarian,' says the shorter man.

Dobson does not reply but waits, and for several seconds longer the drovers continue to loiter, unable to resist looking at Gertie, until the steadiness of his presence and the chiming of the hour appear to persuade them that they ought to move on; their business is done. He watches as they leave – sweat stains darkening their backs, straw stuck to the dirt on their boots – then pulls open the cash drawer and begins dividing the coins into the compartments, and when Gertie brings him the money for the soaps he confirms with a glance that her soldier has gone and quietly says, 'Captain Beckwith has requested more ointment. Perhaps your mother told you?'

'No,' she says.

'He'd like you to make a delivery this afternoon.'

'Oh, good!' she says.

He looks at her sharply. 'There are several jars in the storeroom. Take two of them.'

'Shall I deliver a letter as well?'

'No,' says Dobson, irritated. 'Not today.'

'There's one on the table.'

'I know.' He closes the drawer. 'I need to review it.'

'When shall I go?'

'You can go at once,' he says. 'But be cautious on the road.'

'Shall I go on the bicycle?'

'Yes, of course the bicycle!' he exclaims, then wonders as she turns from him whether it might yet be more sensible to resist Montague's request for another delivery, at least until Sunday, since Gertie is so guileless, an innocent still, and a distraction not just to their visitors on a market day but to the roughs of Riverside Road, whom she will now have to pass on her way to Beckwith House, a mile or so in the distance, and indeed he would stall her but that the bell above the door is jangling once again and he must attend to the needs of his customers: another elderly neighbour, another agriculturist.

a poor woman's suffering

Dobson does not doubt his daughter's appeal to men of every level, for she is an attractive young woman, as physically developed as his wife is diminished – her attributes a clear indication of nature's designs for her – and while it is no surprise that she should have inherited the stature and complexion of her natural mother, who was so very pretty and plump, it is concerning to him that she should leave his house daily for the Beckwiths' factory, sometimes walking as far as the ferry unaccompanied, often coming all the way home on her own, for he has seen the glances, outright stares, the nudges and smirks, and in fact, to begin with, at the start of her employment, he insisted on escorting her in either direction – at least to the jetty and back – except that Gertie was shy of accepting his arm and contrived to meander and dally, slipping ever further behind him, until one afternoon he was struck by a sense of himself not as her father, or even a gentleman, but as a Mussulman, striding ten paces in advance of his juvenile bride.

The thought was unsettling. He found the situation infuriating, and the moment he had the pharmacy door shut behind them he turned on her and roared, his rage as alarming to himself as it was to poor Gertie. She flinched as though he had struck her. Shocked, she began to cry and fled upstairs to her room, and Dobson sat in one of the chairs by the counter and lit a cigarette, then another, and continued smoking until his hands and knees had ceased trembling. Later he joined his family for supper, and nothing further was said, not a single word. The following morning Gertie waited for him to come downstairs as usual, and only left for the factory when her mother insisted she must.

Dobson watched her through the heavy lace curtains. He watched her come home as well.

And now, if she is to be chaperoned at all, it is with a group of other girls who pause by the pharmacy on their way up the street and take her into their number if she is ready – which on occasions she isn't, for Gertie is prone to lateness and they are unable to linger. The day-shift at Beckwith's begins at six thirty, when every route into the factory will be streaming with workers, and where once they would all have been men, excepting the kitchen workers, now they are more than half of them women, and just as the men would clump along with their shirt-tails hanging out, chewing on a hank of bread perhaps, hastily filling a pipe, the girls will still be buttoning their blouses, their boots unfastened and flopping.

Some of them will be smoking, an unthinkable spectacle just two years ago (and they know it).

Among the smokers, Dobson has noticed, is Winnie Barley's daughter, called Mabel, who was formerly a domestic servant to the Beckwiths and now lurks at the rear of the group that calls in the mornings, always at the rear, for she has been to see him twice already this year, and though on the first occasion she had nothing to be ashamed of – her menses were irregular, that was all – she came the second time because she feared she may have been 'caught', and while again her menses were the cause, still she appears bashful, wary of meeting his gaze. She cannot quite compose her face into a semblance of relaxation but is always affecting to have found something interesting to fix upon in the distance, and appears to compensate for her embarrassment with the boldness of her smoking.

Possibly she thinks it is medicinal. That wouldn't surprise him, but it is hardly respectable, and whenever Dobson sees Gertie in her company he regrets the breach caused by the war in his daughter's friendship with the Misses Beckwith, whose influence was more beneficial – and a surer complement to his own – than any she is now exposed to, which will include the example of Mabel's mother, another worker in the factory and another of his regular customers, who was formerly among those who believed that coins or nails soaked in boiled water might act as a purgative to an unwanted pregnancy (of which she has borne several).

This much she confessed to him on the first occasion she sought his assistance, when she was not only young, and quite drunk, having consumed a great quantity of gin, but tearfully remorseful, though less because she was about to bring on a miscarriage than because she had hoped to raise herself above such a remedy, for as she made clear through her tears, she was determined to be a good wife, and a decent, respectable woman – more so than any of her neighbours – and should never have allowed herself to get into such straits.

Since which time he has helped her on three more occasions – twice with oil of pennyroyal, once with apioline, both medicines labelled identically: *Dobson's Female Pills: Traditional Herbal Emmenagogue Mixture* – and while she is distinctly more shabby and careworn than she once was, she remains a handsome woman, upright in her bearing and, in Claude Dobson's opinion, no less self-deceiving or self sufficient

'Mrs Barley?' he says at last, his shop having now emptied again. 'You would like a word with me in private?'

Tight-lipped, she nods. 'Yes,' she says, 'I would.'

'Please. Come through,' says Dobson, and lifts the hatch on the dispensary counter and guides her into his storeroom, past the table and his unfinished letter to Montague, then into a smaller room at the back, which affords some privacy for this kind of business and contains a couch with blankets and pillows, blinds he can pull down, and a solitary armchair beneath a locked cabinet that contains several dozen bottles of his pills for maintaining monthly regularity, as well as certain instruments, the mechanical appliances he might sometimes be called upon to use should his medicinal remedies fail to alleviate a poor woman's suffering.

16
Walter

fight!

A little way down from Mortuary Yard there is a lodging house, a hotel of sorts, which appears to have no name (none is displayed) though locally it is known as the Midden and is somewhere an older son can be sent to bed down, should his home be too crowded, if he isn't too fussy. Ninepence a night it charges, four and sixpence a week, and for this he can expect a breakfast of porridge and tea, and a bunk and a coat peg in a room shared with five others – most of them tramps, itinerants looking for work – the bunks like coffins and the bedding still carrying the stench of the last man to lie there.

It is a dark, shambolic old building, the stairs steep and creaking, the windows filthy with grime, and the frowsy, urinous smell is enough to make anyone retch, though as Walter comes towards it this afternoon he finds a small crowd at the door, a dozen old men and boys jostling each other as if hoping to be allowed in, among them the urchin Walter saw stealing milk on the market just a little while earlier.

It seems there's a kerfuffle inside, and Walter places his hands on the boy's shoulders and says into his ear, 'What's going on?' but the boy need not answer him, and doesn't, since the scene is so clear, almost exactly as Walter might have anticipated – the rip in the sleeve of this fellow's serge jacket, the smell of someone's spent pipe – and peering through the crowd he recognises the red-nosed toper Daniels, who is forever in a scrape of one kind or another, a jester always looking to raise a smile, but a damned nuisance when he's in his cups, never knowing when to leave be. He is merry now, and enjoying this limelight, comically pleading his innocence to Nellie Tuttle, a former neighbour of the Barleys and a sad old toper herself, who is standing in the lobby and accusing him of mistreating her.

'But you know I'm nothing like other men!' Daniels protests, and Nellie hoicks her shawl over her shoulders, adjusts the tilt of her hat.

'Oh yes you are,' she replies. 'You're exactly like other men – and a lot worse. Your hands were everywhere they shouldn't be!'

She is affronted. And it is like a panto at the Hippodrome, a show they have performed many times, though Walter doubts this audience will linger unless Daniels and Nellie should come to blows, in which case a cry of *fight!* will go up and in no time the crowd will double or treble in size since a set-to in Riverside Road is always an attraction, even now, in 1916, and everyone supposedly all on the same side, united against Fritz, the Hun, the filthy Bosch, for just as it is expected that you will help your compatriot, your neighbour, it is also accepted that there will be spats – or worse, genuine batterings – and that the women will be every bit as bad as the men, every bit as rough and foul-mouthed, particularly if they are pitched one against the other and encouraged to scratch and screech and swing each other round by the clothing or hair, regardless of who might be watching them, their own children included, neither of them prepared to let go and no one inclined to step in and put an end to it.

Two females fighting is an ever-popular spectacle, though better still is a knockabout between a husband and wife, so long as she has the upper hand, or they are even. A mismatch isn't much fun for anyone, and as Walter steps back from the Midden he remembers an occasion when he was twelve and his own father caused such a commotion at home – his sisters weeping in the yard and his mother screaming upstairs – that the police were called but couldn't, or wouldn't, go into the house. They stood hammering on the door until Eddie Barley appeared at the bedroom window with the fender from a fireplace and hurled it down at them, swiping one of the constables' helmets clean off, the strap nearly cutting his throat.

There are often such scenes on Riverside Road, especially on a Saturday, when sometimes it will seem that the woman's best hope is for another man to intervene, all chivalrous intent, and lay about her husband on her behalf (or simply for the sport of it), which was what Walter supposed was in store for his father when Joe Orford, the butcher, their landlord, came striding down Mortuary Yard that evening, rolling up his shirt-sleeves while Mabel, who had gone to find him, stumbled along in his wake with his titfer and coat.

The policemen stood aside; the onlookers kept their distance.

A former boxer, still handy with his fists, and conditioned from lifting the carcasses of cattle and pigs, it was Orford's custom in those days to escort his elderly mother on a Saturday to the home of another old widow, Mrs Sarrington, doffing his hat to all and sundry as he went, exchanging pleasantries with his customers, before proceeding to the Turf Tavern or the Waterloo Arms until the time came to go back and collect her, and if he should happen to notice a young fellow up to no good he would not hesitate to clip his ear, just as he would not shirk to make it his business should he see another man ill-treating his wife. 'Now, now, my friend, that's no way to behave,' he might begin, then swiftly settle the matter with blows, a single uppercut sometimes all that was required, although in this instance a few kindly words appeared, at first, to be as much as he intended.

'Come on, Eddie,' he said to Walter's father, the argument having spilled into the yard and Eddie so drunk he seemed barely able to stand, 'you let Winnie alone now, she's all right.'

'But she needs to know who's boss,' Eddie told him, his squat legs unsteady.

'Oh, I think she knows,' said Orford, glancing at Winnie, who was dishevelled and tearful and clutching to her sides the smallest of her children. Don't you worry about that, I think she knows who's boss.' He patted Eddie Barley's chest, and reached a comradely arm around his shoulders. He nodded to the constables. 'So why don't you come along with me, come along to the slaughterhouse?'

'What for? What's there?'

'There's work, Eddie. I could use an extra pair of hands, and there'll be a couple of bob in it for you. What do you say?'

Eddie didn't reply but vacantly gazed at his house, as if unsure where he was, how he came to be out of doors.

'Eddie?'

'What is it?'

'How about you come along and give me a hand?'

'If you like,' said Eddie then, looking into Joe's face, 'I don't mind,' and allowed himself to be guided away – the two constables following – as docile as any carthorse in Callard's stables, and didn't return until late the next morning, when Orford let him out, his bottom lip so fat he could not talk and both his eyes blackened. Somewhat subdued, even sheepish, he placed a few coins on the kitchen table and stayed sober then for several weeks, as sober as he was able.

a pitiful, pitying look

Walter watches as Daniels and Nellie head off for the Crown, linked arm in arm, their differences resolved and their audience already gone, then for a short distance he ambles along in their wake, the afternoon murmurous with flies and midges and wasps, the perpetual hum of the yards and the hubbub that descends from the market on a Saturday, until gradually he finds himself lost to this noise as if in a dream and fails to notice the clip of the cattle coming behind him.

A drover's sharp *hup!* brings him round, and quickly he steps to one side and stands across from the galvanised pails and troughs outside Atkinson's ironmongery – GOODS FOR SALE

OR UPON HIRE, CUTLERY GROUND AND REPAIRED –
and waits for a small herd of Shorthorns to lumber lazily past
him, guided by a couple of drovers, one even shorter than Walter
and as dark as a Romany. Sweat clings to their shirts. With sticks
a yard long they keep the cattle on course, and when the last of
the cows reaches the ironmonger's it turns its soft wounded eyes
upon Walter, allows him a pitiful, pitying look, then drops a fat
splat of manure to the cobbles. All at once a crust of flies settles
over it. The cow keeps its tail raised, twitches it left and right,
and Walter sees its sphincter slowly opening and closing as if it
were trying to breathe, as though gasping for air, and despite the
heat of the sun on his jacket he feels a chill passing through him,
a sudden remembrance.

It comes and goes in an instant and he tugs his sleeves straight,
smartens the skirts of his tunic and crosses the road in the direction of Orford's.

The butcher, he supposes, will be prospering in spite of the
war since his closest rival in the meat-selling line was Gerry
Durham, a German by descent whose name, as everyone knew,
was an Anglicisation of Gerhard Druhm and whose premises
were a target of patriots and hooligans in the days after war
was declared, his windows smashed to smithereens, his produce
stolen, and no one prepared to step over the threshold except
to insult him – or, worse, issue threats – such that Durham's
wife (who was English through and through) had to go into
hiding with their five children while Gerry himself was interned
by the authorities, no one knew where. But then he always did
keep a little to himself, a watchful individual, dour and
methodical – unlike jolly Joe Orford – the kind who might
become a spy, if he wasn't already, and certainly he wouldn't
be missed; not even his best customers would admit to regret
that he'd gone.

Such remains the temper of the times, and Walter wonders, as
he looks through the window of Orford's shop and sees the
polished empty trays, the empty hooks, the surprising scarcity of

everything but customers, whether Joe has made a mistake in not picking up the trade in horsemeat, for Durham was the only butcher on this side of the city to cater to that market, and while the other Germans locally have also disappeared, quite a few Belgians remain and there must still be a demand, perhaps even among the poor of Riverside Road.

'So how about it, Joe?' Walter calls above the heads of the women inside. 'When're you going to start trading in horsemeat? I've never seen this window so empty!' Smiling, he leans against the open door and crosses his legs at the ankle, folds his arms on his chest, and examines the chalkboard hooked up on the wall, where the only cuts listed are British – beef, pork, lamb, mutton and rabbit (*'subject to supply'*) – and wonders if perhaps horse-meat too has become scarce, since so many of the best animals have been shipped overseas.

'Spice on that, dear?' says Orford.

'Lovely, please,' a woman replies, and Joe shakes some powder on a scrawny bladebone of beef and makes his usual unhurried show of folding it into a parcel.

Walter sighs, and steps briefly aside as another woman enters the shop, then shouts, 'You missed a trick with old Jilly, though, didn't you, Joe? Do you remember? You could've turned a few bob out of her, done the slaughtering yourself, sold her off in fucking bits. You missed a trick there all right!' He points a little way along the road, and says to no one in particular, 'She practically gave herself to him. Died right there. The old mare from the ice house.'

That was in 1914, when Walter was sixteen and employed by Cyril Greenland to haul a handcart up and down Riverside Road, delivering three-shilling slabs of ice to the wet-fish merchants, dairymen and butchers who were everywhere then, though sometimes he would also be required to help carry the ice much further afield – to Beckwith House and beyond – which meant that poor Jilly would have to be harnessed up to the wagon, since so many of the younger horses had been commandeered by the military, including the piebald Bella, who had been brought in as Jilly's replacement.

Released onto Crag's Meadow a year earlier to chew grass and canter about for the rest of her days, Jilly was forced back out of retirement and though she wasn't ill-treated, or even overworked, one morning she collapsed as Walter was leading her down from her stable; she simply lay on her side in the street and would not get up again, for all that he threatened and pleaded.

He can still see her. Walter looks to where she lay and remembers the small crowd gathering round her, including Cyril Greenland, who came up from the ice house, and Joe Orford, of course, with several of his customers, a cluster of housewives in shawls and aprons and caps, all solemnly watching the effortful rise and fall of the mare's breathing – her ribs sharply defined in the low sunshine, flies pestering her eyes – and when he glances over his shoulder now he sees one of the Fordham men coming again up Riverside Road from the knacker's yard, tunelessly whistling, his boot-tacks sparking on the cobbles, his hands in his pockets. Walter wipes his eyes on his sleeve, surprised to find he is crying, and steps to one side to let the man through. His name is Chocky, and his trousers are tied with rope, his face shadowed with dirt, and there's a halter tucked under his arm. With the barest of greetings he passes a handful of coins to Cyril Greenland; then without ceremony or sentiment he gives the old beast a kick in the belly and barks at her and as she staggers upright – some of the women turning away, too distressed to watch any more of it – he slips the halter over her head, takes her by the lead-line and runs. He makes her trot to her death.

In next to no time her skin will be leather, her bones boiled for glue, her hoofs made into buttons. The last of her flesh will be minced up for dogs, and though this isn't any of Orford's doing, none at all, suddenly the very sight of him is infuriating, a provocation, and Walter shouts into his shop, 'You're a fucking disgrace, Joe, you really are! You charge us rent on that stinking fucking hole, you squeeze us for every last fucking penny, than

126

you go and pass up a chance on that poor fucking horse! You could've bought her. You could've sold her as mincemeat yourself, a tanner a pound. What's got into you, Orford?'

But the butcher remains quite unable to hear him. However loudly he yells, however filthy his language, Walter cannot get through to him, not even when he continues, 'Orford! You filthy cunt, you shitty fuck, when are you going to lay off pawing my mother and do something about our fucking house? Orford, you cunt!'

He pauses, his temples pounding, fists clenched, then looks around him for something to throw, a cobble perhaps from the road, but catches instead a glimpse of Gertie Dobson rattling by on a bicycle, the sun blaring from her white dress.

Her bottom is plump on the seat, her waist as slender as any chorus girl's, and she is wearing white gloves, a white bonnet, a white ribbon tied in her ponytail, and suddenly exultant – all thoughts of Orford and Jilly forgotten – Walter whistles to catch her attention and when she half turns he runs a little way after her, or tries to, but his legs have no power; he can make no ground, seems almost to be running on the spot, but horribly slowly, slowed right down. Breathless, he stops, and places his hands on his knees and stares at his boots, his muddy military boots, which feel as if he hasn't removed them in weeks – more weeks than he can remember – then pulls himself together and sets off at the double in pursuit of her.

17
Winnie

No one else would display her such courtesy

Beyond Edwards's the monumental masons and Bateson's the builders' merchants and Egerton's the fishmongers there's a turn for Lady's Lane and the Artichoke Inn, after which comes Hope Brothers' hosiers and Batterbee's barbers and the workshop of Samuel Sexton, bespoke boot and shoe manufacturer ('*Motorists' Footwear & Leggings a Speciality*'), followed by Woolcomber's Alley and the Gardener's Arms, Warren's confectioners and Morgan's walking-stick makers, then Talbot's the tobacconists, where a workman on a ladder is fixing a new hoarding to the arm above the door ('*Sure Shot cigars: the leading 2d smoke*') and Winnie Barley is forced to step into the road before turning down Half Moon Alley, passing the yard of Aldrich's grocer's (now boarded), in which stands a row of barrels containing the jam he was attempting to make from winter root vegetables – fresh fruit becoming so scarce – before he took his own life, every one of his five sons having been killed overseas.

Two of the barrels have split and the stinking, treacly mess is swarming with flies in the muggy mid-afternoon heat.

Winnie covers her mouth until she reaches the quayside, then gags on the rank sewer smell of this stretch of the river and spits on a patch of rough tufted grass, a cold sweat breaking out on her forehead, one hand clutching a railing, the other her belly. She is not very well and ought to sit down. Giddily she turns in the direction of Ice House Lane, the next entry along, where she ducks beneath the rickety steps that lead up to Cyril Greenland's abandoned old office – a clapboard shed on timber piers, the windows becoming quite filthy – and continues along the towpath to the end of Ferryboat Lane, where each morning she will wait to cross the river to Beckwith's Engineering, the platform offering just enough room for the thirty-eight passengers that the flat-bottomed boat can accommodate, most of them standing, the others seated on benches beneath a row of ramshackle shelters.

She sat there this morning at six. She goes and sits there again now.

It costs a ha'penny a day to make the passage across, and most mornings she and the other women will go over in silence, anxiously watching the approach of the opposite bank, since it was only this year that the ferry capsized, one icy evening in February, drowning two of the passengers outright, two more of them succumbing to consumption because of being dunked in such freezing cold water, and the ferryman himself falling to pneumonia, which no one would have wished on him – he was a decent old boy, and always ready to offer a hand up if the ferry was rocking – but still, who else was to blame if it wasn't the ferryman? Out of kindness to the women, he had allowed too many on board.

Winnie gazes at the shimmer in the middle of the river, which is where they tipped in and where the current is strongest, though it seems so innocuous now, and scans across to the landing platform and up to Beckwith's railway sheds, their wavering bulk in the haze, and behind them the higgledy-piggledy confusion of factories and warehouses, chimneys, towers and other buildings that comprise Beckwith's Engineering, including Shed F where she works, the letter painted ten feet high on its side.

Around at the front it is more handsome, of course, the part of the site known as the West Gate, where the letters *J. A. C. BECKWITH & SON* form an arch in black wrought-iron over the main entrance, the ornate double gates depicting in metal an unlikely array of delicate things: fleurs-de-lys, sunflowers, rosebuds and tulips, poppy heads. The SON in the company name isn't Montague, she understands, but Montague's grand-father, the firm having been founded before Victoria was queen, and that is the entrance that the current Mr Beckwith will use, coming and going most days in his motor-car, his office some-where concealed in the cluster of red-brick administrative buildings that stand in the shade of two massive old plane trees, the tarmacadamised road lined with fancy gas-lamps, bordered by flower-beds.

Winnie has been through those gates only once, for just over an hour, when the company first issued its call for female work-ers and she joined a queue of mostly familiar faces in a lobby of varnished panels, marble tiles, and long dark paintings of battles – the soldiers in kilts, scarlet tunics, feathered helmets. The smell of beeswax was pleasant, the light tinted by stained-glass windows as if in a church, and there she stood with the other women, all of them dressed in their Sunday-best clothing and talking in whispers as they waited to be summoned one by one to a room whose door remained open, a plain deal table at its centre and two sombre gentlemen facing the applicant, who was invited at last to be seated.

The questions were brisk and concerned her previous employ-ment, her age and marital status, the status of her husband and male dependants – whether employed, enlisted, wounded, miss-ing or killed – and the nature if any of her family connection to Beckwith's. Her father, a foreman, had worked there. His name was still known. That sealed it.

She was shown out through a different door and into a differ-ent corridor and asked to take a seat on a bench where she was offered a cup of tea that she would have accepted but that a gentleman in a frock coat, starched collar and tie, waistcoat and watch-chain, his shoes beetle-black and shining, strode dumpily past her and into an office marked *J. L. Tudor Esq., Clerk of Personnel*, and almost immediately reappeared. He coughed softly, and pronounced her name. Winnie's heart quickened

A coal fire burned in the room, an old leather armchair beside it, and the walls were tidy with framed diplomas and small wood-mounted samples of Beckwith's famous barbed wire and netting, the ceiling so high that the lights descended on pulleys, though this was not, she realised, Mr Tudor's actual office but the ante-room to his office, and the gentleman observing her from the leather-topped desk by the door was his secretary, a Mr Boleman, who required Winnie to sign her name on a document that he pushed towards her, pulled away from her, and promptly concealed in a buff-coloured file.

'Thank you, Mrs Barley,' said Mr Tudor himself, offering his hand. 'I'm delighted to welcome you to Beckwith and Son, Engineering, where I'm sure you'll make a very valuable contribution.' Then, 'Shed F, beginning Monday morning at six thirty, if you would,' and gently smiling, gently touching her arm, he ushered her out and called the next person in.

No one else would display her such courtesy, no one else in her life but Joe Orford.

accidental drownings and suicides mostly

Winnie hears a splash some way downriver, a smooth entry, no explosion of water but a bullet of noise and then silence. She watches until a head emerges mid-channel, one arm coming over, then the other, and seemingly effortlessly the swimmer in his blue costume proceeds coastwards, his head switching this way, then that, his dark hair otter-slick, his legs rhythmically chopping, and as she watches his progress as far as the rowing club – a smart terraced hut painted in maroon and white stripes – she aches to follow him, and gets to her feet, as though tugged, and walks to the edge of the platform.

She leans a little way out, gazing into her reflection, and seems to see the taint of the factory washing across her, for Beckwith's draws off so many thousands of gallons of water a day – to cool the wire after annealing, to rinse it after its acid bath – then pumps the water back into the river, contaminated by chemicals and use, and as she looks down at it, fatly lapping up to the piers, she imagines the surface tilting towards her, the platform collapsing, and herself tumbling over, which wouldn't be at all out of the ordinary in this neighbourhood: she has seen so many bodies passing down Mortuary Yard on the constable's handcart – accidental drownings and suicides mostly – and once even saw her own brother drifting by on the water, his arms spread out to either side of him and a swollen cigar wedged in one hand, his face hideously bloated and pecked at by fishes.

A neighbour had called her to come, and of course there was already a crowd looking on since Ronnie was by that time well known, a joke figure in fact, who had previously worked in Fawley's brickyard, an office boy at the start, but later clerk of all aspects, in charge of the wages, the men's stamps, the company invoices, all the paper paraphernalia, and so it was to Ronnie that the instruction had come to shut everything up one winter when the frost wouldn't melt and the bricks couldn't be made and Fawley's debts overran him; it was Ronnie's responsibility to sack all the men, then sack himself, and lock the office and take the keys along to Mr Fawley, after which he didn't work again, but retreated into himself, obscurely to blame – in his own mind, at least – for the brickmaker's failure.

Reclusive for much of the week, on Saturday mornings if the weather was fine Ronnie would go along to redeem from the pawnbroker's a gentleman's suit of black pinstripe with a black leather briefcase, black umbrella and gold watch-chain, then put on his bowler hat and walk the six miles into the countryside to Raworth Mill station, from where he would catch the next train coming straight back. He travelled first class, the country dust wiped from his best boots, and alighted on platform three to be greeted by the usual urchins asking if they might carry his brolly and briefcase, for which he would tip them a few farthings before proceeding to the restaurant of the Railway Inn, where he would dine from the menu and drink several brandies, then stagger home drunk to his kitchen, chamber and garret in St Xavier's Lane (another of Joe Orford's properties).

That was Ronnie's entertainment of a weekend – sixpence for the train fare, some farthings for the children, half a crown or more at the inn, and whatever it cost to redeem the suit and accoutrements that he would have to pawn again the following Monday – until finally he came to the end of his money, as he was bound to, as everyone expected he must, sooner or later, and one day failed to make the return journey by train but floated back down on the river, his watch-chain, brolly, briefcase and bowler all gone, his pinstripe suit soaked through and inflated with air, and that fat cigar stuck between two spongy white fingers.

He had merely wanted to be better than he was; Winnie could understand that.

she works as hard as any man

The wood railing creaks. Winnie can feel how easily it might give under pressure and as she steps away from it she slips her hand into her skirt pocket for the bottle of pills that the pharmacist gave to her and grips it tightly, so tightly her hand sends a spasm of pain through her wrist and into her forearm, and considers the possibility that she might squeeze until the glass breaks, piercing her hand, cutting it to pieces, as might have happened to poor Walter, her eldest – who is surely not missing, but gone; she is more than ever fearful of that – and as might yet happen to the child she is carrying, if the pharmacist is obliged to use his instruments, if his pills fail to work, when possibly she too will be shredded a little inside, which will be no more than her due, her just deserts, though that at least might be one way out of it, the heaviness of not knowing about Walter, the sadness, and the pain in her shoulders and neck and her head, which is worsening because of the drink, her hangover having come early: she will need to sleep or take another drink; she cannot bear to sober up.

The cries that come from her sometimes are a surprise, as if emitted by some other woman.

Winnie agitates the pills in the bottle, rattles them about, then sighing, she twists out the cork and shakes a couple into her palm, just a couple, and throws them into her mouth and tips back her head and swallows. But two might not be sufficient, so she swallows another, and decides she will take a drink in Ernie Thirkettle's grocer's, where there are tables and chairs and the company is usually kindly, most of them housewives like herself – sharing the sorrow of sons and husbands overseas – who come to calm their nerves with a sip of sweet stout or a measure of gin; besides which, it is the nearest licensed premises to the ferry, popular with Beckwith's employees – the females at least – and she is known there.

Winnie treads heavily back up the towpath and walks along to the next narrow entry, Haycock's Alley, where she palms away the wet, fragrant slap of a bedsheet hanging over the yard, then another, and another, the damp running cool down her forearm, dripping onto her face. It is soothing. She takes her purse from her skirt pocket and pokes a finger at the coins she has kept back from her wages and reminds herself that she has earned this, her spending money, for she works as hard as any man, without yet being a man, and for less money than a man – less, she is sure, than the old boys she works alongside, all of them a little slow-moving, heavily bewhiskered in the old-fashioned way, including Harry Heggarty, who may or may not be retired but appears to have the run of the sheds and to know everyone, including those who have passed on, including Winnie's father.

Most days Harry will come by, nodding and smiling, chatting to this person and that, and occasionally he will pause by her machine to ask after her husband and son. He will perch on the rim of the rubbish bin as if determined not to let himself settle, but always he will settle, for twenty minutes or more, which

Winnie doesn't mind, despite the attention she knows this attracts from the other men, the nudges and winks.

Harry sits with his hands tucked under his armpits – a peculiar posture – his right hand beneath his right armpit, his left beneath his left, so that his elbows poke out to either side and it looks as though he might be imitating a chicken, his crooked arms a pair of flightless wings, which is what she told him just a few days ago, when the spools were running slow: that he put her in mind of the sheds at Crag's Meadow, where she worked for several years, plucking the turkeys and geese for Christmas, sometimes even wringing their necks in the slaughtering shed. She was teasing him, but he didn't seem to catch on, so she described the first bird she ever killed, which ought to have been straightforward, a simple twist of her wrist just as she'd been shown, listening for the *click* as the turkey's neck broke, except that she missed the click and kept twisting and wrung the bird's neck as if it were a towel while Mrs Maudle the forewoman looked on, smirking in her superior way, until the head came clean away in Winnie's hand and she found herself spattered all over with blood, with a dollop of shit in her lap and Mrs Maudle no longer smirking but sprayed with blood too and frantically calling for someone to help her clean up.

The story was meant to amuse him, but Harry Heggarty gravely nodded and told her in turn about Beckwith's old galvanising shop, how it used to be when Winnie's father worked there, even until very recently: he wouldn't have taken a job in that place to save his soul, he said. It was infernal.

'Dim lights, you know – all dark, Winnie, except for the fires beneath the pots, burning away, which'd be all spitting and spluttering. That's what they called them, pots, though they were great big things and the boys would be coughing – coughing out their insides – with bits of metal all flying about, burning their clothes. The netting would feed into the pots and, oh, that used to fly everywhere, and the clothes those men wasted! Clothes and boots. Didn't get an allowance. No extra pay. So we went on strike for them – they wanted clogs and we went on strike for them, marched up and down Balmoral Road – banners, hymns, chests out. And whatsit – Atherton? – gave a speech from the back of a coal-cart. He was a good speaker, clear, you could hear every word – he went down well, he made a lot of sense. A month and a bit that dragged on for, but we won through in the end and the men got their clogs – they got their clogs – because, you see, this Beckwith, he's not the saint he's made out to be. He wasn't then. He isn't now. And here's the thing, Winnie, we went on strike to get the men their clogs, then they opened a new galvanising shed, a new process, all a lot cleaner, a lot safer, so the clogs weren't ever needed, they were never needed – just the men – then the next thing is they were shipped out to France and no strike's going to save them now, is it? That's a lot worse than here, isn't it? A lot worse than any plucking shed, eh?'

Winnie said she wouldn't know – and how could she know; how could any of them imagine? – for even though her machine manufactures barbed wire for the front, and she can picture the damage one of those spikes might cause to a man – perhaps even to her own son – she has no doubt the men's suffering is far worse than she can imagine, so she tries not to imagine, but concentrates as well as she can on her job, which is to regulate the performance of the mechanical knife that cuts the wires aslant to make the spikes, and to adjust the tappet and cam that determine the regularity of the interval between the barbs, and to control the speed of the belt that turns the spool onto which the finished wire is coiled. All of which she can do without supervision, as can the other girls – and they are all of them girls, never ladies, just as the machines themselves are referred to as girls – and when she is on a good run Harry Heggarty won't linger to talk to her but will mime the lighting of a pipe and will nod and soundlessly laugh, then later say, when the machines are turned off, 'You had the old girl running today, you had a pipe on.'

But though she is perfectly competent now, requiring no guidance or instruction, and can do just what is required of her as a man's temporary stand-in – frequently working twelve hours in the day – still Winnie feels very little like a man: his mystery remains, for this is his machinery, his grease and metal environment, his clanking noise, the product of his invention, and she merely sits in his place – or, rather, sits where he would ordinarily stand – and feels the mystery of him, his absence, whoever he is.

She does his work, accepts his wages, and takes a drink or two on a Saturday, just as he would, if ever the war were to end, if ever he were to return here.

18
Gertie

her father's uncommon generosity

In the basket of her bicycle the two large jars of Dobson's Soothing Lotion (Antiseptic & Healing) clink troublingly together as she jolts over the cobbles past Cleverley's wood yard and the turn for Synagogue Lane, at which point the agitation in the heavy frame is communicating so strongly through the handlebars, and causing her fingers to tingle so peculiarly, that Gertie fears she might lose her grip.

Men are smiling at her, she realises, and of course she is going too fast, but her brakes barely work – merely scratch on the wheel rim – so she must slow herself by hopping for several yards on her right foot, coming at last to a stop beside the tiny shop of Mrs Olorenshaw, who makes her own piccalilli and sells only that, where she sits back on the saddle, her left foot braced on the kerb, and peels off the white gloves that she was such a fool to wear on such a warm afternoon.

Gertie's heart is pounding. She lets out a heavy exhalation and shakes her hands, rubs them vigorously together, and looks over her shoulder and nervously scans the many faces behind her, half fearful of finding another with a resemblance to Walter, then notices a stooping old man – his nose lengthily dribbling, his mouth slackly open – who is staring at her from the dark entrance to Albemarle Alley, just over the road. 'Hello,' she says, bunching one glove inside the other. 'Isn't it close today!'

A plip of slobber lands in the dust by the man's boots, and he neither replies nor looks away from her. Gertie smiles at him uncertainly. His ragged jacket, she notices, bears the ghost of the blue and white stripes that distinguish the uniform of the municipal Workhouse, and she wonders if perhaps he has wandered away and got lost, and would offer to help him except that some cattle are coming up Riverside Road behind her. Hurriedly she realigns the jars in her basket and positions her gloves between them as a buffer against breakages, then calls, 'Goodbye!' to the old man as she wobblingly sets off again, past Warminger's coke and coal merchants and the flickering railings of Callard's brewery, where she begins to accelerate and thinks back to the day her father decided she should accompany him on a visit to the Workhouse, almost exactly one year ago.

It was the morning after she had spoken to Sammy Edwards in the stonemason's display room, and Gertie remembers the ominous tone with which her mother informed her at breakfast that she was to go with her father on an 'excursion', a word she chose after a momentary pause and was quite unable to colour with any hint of excitement. Gertie was to dress herself smartly, and her mother would help her, and help with pinning her hair, though she would not reveal where Gertie was going. 'I'm sure he'll tell you himself,' was all she would say, 'when he gets back.'

'From where?'

'From using Mr Edwards's telephone.'

'His telephone? Why?'

'Your father will explain.'

But he said nothing. Gertie remembers sitting up neatly beside him on their hired trap as they trotted down Riverside Road – the railings of the brewery shimmering on one side, the railings of Riverside School coming up on the other, then out past the fancy gates of Beckwith House and over the rattling bridge to the railway station, where the soldiers are due in later today – its outline luminous at that time of the morning – and along the handsome thoroughfare that led up the long rise of stone-built houses on Mount Pleasant, with their lawns and unusual trees, and into the sweet-smelling countryside to the east of the city, and he said not a word to her, though his jaw was working all the while, gnawing away at his thoughts, his brows forbiddingly close, until at last they came to the Workhouse half a mile further on – the Poor Law Institution, now called – where in previous years he had served on the Visiting Committee that had made monthly inspections of the conditions. By that time his only connection, so far as she knew, was to supply the dispensary with its medicines, yet still he remained a significant personage at the Workhouse, as was revealed when they arrived and passed a dozen or so elderly inmates – old ladies in bonnets and shawls, frail-looking men in their striped jackets – who were sitting out on the boundary wall in the sunshine, smoking clay pipes, but got at once to their feet when they recognised him, and doffed their caps and stiffly bowed, just as a little further on another man, not quite so old or so frail, paused in his labours and pinched the brim of his cap, partially lifted it, though he looked quickly away when he became conscious of Gertie's attention. He returned to his work, whitening the decorative rocks beneath the elms on the driveway, and quietly her father rebuked her: 'Try not to gawp at him, Gertie.'

Their horse tethered securely, Father helped her down from the trap and led her briskly up the path to the porch of the main building where he gave the bell-rope a vigorous tug and went through the heavy oak door without waiting to be admitted, the bell loudly resounding in the wood-panelled vestibule, and when a red-bearded attendant promptly appeared, buttoning his jacket over his belly, he too touched the rim of his cap and said, 'Mr Dobson, sir.' Then to Gertie, not quite meeting her gaze, 'Miss.'

It appeared they were expected. From a doorway to their left stepped a white-aproned, bosomy little body – smiling, stern-eyed – who offered her hand first to Mr Dobson, saying she was delighted, then to Gertie, saying not a word, though her gaze lingered on Gertie's face, as if to fix it in her memory, and swiftly appraised her appearance, her shapely figure in her cream cotton frock.

'Matron,' said her father, and took from one pocket a pouch of tobacco and from another a few penn'orth of sweets, and said they were to be awarded to whomever might earn them, his voice half obscured by his beard, swallowed back, it seemed, by some sort of reluctance or discomfort: he wasn't a hard-hearted man, of that Gertie felt certain, but he was awkward in his compassion, and perhaps uncomfortable to be seen to be charitable when he had so often railed against encouraging the indigent, as he called them, in their dependence on others.

Matron expressed her gratitude, and passed his gifts to the attendant, who accepted one in each hand and held them ceremoniously until Matron suggested that Mr Dobson and his daughter might like to follow her. 'This way,' she said, and guided them down one long corridor, then into another, their heels clacking on the stone flags, echoing ahead of them, a smell of carbolic masking something altogether more unpleasant, which arrived sharply to greet them at the door to a wide, high-ceilinged day room in which sat a dismal array of seemingly emaciated old women in Bath chairs and settles and rickety garden chairs, some draped in brown blankets, some drooling or keening, and all of them facing the fireplace – which was lit, though meagrely, and enclosed by a vast iron-mesh cage – apparently unaware of Matron or her visitors, who proceeded past them, across a floor scattered with bits of straw matting, then into a corridor identical to the one they had just left, except that it was populated by half a dozen young women, none of them older than Gertie and all on their hands and knees with cloths and scrubbing brushes, blocks of yellow soap and pails of grey water.

Motioning towards an alcove in the wall, Matron indicated to Gertie and her father where they might stand, and for several minutes they quietly watched as the girls scrubbed the already unblemished tiles, until Gertie's back began to ache with the effort of being so still, and finally Matron clapped her hands and barked, 'Stand!' Which cumbersomely the girls did, each one of them displaying a huge, surprising belly beneath her grey tunic, and all of them flushed and conspicuously damp about the brows and under their arms.

'Do you see?' asked her father, in a low, confidential tone, which nevertheless could not fail to be audible in the echoing corridor. 'These girls allowed themselves to be distracted by young men in khaki – they had their heads turned – and this is the outcome. This is where it must lead. Do you understand me, Gertie?'

He was glowering, and she swallowed and said that, yes, she did understand him, and with a satisfied nod he turned on his heels and led her back in the direction they'd come – Matron now hurrying along in their wake, chubbily failing to keep pace with them – and not only signed the visitors' book with unusual energy but handed the attendant a couple of pennies, and it was this as much as anything else she experienced that morning that remains in Gertie's memory – her father's uncommon generosity – since the true purpose of their excursion remains somewhat unclear to her, given that she is so easily distracted, and always has been – as he himself so often reminds her, and is in addition no stranger to such damp, aching drudgery as they observed that day in that corridor.

Gertie has ample experience of just that nature of work, which her father surely ought to have known since it was he who paid for her education, and chose the institution she attended, in order that she need not be molested, as he once put it, by the likes of the imbeciles and ruffians in the school on Riverside Road.

she was clumsy and dropped things

Jeremiah Beckwith's Academy of Housecraft and Manners for Girls wasn't much further from the pharmacy than her previous school, but took Gertie in the opposite direction, towards the centre of town and the narrow streets around the cathedral, and she was happy to be sent there since she liked to wear a uniform and enjoyed being taken for a young lady in her sailor's straw boater and pleated blue tunic. The school had been founded by the previous Mr Beckwith – the grandfather of Edwina and Emma – and provided for two classes of pupil, the fee-paying Schoolgirls, of whom she was one, and the charitably supported Housegirls, most of them orphans or the surplus females of poor families. And while the Housegirls did receive some rudimentary schooling in the three Rs – just as the Schoolgirls were educated in the fundamentals of domestic science – their education was mainly an apprenticeship in all aspects of service, everything from the duties of the scullery-maid to those of a lady's maid.

The Housegirls would do the work about the school that in any other establishment would be the duty of hired hands, which included changing the bed linen of those Schoolgirls who lived in, and washing and mending their clothes, including their underwear, and waiting upon them at table. Every morning when Gertie and the other day-girls arrived they would join the boarders for a breakfast of toasted white bread served with strawberry jam in one silver pot, marmalade in another, and tea poured from pink china pots to pink china cups, the table having been set before most of the Schoolgirls were even awake. The Housegirls were required to rise an hour earlier, and would go to bed an hour later at night.

Gertie enjoyed the deference of the Housegirls, on those occasions when deference was required of them, and suffered no embarrassment at receiving their little courtesies, since all of it seemed to her exactly like a game – she knew they were pretending – and, besides, she would regularly be set to sharing chores with them as a punishment for her many misdemeanours (her lapses in concentration in the classroom, her failures of deportment), this in addition to the chores that were already a part of the Schoolgirls' curriculum, for no one expected them to become mere ladies of leisure: their best hope, they were told, was to be taken in marriage by a superior professional man, who would

143

naturally depend upon a small number of servants for support (though perhaps only as few as one or two), and might therefore require his wife to have some personal acquaintance with the drudgery of housework, and so in addition to their uniforms the Schoolgirls were required to be kitted out with hard-wearing work clothes, such as the Housegirls would wear in the mornings – blue and white things – and thus attired they would be set for a few hours each week to cooking, scrubbing, washing or polishing. Collectively they might wash and dry the crockery after their midday meal, for instance, and it was there, not in her stumbling performance in class, but in her clumsy execution of the simplest domestic task, such as drying the dishes, that Gertie received the most reprimands and punishments. She was clumsy and dropped things.

Nevertheless, she excelled at needlecraft, appeared to have a gift for it, and so it was that the headmistress of Beckwith's Academy – a stern little person named Mrs Aspinall – arranged to have her apprenticed to the drapery department of Theobald Osgood and Sons, the largest and finest of the city's emporia, whose motto declared *Premium Quality In All Goods For All Classes* and whose reputation attracted ladies from both the city and the county to have their clothes made or adjusted in the style and to the standard advertised in journals such as *Home and Hearth* and *The Queen*, the Misses Beckwith sometimes among them.

Gertie was to begin her training in a section called Ladies' Dress Embroidery and Textile Embellishment, where she was given to understand that it was considered almost as much a distinction to work in such a high-class establishment as it was to patronise it with one's custom, and that she wasn't to wonder that her father was required to pay a five-pound premium to have her bound over to learn the intricacies of the trade, or that she would not receive a penny in wages for the first year of the arrangement, and a mere three shillings a week in her second year, or that her father would have to provide her with pocket money, too, out of which she was to buy her own stockings, hair ribbons and pins, and the 'cooking sleeves' she wore over her dress sleeves. She was to consider herself fortunate to be in such a position.

But her father did soon begin to wonder at the details of the arrangement – reputable establishment though it certainly was – and to suspect that Gertie might already know far more in the way of fancy stitching and the like than Osgood's would ever be able to teach her, and so he was, to her relief, uncommonly serene when she relayed to him the news – barely six months into her employment – that the Misses Beckwith had suggested she might become their private seamstress and companion, employed from the outset at five shillings a week to improve upon the garments that they ordered from Manchester and London through the pages of *The Lady* and *The Queen*, her job being to introduce, and sometimes remove, additional tucks and darts, sequins and beads, lace and frills and bits of elaborate hand-stitched embroidery.

Such an accommodation, her father agreed, with such a class of person, would be far more profitable and germane to her education, and far more advantageous to her socially, than any number of years on her knees pinning frocks for the clientele, however refined, of Theobald Osgood and Sons department store, so she was permitted to hand in her notice at once and to make her first auspicious journey to the home of the Beckwiths – which she can now glimpse through the trees beyond the last few dwellings on Riverside Road – where she was to remain for the next two and a half years, even during their period of outspoken suffragism, and the first twelve months of the war, during which year she assisted in their efforts to encourage recruitment, until at last they decided it would be unpatriotic to continue to indulge themselves in fancy hats and frocks at a time of national emergency, and would no longer require Gertie to mend or refashion their existing wardrobe either, since they were committed to joining the war effort in France and to dressing in uniform, and therefore suggested that she might like to contribute by taking up a position in their father's factory instead, to which Gertie gladly agreed, Osgood's drapery department having meanwhile moved over to the production of fine embroidered badges for the officers of the Army and Navy, such was everyone's dedication at that time to the cause of King and Country.

19
Montague

almost the worst of it

When at last they got him out — despite the confusion, the calamitous collapse of that stretch of the line, with men lying dead all around him and the bombardment continuing — Montague was removed at some lick by his bearers to the Regimental Aid Post and the Advanced Dressing Station, then onwards by ambulance train to the Field Hospital and from there to the General Hospital — all of this in under three days — after which he was deemed unfit for an immediate return and discharged to a convalescent home near Dieppe in order to gather his strength (or his wits) before the crossing to England, at which point he might have been dispatched to another hospital or to a Rest Station — such as a man of his rank would ordinarily be assigned — but that Beckwith House was itself about to be established as an auxiliary hospital, which enabled his father to plead the appropriateness of his being allowed home to recuperate. And perhaps it ought not to come as such a surprise to Montague now that the Board should wish to return him to his commission — as must surely be their intention — since his treatment by the authorities thus far has been so charitable, even indulgent, given the absence of any visible wound, any definite affliction other than funk.

'That is how they will view the matter, Miss Dobson,' he whispers, turning about in his room, her image quite clear in his mind. She will be dressed in pale blue, a simple silk garment with ivory trimmings, such as he saw her wearing once previously. 'A clear case of the funk, not far short of cowardice. I think we can be certain of that.'

He nods, clasping his hands behind his back, and slowly paces past the end of his bed.

'Of course, they might not return me to front-line duty at once: I might be offered a desk job, something less taxing. It will depend on the doctor they appoint to examine me, and whether he decides my symptoms are all in the mind.'

'But I can see them,' she might say. 'Your symptoms are visible.'

'Yes, indeed,' he agrees, and pours himself a drop of water from the carafe on his dressing-table. It is tepid, unpleasant. 'What I mean is, I will be assessed from a psychological perspective, on the assumption – it's a plausible hypothesis – that my physical symptoms are the manifestation of a nervous instability. And if they decide that they *are* the manifestation of a nervous instability, then they will have reached agreement that I am hysterical, an hysteric. Men are not supposed to be hysterical, Miss Dobson. It's a somewhat shaming diagnosis, particularly for an officer.'

Montague turns and faces the chair in which she will be seated. The sunlight is falling across it, glistening in the silvery stitch of the upholstery, and as he gazes down on the fabric he contemplates the possibility that the Board might therefore decide to discharge him – not dishonourably, but dismiss him all the same – or, worse, consign him to some asylum or other to regain his composure in the hope that his carapace might begin to recede, and with a deep breath he continues: 'For which reason, on reflection, it might be better that I should return to duty. Given the opportunity, it might be better that I should re-enter the fray . . .'

'Oh, but you can't!' she will object – or perhaps something less exclamatory, since he believes Gertie Dobson to be more naturally reticent than either of his two sisters, such is the impression he has gained from their limited acquaintance;

and while he does not doubt that she will be raw, as yet unpolished, lacking the graces of Edwina and Emma, he is certain that she is honest, and wholesome, and straightforward. 'But do you actually want to go back?' she might ask him. Or, 'Would that be such a good thing, do you think, given your condition?'

'No, I do not want to go back,' he admits. 'No, of course not. It would be quite mad of me to want to return.' He smiles, a reflex, and feels the rubbery stiffness in one side of his face. He touches his cheek. 'A desire to return to the war would be the surest evidence they need that I am mentally unstable and not entitled to go.'

Politely then she might laugh – or perhaps laugh and immediately apologise for her insensitivity, in which case he would be able to reassure her that there is no need to be sorry, since the paradox is amusing after all, and one recognisable to most soldiers; besides which, he is conscious of his own far more shaming capacity for laughter in the midst of such awfulness as he doubts he could begin to describe to her.

'How so?' she will ask him.

'I'm sorry, Miss Dobson?'

'Shaming?'

Montague looks away to the fireplace, where there is a strand of cobweb in the empty grate, a coating of dust on the tiles, and quietly says, 'I wouldn't wish to burden you, Miss Dobson. That would hardly be fair of me.'

'Please, I am listening.'

The sunlight remains steady, the afternoon still, with barely a sound to be heard from the house or the grounds, and all at once the silence begins to seem ominous, pressing like dread on his nerves. Suddenly agitated, Montague strides across to the door, touches the doorknob, then turns and strides back. He lowers himself to the edge of his bed and leans forwards, his elbows resting on his knees, his hands firmly clasped to steady their tremor, and attempts to breathe evenly.

Minutes pass. He frowns; he clears his throat.

'Let me offer you an example, Miss Dobson,' he whispers at last. 'The day recurs in my mind rather like a dream, a persistent bad dream. One of a number of them. It was a Sunday, and we had been ordered to advance on the enemy line, about three hundred yards distant' – he gestures past his balcony, beyond the tops of the trees – 'but first we had to endure a bombardment, a barrage of shelling from our own side, our own artillery, that was intended to subdue the enemy, to weaken his resolve, though you must understand it was no less of an ordeal for our own men – including myself – since we were required to submit to this terrible, terrifying noise just as the enemy was, for hour upon hour, and not just the screech of the shells going over, but the shells coming in – because it was bound to provoke a reaction, you see, a retaliatory barrage.'

Tentatively he touches his hands to his ears, and explains, 'One would feel the concussion in the air when the bombs detonated, and the flash, the sudden heat. Great plumes of earth would go up and come showering down, and there'd be bodies and parts of bodies going up too – one saw such dreadful sights – after which came the shrieks of the men who'd been hit, and the rats, too, since they were everywhere, the higher-pitched screams of the rats. It was a great industry of killing, Miss Dobson, and of course it wasn't only the landscape that disintegrated, but some sense of oneself. The map of oneself, as it were, ceased to make a great deal of sense, because the pounding was so relentless, you see.

'The percussion would seem to begin in the soles of your boots and reverberate upwards, and it struck the inner ear like a hammer on a bell, like the clanging of a bell, and not only that – it's a peculiar thing – but the men's helmets picked up the vibration and began vibrating to a slightly higher pitch that sounded as a *ping ping ping* at the extremity of one's hearing – it seemed to buzz in one's jaw, in one's teeth, rather like a current of electricity.

'So of course one shouldn't be surprised that some of the men lost their nerve. Some of them were bound to weaken, including one particular fellow I remember – a biggish chap, a sturdy upright chap in ordinary life, I shouldn't wonder – who took leave of his senses entirely and became completely demented, yelling nonsense and waving his arms about and clambering to leave the trench before the signal, which only served to add to the distress of the other men, so it was a blessing in fact that he was shot; it was a relief to everyone.'

Stiffly Montague gets to his feet, concealing his hands in his pockets, and looks away to the door. 'It was a relief to everyone, Miss Dobson,' he repeats, 'but still the bombardment went on, and all the while, alongside the assault on one's senses, there was the fearful anticipation of having to go over the top, which tight-wound the nerves to another kind of unnatural pitch, such that I'm sure every man there became so coiled with anxiety he could hardly wait to spring up, even if that meant placing himself directly in the line of fire. Which is precisely what happened. The bombardment, for all its fury, was rather a failure. The enemy endured – doubtless he had better defences, concealed underground, than our commanders had anticipated – which meant we were required to advance on him with nothing in our favour, you might say, except that we were Englishmen.'

Montague grimaces, and coughs, and says out loud, '*Come on, if you know you are Englishmen!*' But the sound of his voice in the emptiness of his room seems absurd to him and, whispering, he says, 'I heard that shouted by a chap along the line, Miss Dobson. He was doing his best no doubt – more than his best, I suppose – and one ought to admire his backbone, and his patriotism, but it didn't take him or his men very far. He was cut down almost at once. Because the Germans had no choice but to shoot at us. What else could they do? And how could they miss their target? Our bombardment had ceased, and here we came, scrambling over the parapet, hundreds of us, with hundreds of yards to traverse before we could engage with the enemy, and nothing to shield us from his guns, nothing whatsoever.

'It was like walking into a gale or a blizzard of bullets – one heard the zip of them – and everywhere men were falling, more of them falling than continuing on, it seemed to me. I saw chaps stumbling over the bodies of chaps who had already fallen, and others tumbling onto the remains of men who were still there from the last big push, the putrefying parts of other men – previous men – who had turned black, or green or yellow. Such hideous colours – and of course one would have no choice but to leave them. One would have to press on.'

Montague measures four strides to the window and gazes down on the tents, the duckboards descending to the lawn, the spike of the flagpole. He swallows. 'Unfortunately, by this time the enemy's artillery had also begun to find its range, and the noise was again becoming horrendous, which turned everything into a sort of dumb show. There was the smoke, of course – which was choking – and the showers of dirt, the clods of earth flying about, not to mention the body parts, and in the midst of all of this one saw men frenzied with fear, hideously screaming, or desperately wounded, their faces stricken with terror, and yet there wasn't a cry to be heard. It was silenced by the cacophony that contained it, you see, as if the noise itself had become a different kind of silence, and I remember feeling oddly as if I had passed into a dream in which the person whose body I inhabited gave orders, and gestured, and fired, and stumbled on, and then – the strangest thing – I came upon a man, a corporal, who had chosen to kneel down and pray. I had to step around him. His head was bowed. His hands were clasped in his lap – like so – his eyes were closed, his rifle laid down beside him, and I did nothing, though I ought to have reprimanded him – I ought to have ordered him to fight on – but I didn't, I left him to his prayers, and that is how he remained, not just for the duration of that attack, but all through the shambles that followed it, our chaotic retreat. And then for hours and hours afterwards he remained on his knees, Miss Dobson, sending his prayers up to heaven. Because he was dead, do you see? He had been dead all along. That was simply how he had fallen, onto his knees.'

The sun is warm on Montague's neck, the back of his head, and distantly he seems to hear a rolling of thunder, some vibration in the atmosphere, a quickening in the trees around the lake, and with a shiver he steps away, begins another halting tour of his room. 'We could see him quite plainly,' he whispers, 'those of us who were left, pinned down in our trenches and bolt-holes. And it just so happened that I was looking straight at him when a shell landed – not a direct hit, but near enough that the blast or a fragment could fly out and take his head clean off his shoulders. That is what I saw. And still he knelt there, this dogged Christian, and I'm ashamed to say I felt not the slightest shock or revulsion at the sight of him, or even pity for the poor fellow – whoever he used to be – but something close to elation, Miss Dobson. Joy, exaltation . . . certainly hilarity. That is when I started to laugh, I'm afraid. I found the sight of him quite hilarious.'

Grimly Montague refills his glass. 'Quite hilarious,' he repeats, and holds the water up to the light, looking for contaminants, green spores that might explain its peculiar tint and mildewy taste, but it is clear. 'Except that there was no humour in it, none whatsoever, simply hysteria, though I dare say there was also a degree of relief – to have survived, you know. Because the conditions did not favour survival.'

He sips, and dabs at his mouth with his handkerchief. He has made himself hoarse. 'No, not at all. The conditions did not favour survival, but neither did they particularly reward it, Miss Dobson. Which may also be a paradox – a curiosity anyway – that sometimes one would regret coming through, because the aftermath could be so much worse than the engagement itself. The landscape would be all blasted about, of course, a dreadful quagmire, as it was on that day, and yet it was also alive with movement, all wormy with men crawling and wriggling about – the mortally wounded, you know, dozens and dozens of them, Germans as well as our own, all mixed up in the mud. And then there was the shelling and shooting, which continued – the danger hadn't really gone away – and so the burial squads were not able to retrieve the dead, and the medical chaps weren't able to tend the wounded – they simply had to be left there, crying and moaning, because there was no possibility of anyone being able to clamber out, not if they wished to preserve their own life. Besides which, the trenches were also full of men in need of attention. And you must understand, it wasn't only these poor men that one had to listen to: it was the weeping of the others, the survivors – the sound of so many men sobbing like children. How about that, Miss Dobson? That was almost the worst of it. The sound of those men crying.'

Montague glances across to the chair and supposes that Gertie's eyes would also be welling with tears, softly gleaming in this late-afternoon light, but she would not flinch at his news and he would not be tempted to spare her, for she would not wish to be spared. 'Go on,' she might say, accepting his handkerchief. 'Please, do go on. I believe there was worse for you?'

'Yes,' Montague says, 'yes, there was worse,' and stands at her shoulder, just behind her, and rests a hand on the curved mahogany rim of her chair. 'I had another half a year of it yet to endure,' he says, and flexes his fingers, extends them as if into her dark hair, touching the nape of her neck, and supposes she might twist around a little to face him, and perhaps place her soft hand over his – which is reptilian, of course. His own hand resembles a claw, seemingly bloodless, quite unable now to manipulate a pen, the nails fractured and yellowing, and with a sigh he tilts back the chair, and lets go; he allows it to fall with a sharp clack to the floor, then straightens his shoulders and retreats once again to stand in the shade by his bed, from where he is able to see himself in his mirror, alone in his room, and after some moments he decides to sit down, in case he should fall too, since he appears to be shaking so badly.

20
Walter

Plucky little Riverside!

> *Campside cowards!*
> *High Street roughs!*
> *Plucky little Riverside!*
> *Kicks 'em in the dust!*

Walter remembers this ditty as he heads along Riverside Road in pursuit of Gertie Dobson, and for a few carefree moments he lifts his knees, swings his arms and stamps his feet as he goes, recalling how the boys would play soldiers when they were younger, the city mapped out in their minds as a patchwork of territories, each at war with the rest, everyone a belligerent and no thought for alliances. Softly he chants the rhyme to himself, and soon finds he has a companion, a comrade, marching along-side him, a little old chap by the name of Charlie Champion who used to live in Callard's Yard and always did dress himself in the style of a soldier, with regimental whiskers and a fading blue uniform that might once have come from the circus, his chest decorated with more medals than there have been campaigns in the last fifty years – which is how long he usually claims, salut-ing, to have served Queen and King and Country.

The last Walter heard he was poorly, on his way out, and is encouraged to find him seeming so well. 'Hello, Charlie,' he laughs, 'I see you've come through again,' but though the medals are obviously fakes, and Charlie is clearly a clown of some sort, he is serious, rarely smiles, and doesn't smile now, but salutes and whips off his cap and holds it out for a tip. Apologetically Walter pats his tunic pockets, and shows him two empty hands. 'Sorry,' he says, and Charlie briefly stands with a loud stamp to attention, still saluting, then falls in step a few paces behind him.

Which has always been Charlie's style. Depending on the season he might sell lucky primroses gathered from the countryside, or watercress, or lucky lavender, and in winter there will be cough sweets and chestnuts, but largely it seems he makes his money simply by parading up and down Riverside Road, singing songs and saluting and proffering his cap, and whenever there's a gala day he will be there, not just on a Saturday for the market, but on those red-letter days that come around only once in a year – for instance, Empire Day, when Charlie Champion will behave as though he were as important a personage as the Lord Mayor or Sheriff, arriving to announce the half-day school holiday, and will stride up Riverside Road ahead of the municipal landau as it makes its way first to the Infant and Junior Schools, then to the Girls' and Boys' Schools, accepting the applause of the crowds, plying with his cap for their coins.

And, of course, when war was declared he was everywhere, including the scrimmage outside the Corn Hall on August the fourth, where the front page of the *Mirror* was posted in a glass-fronted display case and he and Walter rubbed shoulders in the jostle to look at the news, though Charlie alone among that heaving crowd seemed less concerned with what the paper might say than simply to be part of such a comradely body of men, caught up in their enthusiasm, even elation.

Huge Crowds Cheer Their Majesties at Palace, reported the *Mirror*, and they cheered too at the rallies on City Parade, the Cattle Market and outside the Guildhall, dozens of men raising their caps, bowlers and boaters to the summer sky and giving three cheers for the King – Charlie Champion saluting – and all of this so out of the ordinary it was as if some spirit of comedy had spilled from the Hippodrome, or as if the war had already been won, such was the sense of celebration, the great stir of excitement, the carnival air.

'Do you remember all of that?' calls Walter over his shoulder, as they make their way towards the Boys' School, a scraggy Jack Russell hastening past him, its eyes white and bulging. 'Charlie?'

'I do, yes,' replies Charlie, who is further back than Walter realised. 'I remember that well.'

This was at the beginning, when every day seemed a gala day and the flags and banners in town were newly unfurled and their colours so startling, and stirring – for instance, the one that was strung across the entrance to the Artillery Barracks in St Saviour's Street. COME AND JOIN THE HAPPY THRONG, it said, and countless men did, or tried to, especially the young ones, some of them plainly too young to enlist, Walter Barley included. They flocked in their droves to the meetings, listened rapt to the speeches, heartily chorused the songs – 'Land of Hope and Glory', 'Rule Britannia', all the usual bull – then queued to step up to the platform to sign over their lives beneath an image of Lord Kitchener stabbing his finger, after which the lucky recruits (the ones who weren't turned away) would be marched to Crag's Meadow behind a military band, a smiling drill sergeant alongside them, groups of onlookers cheering. The men would be wearing their civvies – clerks as well as labourers, scholars as well as apprentices, some sporting bow-ties, some smoking clay pipes – while Charlie Champion would be there in his uniform, his tin medals glinting, patting their backs and saluting every farthing they pressed into his palm.

'But you didn't take the King's shilling, did you, Charlie?'

'They wouldn't let me,' Charlie replies, his voice becoming small in the distance. 'I was already serving His Majesty. You can't take it twice.'

'No, I think you were too fucking old,' Walter corrects him, and hears a drill sergeant's barked orders coming from the schoolyard ahead of them, then the scuff and stamp of men's boots as they come to attention, and automatically he straightens his shoulders, lifts his chin, and prepares to fall in if required. 'You were too fucking old,' he repeats, 'and I was too fucking young.'

But Charlie has now made his retreat, disappeared entirely from view, and when Walter arrives at the railings, the shadows of the spikes falling across him like bayonets, he finds himself alone, the only spectator as two dozen conscripts are put through their paces, all of them middle-aged men in shirt-sleeves and waistcoats, a few bearing shotguns, the rest holding sticks, and every one of them red-faced and sweating.

Walter recognises Jim Cotton the blacksmith, and Lincoln the pawnbroker, the lathe-turner Sinsell, and several others from the yards and shops along Riverside Road, including old Patty the poacher, a friend of sorts of his father, who will spread his nets most Sunday evenings at the top of Slaughterhouse Lane, right under the noses of the constables, checking for holes, and is renowned for his fists, having laid out half a dozen much younger rivals – Campside cowards, High Street roughs – in the woods in and around the Beckwith estate, flattened them one at a time without removing his overcoat, in which were concealed that evening's rabbits and pheasants: he is such an enormous old fellow, a single blow was all that was needed, and down they each went (though in another version he was ambushed outside his own privy, smoking a pipe and dressed in his braces and vest, while in a third it all occurred in the bar of the Wellington Arms).

'Good on you, Patty!' Walter shouts, cupping one hand to the side of his mouth. 'You go and give old Fritz what-for!'

But, of course, the poacher does not look around or break stride. Dutifully he turns and turns about – shoulders arms, presents arms – and Walter senses the great air of resignation in each of these men, for they are not the likely lads of one or two years ago, but their fathers and uncles, and while they won't know what is ahead of them, not the truth of it, they will have heard enough to expect the worst, whatever that might mean to them. Walter follows their progress from one end of the wide expanse of playground to the other, where they become momentarily lost in the heat haze and mica-sharp glint of the sun on the bitumen, and has the fleeting impression that he is looking at ghosts, at a memory of men, and urgently grips a railing in each hand and hoists himself onto the low perimeter wall – as onto a firestep – and tries to shout at them to take cover, to keep their heads down, but the words will not come – they catch in his throat – because by now it is hopeless, it is too late, and he drops disconsolately back to the pavement as several of the men turn the wrong way, go left instead of right, and it all becomes a bit of a mess-up, a shambles.

The next command is a weary 'Fall out' and immediately the men take another right turn, another few paces, then allow their shoulders to sag, their arms to stop swinging, and traipse off in twos and threes towards the largest of the school buildings, its steeply pitched roof reminiscent of a small church, the whitewashed wings to either side as plain as any barracks. The burly, bewhiskered sergeant flaps out a handkerchief and wipes his neck and brow, then marches briskly after them, and in moments the playground is deserted, the buildings and boundary walls seeming to recede into the distance, everything quiet.

some rough stuff

Walter shivers. Despite the muggy afternoon heat, and the sunshine, he feels a chill at his neck and down both his arms and he turns up his collar, hugs himself in his tunic, and remembers the ice slides the boys used to make here in the winter, and the tussling queues of his classmates waiting their turn to go while the others – the ones who had already been – buffed up the ice with their caps so that it would shine almost like glass, and then the pile-ups when one of the boys set off too soon and the rest of them suddenly followed, all yelling and shoving. Squinting through the railings at the glare on the playground, he recalls the rough-and-tumble of it, the great exhilaration before Dr Westmoreland came to the main doors with his whistle, the initial blast requiring everyone to halt and stay still, which they would, heaped one on top of another like sandbags, like the bodies of the dead, though grinning, since it wasn't such a bad thing, then, to be caught out of doors in the midst of some rough stuff. The school day hadn't yet begun, after all, and it was what was expected and encouraged of boys, though woe betide any of them who dared to laugh or move before the second blast of the headmaster's whistle, which was their signal to jump to and smartly file through to their morning assembly, where they would sit alert and cross-legged on the waxed wooden floor, their hands on their knees, pinked with the cold, and if any boy's socks should be down round his ankles, or his collar awry, he would have to hold out his hand and take a strike of the cane from one of the masters whose duty it was to line them in rows, evenly spaced.

The school was a six- or seven-minute sprint from the Beckwith estate, and often in his haste not to be late Walter would have to haul himself up and over the railings, still hungry after his meagre breakfast, and race to reach the hall before his classmates had assumed their positions, and though he is so much less agile now than he was then, he takes a short run at the railings and finds he is still able to heave himself over without getting spiked and to land without hurting himself. Clumps of mud fall from his boots, and he looks quickly around to see who might have observed him, but there is no one, and keeping his head down he hurries across the schoolyard to the side entrance, conscious that he must not forget Gertie, that his time in this place cannot be long.

discipline was paramount

Riverside School for Boys was always known as a rough school, even as a school for the criminal, there being so many scoundrels, vagabonds and thieves in the vicinity, but whatever the short-comings of the boys who attended, few would leave, warned Dr Westmoreland at the start of every year from his dais in the hall, without a sense of right and wrong, and a sense of the pain of the penalty for doing wrong; nor would they leave unable to read and write, and even those who struggled with words would be encouraged in their native knowledge of the value of money at least – twelve pence to the shilling, two hundred and forty pence to a pound.

But to Walter's mind what Riverside provided above all was a schooling in the discipline of forming straight lines, of lining up in single file at the doors from the schoolyard, then assuming double file in the corridor leading through to the hall, then in class formation for prayers and hymns, and out you had to file afterwards, brisk pace, no running or straggling, no bunching in groups.

Discipline reigned. Discipline was paramount, and in their classrooms for the rest of the day the boys would sit in their regimented rows with their hands on their desks – chests out, chins up – and chant their alphabet, their tables, their *doh ray me*, while the master patrolled the aisles, or stood with his back to the fireplace, and if you should lose your way you would receive a whack on the skull, or else be required to hold your hand forth and take a swift tingling cut of the cane. There would be three on each hand for insolence, and straight along to Dr Westmoreland and his longer, thicker cane for any more serious misdemeanour.

Unsmiling, grey-bearded, his left leg somewhat withered, the headmaster wore his black cape and mortar board and carried his cane not merely throughout the school day but on the long walk to and from his home at the crest of Mount Pleasant, from where he claimed to look down on the school and the warren of streets that surrounded it, just as he looked down from his dais at the boys every morning, and no matter how often he was called upon to dispense the same discipline, there was never anything fabricated about Dr Westmoreland's fury: still his eyes would glower, still he would bristle with indignation, and his blows were always in earnest, his outrage undiminished. He would make you bend over. He might make you drop your trousers.

All of this Walter recalls as he treads cautiously along the squeaking corridors, looking into the classrooms for Patty and the other men, but finding only rows of empty benches and desks, the sun slanting through the high windows onto wall-maps, potted palms, scuffed wainscoting. Everywhere is deserted, expectant, and when he comes upon the headmaster's office he pauses a moment to listen at the door, then tries the handle, but it is locked; it won't give, and while he doesn't doubt that Dr Westmoreland will be too old and too lame to fight in any war, he wonders which of the other masters will have rallied to Kitchener's call, and which will have got their comeuppance – the meanness beaten out of them, or better still: bits blown away – for instance, Mr Elliott, whose speciality was to twist the hair at the nape of your neck, a truly excruciating pain that would bring tears to your eyes, and bring you out of your seat, trapped and contorting and trying not to make a sound since you weren't to yelp or whine or he would only twist harder. He was a brute to the boys, but no worse than Mr Eastwood, who would tour his classroom constantly, silently, and cuff your ear on the merest of pretexts, or none at all, just when it was least expected, cupping his hand for impact and causing an ache – and sometimes deafness – that would last for the rest of the day.

But crueller than either of these, Walter recalls, was Mr Cronin, a jack-a-dandyish man whose delight was to take your hand gently in his and softly stroke it open from the heel of the palm to the tips of the fingers, and if your fingers should begin to crawl back in fear of what was to come then very gently and softly he would stroke your hand open again, and you were not to look at him, or close your eyes in anticipation of the pain: you were expected to witness your punishment, to concentrate on your hand as Mr Cronin pinched the tips of your fingers together and smartly struck *once* with his cane, then a pause as he moved your hand an increment to one side, and *twice*, and another pause, another slight shift, *and three times*, the last always the sharpest, as sharp as a dose of Dobson's smelling salts, the pain stinging to the top of your nose and bringing tears to your eyes, though you were not to begin crying, as Walter's friend Jack Cockey once did, since Mr Cronin would drop your hand with the merest hint of a smile and calmly resume his lesson, confident that he needn't humiliate or excoriate you any further, secure in the knowledge that your classmates would see to you instead – in the schoolyard or on your way home – making chicken noises, blubbing noises, shoving you and laughing, which was what they did to Jack Cockey, and while Walter wasn't among Jack's tormentors, neither did he attempt to stop the taunting of the others: he allowed them to bully him.

And he is sorry about that, now; Walter is sorry about so many things, and would apologise if only he were able to find Jack Cockey among all the other boys sitting cross-legged in the hall as he hurries down the corridor to join them, his lateness conspicuous to everyone through the glass partition and plainly advertised on the clock above the door: the time is now five minutes to nine and Walter has no choice but to wait outside as Mr Eastwood clunks through the opening bars of a tune on the piano and the boys begin to drone out their first hymn – though altogether too drearily for Dr Westmoreland, who hammers on his lectern with the crook of his cane, bringing a halt to the performance and demanding, 'More gusto! More gusto, you boys!'

Then, 'Mr Eastwood,' he says, and they start over as Walter looks anxiously in from the corridor, where he will have to remain not just for this hymn, but all through the morning assembly, which will proceed with Dr Westmoreland's sermon, followed by the Lord's Prayer, then this day's announcements, before the boys are required to bow their heads and say a silent prayer – their hands pressed together, fingertips touching their chins – after which the last hymn will be sung and finally Walter will be required to enter the hall and take his punishment from Dr Westmoreland in front of everyone: a strike on each palm from the cane, and two additional strikes if he should cringe or cry out.

But when at last Mr Elliott opens the door and smiles as he beckons him inside – his face bloodless, as pale as any pig in Orford's abattoir – Walter finds he is tired of Dr Westmoreland's cruelty, no longer in awe of this awesomely angry man, and though he approaches the dais when he is summoned he resolves not to allow the headmaster to punish him, and does not raise his right hand – palm upwards to shoulder height – as is required, as he has done in the past, but keeps both his hands clenched behind his back, his arms crossed at the wrist, and while he will not look the headmaster in the eye – he isn't that brave, or insolent – he refuses to hear him when he says, 'Hand.' Then, 'Hand, boy!'

Stiff-armed, and facing directly ahead, Walter takes a blow to the shoulder, then another, but will not surrender his hands, even when the headmaster steps down from his dais, lame as he is, and strikes at Walter's arms, then at the back of his thighs, and suddenly loses his temper and grips Walter's hair so tightly that Walter can hardly resist for the pain of it and must drop to his knees, forcing the headmaster to kneel beside him. With the other boys now becoming excited – some of them standing, calling encouragement – Walter curls up on the floor and tries to make himself small, still clenching his hands, and makes not a sound, barely dares even to breathe, as Dr Westmoreland lashes out at him wildly, thrashes him repeatedly, until his fury is all spent, his heart and energy gone.

No other boy will ever provoke the headmaster so badly. And no one now can ever again accuse Walter Barley of cowardice.

21
Gertie

everything so marvellous

The only maid to have been retained by the Beckwiths is the oldest and least suited to the work in their factories, poor misshapen Eileen Thomas whose face, Gertie remembers – it was Miss Emma who said it – resembles the flat of a pan in its lack of expression and who betrays not the least glimmer of recognition or pleasure at finding Gertie Dobson standing again at the top of the steps to the Beckwiths' front doors. Under Eileen's steady scrutiny Gertie feels herself reddening, and holds up the jars of Dobson's Soothing Lotion (Antiseptic & Healing) and brightly announces, 'Mr Montague ordered these. I'm making a delivery from my father.' But Eileen does not respond, and Gertie suspects she ought not to have revealed the labels on the jars, or perhaps not the cause of her coming, and helpfully adds, 'My father is Captain Montague's pharmacist.'

Eileen nods and looks to Gertie's bicycle, which is propped against one of the pillars supporting the porch, her gloves bunched inside the basket, her bonnet hooked over a handlebar, and then, as if this were all the confirmation she required, shuffles backwards and sideways and holds open the door.

'Captain Beckwith asks would you kindly mind waiting in the Guest Hall, miss.'

It was improper to call him 'Montague', Gertie supposes, and in a fluster she attempts to offer the jars to the maid. 'Maybe I should just leave these with you, Eileen? Do you think? That's all I came for, to deliver his ointment.'

The maid allows a glance at the jars but stiffly declines to accept them, and ignores the familiarity of first names. 'If you wouldn't mind waiting, Miss Dobson. Captain Beckwith is expecting you. He will be with you quite shortly.'

'Yes,' Gertie concedes, 'sorry,' and steps over the threshold into the cool of the hallway.

'This way, miss.'

They turn past the central staircase, the newel post crowned with an oversized acorn that Gertie touches as she always does, then says in the manner she learned from the Misses Beckwith, 'I don't mind taking myself along, Eileen, if that would be a help to you. I think you're all on your own now, aren't you?'

By way of reply Eileen turns her torso slightly around as she walks, since it seems she is unusually fixed in the spine, as well as short-necked, and can only look left or right by rotating about at her waist, but still her face is inscrutable and she says nothing. She continues ahead, as she is obliged to, for Gertie is a guest, a caller to the front door who has been invited inside by the Captain himself, and there can be no possibility of allowing her to find her own way, however well acquainted she might be with the house, though in fact, Gertie realises, the hallway and passage are not as they were, for while the fixtures are the same – everything so marvellous and not a plain piece of panelling anywhere, the wainscoting ornately carved in relief with griffins and ribbons and scrolls, the door frames decorated with shields and floral bouquets – the pictures have all been taken away, leaving a shadow of themselves on the wallpaper, and whereas before there were sideboards and tables and all manner of ornaments in ceramic and glass, now there is nothing but the echo of their footsteps on the marble-tiled floor, from which, Gertie notices, the red patterned rugs have also been lifted.

Eileen opens the door for her. 'If you'd care to make yourself comfortable, miss, I'll bring you some tea.'

'You don't need to, Eileen, really, I wouldn't want to put you to any trouble.'

But Eileen surprises her with a smile, and says, 'You make yourself comfortable, miss,' and lightly caresses her arm, as she might her own daughter's.

'Oh,' Gertie says, 'yes, all right,' and stands and stares as the door softly closes and Eileen's footsteps recede along the corridor, then turns with her two jars and surveys the Guest Hall, whose walls are crowded with pictures, more than ever there were – gilt-framed portraits in oils, landscapes, watercolours, drawings – while several others she recognises are stacked against the wainscoting alongside a dozen or more rolled-up rugs, a thicket of floor lamps all missing their shades and several tea chests that appear to be packed with straw. The heavy old grandfather clock that stands beside the bookcase now has three smaller companions, though each is showing a different time and only the smallest is working; the others require rewinding.

The time is ten minutes to five.

This was always Gertie's favourite among the Beckwiths' many rooms, with its high arched windows and Gothicky tracery and its great miscellany of furniture – armchairs like miniature thrones, wicker chairs from the garden, shabby old sofas, and tables of various sizes on which books were piled and flowers spilled from vases – but now it seems the Guest Hall has become a place of storage, the existing furniture overlaid with sheeting as a protection against dust and the times, some of it supporting the many additional items that have been brought down here from elsewhere in the house, including the cream satin couch that was formerly in Miss Edwina's bedroom and which is now lopsidedly stationed on top of two other sofas. But there is, she notices, a circuitous route through all of this clutter to the companionable arrangement of armchairs by the french windows that face out to the sunken Italianate garden and the driveway to the house, which was where she used to sit with the Misses Beckwith, quietly at work on her sewing as they talked and talked – 'debated', they called it – their voices reverberating beneath the high ceiling, a pot of tea and a cake-stand on the table between them.

Gertie navigates her way to there now and cautiously sits in her usual place, straight-backed, a jar supported on each knee, but soon decides she would be more comfortable standing and deposits her jars on the table and steps a little nearer the windows, where the sun slants warmly across her and she is happy for a few moments to imagine a stranger approaching the house and looking up and assuming her to be one of the Beckwiths – a cousin, perhaps, of Emma and Edwina, or even the fiancée of Captain Montague – but then senses that she is indeed being watched, observed by someone outside, and widens her eyes as though to see in the dark and carefully scans the trees that hide the house from the road, the rose bushes immediately below her, then the ornamental pond with its mossy cherub on a plinth, and the flower-beds and the lawns, but nothing moves, no one appears to be there, and she assumes she must be mistaken, though nevertheless she retreats to her seat, where she will be less conspicuous, and quickly retrieves her jars of ointment from the cherrywood table just as Eileen comes back through with the tea-tray, a solitary cup chiming in its saucer, a silver teapot gleaming.

'Is Mr Logan still the gardener?' Gertie asks.

'He is, miss.'

'Does he have help?'

'Not now. Sugar, miss?'

'Two, please. Is he here today?'

'He was, earlier. He's gone now.'

Eileen pours her tea, which is too weak, and Gertie, who is accustomed to being waited upon in this place and knows better than to interfere, looks back towards the garden and glimpses the smallest of movements – a bumble-bee feeding from a foxglove, dipping into the flute of one flower, rising to the next – and realises then that there are others, any number of bees, and is surprised at herself for not noticing them sooner. The air outside will be humming with their noise, and thick with the scent of the flower-beds.

'Milk, miss?'

'Just a little,' says Gertie, and is distracted by a flash of white as a bird of some kind flies over the pond, followed at once by another, after which she becomes aware of several more birds, settling on the walls around the garden, hopping on the lawn. 'It must have been me who scared them away.'

'Miss?'

'When I stood at the window.'

Eileen's face registers neither interest nor puzzlement, and with a stiff nod she turns and makes for the door, then pauses half-way, standing between two stacks of chairs with her tray awkwardly hitched against her hip, and says conversationally, 'You'll be working in the factory now, I expect.'

'Yes.' Gertie smiles, then adds as she always does: 'Just like a man!'

'And Mabel Barley?'

'She works there too, yes.'

'Alongside you, miss?'

Frowning, Gertie says, 'Yes, nearby. We're friends.'

'I think of Mabel the most,' Eileen informs her. 'Of the ones who were here, I think of her the most. She was a good girl. You'll remember me to Mabel, the next time you see her?'

'Yes, I will, if you like.'

The maid is silent, fixedly gazing at Gertie, then says, 'It was Mabel's brother used to clean the family's boots.'

'Was it? I didn't know.'

'At one time. Then he delivered the ice, didn't he, later on?'

'Did he?' asks Gertie, politely.

'He did,' says Eileen, as if to herself, and turns to depart. 'He was the one who delivered the ice. I used to give him the keys to the back. Until the last time.'

'Walter,' offers Gertie, remembering.

'That's right, miss,' says the maid. 'Walter, who then went and enlisted.' She touches one of the stalled clocks by the door and glances at the dust on her fingers. 'He'll be dead now,' she says, and hesitates, then appears to decide against saying more. Quietly she shuts the door after her.

a respectable distance

The glazed door to the terrace swings open and Gertie takes a sudden step backwards. 'Oh!' she exclaims, and holds her cup and saucer away from her dress. She looks down at herself, then at the floor. Nothing was spilled.

'Miss Dobson. I'm sorry. I startled you.'

'No, it's all right,' she says, and offers a laugh, but Montague has never seemed comfortable smiling, and is in addition more badly afflicted than she remembers, his forehead and throat and all of one side of his face now nearly as red as her father's rubber gauntlets, but everywhere peeling, his complexion in places like candlewax. Carefully she places her cup on the table and stands demurely before him, her hands clasped, her expression attentive. Tall and very thin, he appears almost to be leaning over her, though he is standing at a respectable distance, and when he doesn't say any more she adds, 'I mean, yes, you did make me jump, just a bit. I didn't expect you to come in from outside. I thought' – she gestures away to her right – 'I was expecting you to come through the hall door.'

'Element of surprise,' he says, and removes his boater, drops it onto one of the armchairs. 'Too long a soldier.'

He is joking, Gertie feels sure, though she can find no hint of humour in his mouth or his eyes, which are red-rimmed, steadily returning her gaze. Possibly she ought not to examine him so closely – it may not be polite – and struck by this thought she picks up her two jars of ointment and thrusts them towards him. 'You ordered these,' she says.

'Yes, I did,' he confirms, and allows her to place a jar on the palm of each of his hands. Still looking at Gertie, he jogs them a little as if to estimate their weight, and she cannot help but fix on the sorry state of his fingers, which are as tight and red as a turkey's claws, the nails quite appalling. He also appears to be trembling.

'You have the shakes,' she says, with surprise.

'I do,' confirms Montague, looking down.

'Like my mother,' she adds.

'I wouldn't know about that, but yes, I do.'

'Does the ointment help you?'

'To stop the shaking?'

'No. I mean—'

'It relieves the discomfort, yes,' he says. 'Temporarily at least.'

'My father *concocts* it,' says Gertie, and widens her eyes at him, her comical face, 'in his laboratory.'

Montague studies the labels on the jars, then turns them towards her. 'Evidently,' he says. 'He has his name on them.'

'I mean he mixes the ingredients himself, to his own recipe.'

'So I understand. You must compliment him when you return.'

But Gertie cannot be sure if this is meant sincerely, and doubts she would know how to compliment her father in any case, and finds she is lost for what to say next, though she is sure there was something. She looks down at the cherrywood table, the cold remains of her tea.

'Miss Dobson, forgive me, would you care for more tea? A fresh pot?'

'No,' she says, 'no, thank you.' She touches the fine polished grain of the table-top, then the lid of the teapot, and wonders if Montague is waiting for her to leave, is perhaps puzzled or annoyed by her continuing to linger. She takes a deep breath. He has brought in the scent of the garden. 'I'm sorry. I'd better be on my way.'

For a moment he doesn't respond, and looks beyond her, as if contemplating the fate of the furniture stacked around them, then says, with some deliberation, 'No, Miss Dobson . . . There's no need for that. If you would like to stay a little longer, I should be very glad of your company.'

He waits. He is dressed as though for tennis or a regatta – with men's apparel Gertie can never be certain – in a striped cream and white blazer, white cotton trousers, and she wants to object that she is hopeless at games, if that is what he has in mind, but of course he hasn't asked her; he has made no suggestion of any kind, and she says, 'Yes, I would like to.' Then immediately, because she is flustered and is starting to redden, 'I was wondering, since the house is to be a hospital now – and all of these things have been brought down – where will Miss Edwina and Miss Emma have their rooms, if they decide to come home?'

'Why would they decide to come home?'

'To nurse the wounded.'

'I shouldn't think they'd do that.'

'Oh.'

'No, I shouldn't think so at all.'

She looks at him, his peculiar stiffness. Moments pass. She cannot think what she ought to say next.

'Two reasons,' he concedes then. 'One, if their letters are anything to go by, my sisters are having far too jolly a time of it in France to want to return. And two, they would consider it mere frivolling to be back in England, helping chaps to convalesce in what used to be their garden, after all.'

'In their garden, yes,' Gertie nods. She looks out past the stone balusters of the terrace to the pond and the cherub and sees in her imagination the slobbering old man from Albemarle Alley, and a dozen just like him, all bandaged and walking with sticks. She cannot picture the Misses Beckwith tending such men, or indeed any men; not here.

Montague coughs, and says with the faintest of smiles, 'I don't mean this garden, of course. This particular part of the house will remain with the family – and there are still plenty of rooms my sisters can use if they choose to come home on leave, or else they can stay with Mother in London – but Father has relinquished most of the rest of it, including the grounds at the rear. The gardens round there are full of tents. Did you know that? Hospital tents.'

'No.'

'Ah,' says Montague, and places the jars of ointment on the table, and with a sudden jauntiness adds, 'Then I wonder if you would like to accompany me on a tour of inspection, Miss Dobson?'

'To see the tents?'

Montague picks up his boater and crooks an arm for her. 'To see the tents,' he confirms. 'Before the wounded arrive.'

'Is that allowed?'

'Of course. Why not?'

'Well . . . yes,' she says, 'yes, all right,' and tentatively cups a hand around his upper arm, the merest pressure of her fingers on his sleeve an unfamiliar thrill to her.

'After which,' he continues, 'we might walk down to the lake, if you like. It'll be cooler there, and it's quite pretty this time of year. Would you like that?'

And thinking of poor Sammy Edwards, who once offered to reveal to her the workshops behind the stonemason's display room, Gertie smiles and says, 'Thank you, yes, I would,' and allows Captain Beckwith to guide her out to the terrace, the air as scented and moist as if they were entering a tropical hothouse.

22
Walter

'it burns a lot of water'

A yard by a yard and six inches thick, a three-shilling slab of ice was as much as a boy of Walter's age and physique could be expected to heave up a hill on a handcart as cumbersome and heavy as Greenland's. And there were a great many hills for him to climb; the side-streets round Riverside Road have always been known for their steepness.

On the far side of the river is the flood plain, which is flat for a quarter-mile stretch before the land starts to rise, and that is where Beckwith's Engineering has its Works and where the new flour mill has been built, but on this bank the rise begins at the riverside, every alley on the slant, all the streets winding upwards, with Italians making ice cream and butchers and dairymen and wet-fish merchants to be found at every turn, and all of them requiring ice – in the summer especially – as do the very big houses, the likes of the Beckwiths', the Osgoods' and the Pettifers'.

The ice comes in by barge from the coast and goes now to Randall's on Steam Packet Wharf, though for many years the business belonged to Cyril Greenland, a grizzled barrel of a man with side whiskers in the style of Isambard Kingdom Brunel, his moleskin breeches patched at the knees, a dusty bowler tipped back on his head, who died eighteen months into the war, suffered a heart-attack and passed away in his bed, as men of his age are still able to do.

His premises remain at the foot of Ice House Lane, a wooden structure overhanging the river with a set of rickety steps leading up to his office and the cockpit from which he used to operate the grapple and chains that lifted the blocks from the barge and swung them into his store, where two other men would saw them into the slabs that Walter, from the age of fifteen, was employed to deliver to various businesses locally for sixpence a day, as well as accompanying Cyril on his creaking four-wheeled cart when he made his once-monthly deliveries to Beckwith House and certain other grand estates in the countryside beyond.

But this was only ever the work of the summer. Come the autumn Walter would need to look elsewhere, though of course on Riverside Road there would always be openings, especially for boys who were known to work hard, as he found the day he followed a stranger into Meek's Yard, a podgy clean-shaven fellow four or five years older than he was, and with much the same mission in mind.

Winking at Walter, as though they were already confederates, the young man knocked with one knuckle on the door to Meek's office – *Meek's Steam Navigation Company* etched into the glass – and raised his eyebrows and made a small *o* with his mouth when a voice called him inside. Removing his cap, he left the door ajar. Walter squinted in after him.

'I'm wondering is there any chance of a job.'

'Who are you?' asked Meek.

'John Skip. I live along Spencer Street way.'

'Long walk to get down here, isn't it?'

'Yes,' said Skip.

'That'll be why you pitch up mid-morning, I suppose.'

Skip said nothing. Possibly he had been traipsing from one place to another since breakfast, and possibly Meek realised as much, for then he asked him more kindly, 'Have you worked the lighters before?'

'I haven't, I'll be truthful, but I can turn my hand to most things. I reckon I could pick it up, given a start.'

Meek tilted back in his chair and looked across his right shoulder, past the bend in the river to where his vessels would be dredging the channels, conveying produce to the coast, bringing cargo in from the docks, and said at last, with a sigh, 'No, I'm afraid there isn't much chance of a start at the moment, John – we haven't a lot to do. But Spencer Street you say? What number?'

'One two nine.'

'One two nine,' repeated Meek, jotting that down; then: 'I'll tell you what I'll do, John. I've got your particulars. Anything comes up, I'll send a boy right along for you.' He pointed with his pencil at Walter, looking in through the gap in the door. 'Perhaps I'll send that one there.'

'Thank you,' said Skip, replacing his cap, edging away. 'You won't be disappointed in me.'

'No doubt,' nodded Meek, and Walter stood aside as Skip came from the office, his face flushed, for a moment disorientated. He turned in the direction of the river, then checked, and with a friendly pat on Walter's shoulder he strode purposefully back up the yard, looking in each of the other windows, and pausing by Compton's seed merchants, where again he tapped on the door, and waited for a call, and again stepped inside.

'Well?' said Meek. 'What is it?'

Walter removed his cap as Skip had done, and held it with both hands by his crotch in the same manner, and said, 'Me too, I was hoping for some work.'

'You heard what I said, we don't have a lot to do.'

Smiling, Walter said, 'I don't want a lot to do,' and that made Meek laugh.

'Barley, isn't it?'

'Yes,' said Walter.

'You've been hauling ice for Cyril.'

'Yes.'

'What happened?'

'He doesn't need me in this weather. He says to come back in the summer.'

Meek looked him up and down. 'I remember you with a barrow, when you were a youngster. Am I right?'

'Yes,' said Walter, 'I still have it,' though the wood had rotted with the damp from the manure he used to collect, and from being left out in the rain by the privy.

'Mortuary Lane?'

'That's right. Number eight.'

'Okay,' said Meek, and made a fist of Skip's details, dropped the paper into a basket. 'I'll give you a shout when there's something. That's if you want something?'

'Yes.'

'Okay. On you go.'

And Walter left, passing John Skip at the exit from the yard – the last he would see of him before the start of the war – and was summoned the very next morning, woken just after six by his mother calling upstairs: 'Walter, come down, there's a man to see you!'

'What about?' said Walter, descending.

'Meek wants you,' said the man.

'Will you take breakfast?' asked his mother.

'No, kindly,' said the man, 'I'll wait here.'

And there he stood with his hands in his pockets, leaning into the door frame and quietly whistling through his teeth as Walter managed a slurp of tea, a bite of dry bread, and pulled on his boots, his jacket, and joined him.

His name was Rivett, and he walked briskly, half a stride quicker than Walter.

'Where we going?'

'Upriver a bit.'

'What to do?'

'Dredging,' said Rivett. 'Beckwiths' lake maybe.'

'Beckwiths' lake?'

'Maybe,' said Rivett, though in fact it turned out they were required to work several months on the river before that, since Riverside Road is twenty-odd miles from the coast and constantly the waterways require to be cleared of the silt that clogs the beds and narrows the bends and not only makes

179

navigation more difficult but floods far more likely. Among the vessels that Meek will lease out fully manned to the river authority are a tug called the *Badger*, on which is mounted a steam-driven crane, and two lighters named the *Fox* and the *Vole*, one carrying coal to fuel the grab – 'It burns a lot of water,' said Rivett – the other left empty initially for receiving the mud, and that was the best of work, to be out on the wide placid waters so early each day, flanked by the rustle of reed beds from which emerged moorhens, swans, coots and geese, herons and ducks, the river plopping with fish, the trees shedding their leaves, and then the growl of the machinery as they set to, the thrum of the engine, the squeal and clanking of those gears and pivots and chains.

It rained, then it snowed, and while Rivett worked the boiler below and the skipper the grab, Walter sweated out in the open, in the steam and smoke and damp winter air. He did whatever was assigned to him, most of it hard physical labour, more than most boys of his stature and age would be able to manage, but orders were orders; Walter never shirked. He did as he was told, and what pleased him most was to punt the *Badger* when the water became too shallow or too dense with weeds to risk the propeller.

Standing first at the prow, he would angle the pole into the riverbed, then lever hard in the direction of the stern, and as the tug slid slowly forward beneath him he would walk the gunwale half-way, working his hands down the shaft till it was past the perpendicular, when often he would have the even more strenuous task of releasing it from the mud so that he could return to the prow and start again. But he was adept at it, and they made decent progress, the tug pulling the *Fox* and the *Vole* in its wake, which was how in the end they navigated the narrow, tree-shaded channel that brought them in from the river in February, dredging the bed as they went, until at last they emerged to the wide, flat surprise of the lake on the Beckwith estate.

Meek had the contract to deepen it by a fathom or so. It kept them busy all spring and they saw no one, not a servant or gardener, least of all any Beckwiths, though Walter did look. He kept an eye open the whole time.

the fortunate ones

After a winter working for Meek, and a second summer hauling ice for Cyril Greenland, Walter fancied himself a man, robust enough to withstand the rigours of the fighting in Belgium and France – whatever those rigours might turn out to be – and went along to St Saviour's Barracks one afternoon in the early weeks of the war, where the burly, bewhiskered sergeant on duty took a different view of him, having seen so many other men clamouring to be part of it – more men than the Army had kit for, or barracks to bed them in, or weapons to arm them with; more men than would surely be needed to bring the Kaiser to his knees.

'You need to grow a bit, sonny.'

'I'm eighteen,' Walter lied.

'Nineteen is the minimum. Come back when you're nineteen.'

'The war'll be finished by then.'

The sergeant took a folded handkerchief from his pocket and tipped back his cap, dabbed the sweat from his brow and, with one appraising eye on the next man in line, he said, 'Don't you believe it, my friend.'

'What about later?' grinned Walter. 'I could come back tomorrow. I'll be nineteen by then.'

But this sergeant at least was having none of that, and whacked him hard on the arm. 'No, fuck off now,' he said, and gestured in the direction of the exit, 'get yourself home to your mum.'

And after a moment's hesitation, his eyes smarting from the blow, Walter did as he was told; he turned and marched away and passed on the far side of the hall a few of the fortunate ones, all in civilian attire, their hats and jackets removed, their right hands raised as they repeated the oath that was being read to them by a uniformed officer so many inches taller than they were and so much straighter in bearing. None met his gaze – none noticed him – and as Walter emerged from the dark of the barracks to the sunshine of St Saviour's wide thoroughfare he met a queue of cheerful men still waiting to be taken inside – John Skip standing with them – and burned to be asked how he had fared, to account for himself, but these men were in such high spirits, on the cusp of something auspicious, that Walter slipped by them unseen, sorely disappointed, and a little ashamed, though not yet resigned to missing out on the show.

St Saviour's wasn't the only recruiting station.

nothing about the Army was straight

Many a time as a child Walter had climbed the hill with his pals to the cavalry barracks on the outskirts of town so they could gaze through the gates at the Hussars in their brilliant blue tunics as they performed such intricate drills on their gleaming high horses, and always, he recalled, there would be a guard at the gates – not necessarily armed or even correctly attired – including from time to time a tubby old boy in shirt-sleeves and braces who would give them the lend of a couple of smokes and stand and pleasantly natter as the horses turned through their figures of eight: a recruiting sergeant, no doubt. Walter realised that now, for nothing about the Army was straight, and as he made his way there in early September, determined to enlist at the second attempt, he imagined returning to Riverside Road amid a scene of celebration such as accompanied the men who crossed the market most mornings on their way to Crag's Meadow for their hour of physical jerks, marching almost in step in their Homburgs and caps, bowlers, suits and bow-ties, their coats slung over their shoulders, and a solitary drill sergeant potting the pace alongside them while crowds of well-wishers gathered to applaud and offer them cigarettes and chocolates, including Charlie Champion of course, but many women besides – sweethearts and sisters and mothers – since it seemed that every female in England (excepting Walter's own mother) was fully in support of the war.

Certainly they were more enthusiastic for the cause than the men he had the misfortune to join that day in the hall at the cavalry barracks, most of them servants from one of the numerous estates on the coast, who had been delivered by train that morning at the expense of their employer, a peer of the realm, who considered it his patriotic duty to sacrifice his butler and footmen and numcrous gardeners and estate workers to the needs of the nation (though not his horses, he was firm about that). This at least was the story the servants gave Walter when he joined them in a queue so much less animated than the one at St Saviour's, and while every one of those men was passed fit for service, despite their reluctance, Walter alone was refused, and could hardly affect to be disappointed since he would not have wanted to spend another minute in such miserable company, whether in Flanders or France or six feet under the ground.

as if he were a woman

Refused a second time, Walter resolved to wait until he was older since he had shown himself willing, no scrimshanker or coward, and while he wasn't alone in wanting to go because his pals were all going, and because Kitchener and the King had invited him to, and because so many young women were sporting regimental favours in their hats and lapels, and because certain young women were pressing white feathers on the men who remained, and because the Germans were slaughtering blameless women and children in Belgium – and because it might soon be all over

– he would have been happy to ignore the new canvas banner that appeared on the railings outside St Saviour's Street Barracks the following spring – *STILL OPEN AND RECRUITING!* – and the new poster that went up everywhere a month or so later – *WOMEN OF BRITAIN SAY 'GO!'* – but that a company of Scotchmen came to be billeted among them, two hundred Celts in grey kilts who spent a fortnight living out of the Corn Hall and got around on Army-issue bicycles, *tring*ing their bells as they passed down Riverside Road, their white thighs flashing by and the children all gawping, their mothers nudging each other and cackling.

They were a popular sight, an uplifting spectacle, though they could also be raucous, gathering in the rowdies round about to fight among themselves and get drunk and sing such stirring and sorrowful songs, and it was in one of those dives that something must have been said to Eddie Barley – something friendly – since he came home one evening all smiles and slung a heavy arm around Walter's shoulder and drew him into the sour-sweet fug of his breath. 'Come along with me, son,' he said, and stroked Walter's belly as if he were a woman, and softly belched and said, 'let's us two go and do our duty like these Scotchmen, eh? You and me, come on, what d'you say?'

Walter said nothing – he hardly dared breathe – and Eddie flared; his eyes briefly blazed as he pushed Walter away.

'Oh, fuck you, then. I'll go and fight the fucking Krauts on my own.'

And though Walter called after him as he stumbled from the house into the darkness of that midsummer's evening – 'It'll be shut, Dad, we can go in the morning!' – Eddie wasn't listening and wouldn't come back, not that evening at least, perhaps not at all.

Neither Walter nor his siblings nor their mother had any idea where Eddie slept when he went missing, as he periodically would, and neither were they ever much surprised by the sorry state of him when eventually he returned – sometimes weeks later, bearded and hungry and in need of a wash – but when the following morning Walter climbed the half-dozen steps to the hall at St Saviour's, wearing his bowler to make himself seem taller, and determined again to enlist, he hardly expected to find his father already installed at the head of the queue, still less to find him shaven and wearing a collar and tie.

The clamour of the previous August and September was by then gone, but still the hall was thick with the noise and rank smell of dozens of men, and once his eyes had adjusted to the gloomy interior after the brightness outside, Walter confirmed that no one else in that hall was smarter, more crisply turned out than Eddie Barley, and as he waited to present himself once again at the recruiting sergeant's desk – puffed up with an odd sort of pride in his father, feeling two inches taller at least – he began in his imagination to anticipate the adventure that was in store for them, some rifles and ammo and a ship out to France, a few Hun to knock over and a month or so of fine French sunshine and fillies and wine, and even sooner than that – his mind now aswirl with red, white and blue bunting – Walter imagined the sergeant's hearty hand on his shoulder, and the weight of the King's shilling in his pocket, and the moment of bursting through the door to his mother's kitchen and flinging his coin on the table and announcing, 'I've enlisted! I signed up with Kitchener's Army!'

He pictured all of this as he stood in that line – and pictured as well Gertie Dobson's delight if she were to see him in khaki – but what he failed to anticipate was the obligation on every new recruit to submit to a medical inspection, so when he arrived before the sergeant and saw a group of men disrobing behind a single, inadequate screen – his own father among them – and realised that he too would be required to strip naked under the gaze of that room full of men, many of them also unclothed, and none as young as he was – with tattoos on their biceps and fore-arms, and body hair, and darker, fatter penises, such as his father was now displaying – his courage deserted him and he mumbled an apology, confessed to being under age, and turned and hurried from the hall.

Which was the first and only occasion on which he disobeyed a command, the sergeant calling after him to come back at once, to come back and be a man.

23
Winnie

a cheerful fellow

Winnie's husband wasn't always an inebriate, the sorry case he'd become by the start of the war, and even when he had taken a drink he wouldn't always be trouble; sometimes the opposite.

After a few pints in the Crown he might come home with a bag of bread rolls, or a pheasant or a rabbit he had bought off Patty the poacher, and often then they would see the best of him – buoyant, big-hearted, and more inclined to sing or dance than to shout – but even so, Winnie had learned to be watchful, as had her children, for no matter how merry he might seem to them they always knew to be wary, and to indulge him, since his moods were so uncertain and so apt to turn on the least provocation. His rages were sudden. He might strike out at them sometimes simply for being within range.

Yet at the start, in his prime, he was a steady, dependable man, more often in work than out, more often sober than not. He was a 'clicker' – one of the élite of the boot and shoe trade – a skilled craftsman who cut the uppers from the leather and worked as many as fourteen hours a day, six days in the week (if there was a rush on, if there were orders), and when he was employed in Theo Thompson's – the biggest of the manufacturers locally, whose name is known wherever fine footwear is worn (or so runs the legend on their boxes and advertisements) – Winnie would take his meals to him at the factory, and take the children along with her too (Walter then seven, Arthur still cowled in her shawl), since Eddie wouldn't want to abandon his bench to come home, his wages being paid by the piece, and if she thinks back to that time she remembers a cheerful fellow, lustily devouring the bread and dripping or cheese that she'd wrapped for him and savouring his bottle of sweet tea, but saving the crusts and syrupy dregs for the children, who loved him for it.

They all loved him then, Winnie more than was wise, though it was only on a Sunday that she would be able to show it, once he had supped for an hour or so in the pub and the children had been sent to their Sunday School, leaving their parents to spend the afternoon together in bed – their weekly nap, as they called it – Eddie yawning in anticipation, perhaps slapping her haunches as she tidied up after dinner, his cheeks flushed, eyes glinting, though in time, the more children there were, the more she would have to resist him, insisting that a little affection was all that she wanted or was prepared to allow him.

And sometimes he would oblige her and lay off, sometimes not, though increasingly anyway he was becoming incapable: after William died, his sessions in the Crown began a lot earlier, and lasted much longer.

Of course, in the shoe trade the living was always uncertain, good times followed by bad, and when the orders were done and dispatched the men might well be stood down: not sacked, not necessarily, for the factory retained their cards, and they would have to sign on at the union offices and wait for the factory to call for them, which might be days or weeks later, and in the interim what else could they do but idle about in the alleys and courtyards and pubs? Few of the men would be welcome at home, and there was no point in pestering the foreman, who would shake his head at them – nothing doing – and so they would loiter, and gamble, and drink, and it was in those slack times that Eddie became such a stray, disappearing for days at a stretch, so when finally there was work for him she wouldn't always know where to find him, or if indeed he was ready to go back to his bench, if he could be trusted to take up his knife again after a week or more of living on beer.

Eddie lost so many good jobs because of his thirst.

But then the mile length of Riverside Road has always been boozy with pubs – one for every Sunday in the year, more or less – and there have always been boot factories too, so many of them a man could be sacked from one place and cross the street and be taken on straight away by another, which suited him perfectly, and while some such as Thompson's were sizeable concerns, others were much smaller, little factories made out of two- and three-roomed houses, for instance Hadleigh Pitt's, where Eddie worked for a while, or Billy Goldstein's, the last of the shoe places to give him a start, which was burned out by a fire, completely gutted six months into the war, because one of the boys left his cleaning rag to dry near the stove and it ignited, being saturated with paraffin, which set off all the other rags and shorted the wires, and while no one died or got hurt, several of the men took that as their excuse or hint at last to enlist, though not Eddie, not at that time.

For half a year more he hung on, picking up odds and ends where he could, and though he has now gone from her life, Winnie could not in truth say she is sorry. It is her son that she yearns for, and while Eddie did come back to them once – three months ago – the mud of France still caking his boots, his puttees and trousers stiff with dried dirt, she hopes that will be the last her children need see of him. 'Got given some leave,' he grinned. 'Get the bed warm for me, Winnie.'

she hasn't the muscle

Pests of all kinds are a common thing. Open the oven or one of the closets and a mouse might appear, momentarily startled, then gone. They skitter across the scraps of linoleum, shoot up the rough-rendered walls, and wherever there's food there will be droppings, and bugs, such as the weevils she finds in the pantry and the cockroaches that inhabit the cracks. The brick flooring downstairs is uneven, and though she scatters sawdust to clog up the gaps, it's a devil to sweep, and still the cockroaches will find a way out, though James at least likes to collect them.

He is crouching down now by the skirting, constructing some kind of trap from the cardboard the girls use to make match-boxes, and though he ought not to – it isn't his cardboard to waste – Winnie says nothing, but blearily sits at the table to watch him. He seems to be using a piece of shrimp as his bait. He ought not to be wasting their edibles either.

She lights the first of a new pack of Woodbines, and quietly says, 'Where is everyone?'

James shrugs. 'Station.'

'The railway station?'

'They went to see the soldiers.'

'All of them?'

'Think so.'

'Didn't you want to see them?'

'In a minute. I'm doing this.'

'Have you eaten?'

'A bit.'

'What about Mabel? Did she go?'

But he is far away, concentrating, and as she draws on her cigarette she gazes around at the kitchen, which is dark despite the yard door being open, and so much shabbier than it used to be, for always there are things to be done, which are not being done, and while the children do try to be helpful, they are clumsy and forgetful and need constantly to be told, then reminded. Harold, for instance, has yet to empty the scraps into the midden, and the old newspapers she left for Elsie to tear into strips for the privy are still lying on the hearth where she dropped them. She looks down at the dark print – her head beginning to spin from the drink she took in the grocer's – and notices then that Dot has at least attempted to blacklead the fireplace, but hasn't quite managed to bring up a shine – she hasn't the muscle – so that will need doing again.

Winnie sighs, and accepts that it might as well be left as it is, for Dot has done as best she can, while she is too weary to do it herself – or even to mention it – and with another, heavier, sigh she gets to her feet and flattens her cigarette on the edge of the sink and drops it into the scrap bucket. 'I'm going to have a lie-down,' she says, and steps carefully around her son, her head thick with gin, a spreading pain in her abdomen, and opens the door to the stairs. Slowly she ascends in near darkness to the room she shares at night with the little ones, Elsie and James, where she lowers herself to the bed, curls up on her side, and stares at the window, the blue-black of the sky, the storm that is coming. She presses a hand to her belly, and winces.

he slumped as if shot

Co-ordination was a problem for him, she remembers. In his drunkenness and fatigue, and with the burden of carrying so many things – his dirt-encrusted greatcoat and tin helmet, his haversack and water bottle, mess tin and pouches, bayonet and trenching tool – Eddie could not seem to get himself straight. Repeatedly he had to shrug to hitch his rifle back onto his shoulder, and appeared amused by his own foolishness, wheezily laughing to himself as he rooted about in his kitbag, which he had lifted onto the table, tipping over her teacup and spilling the dregs on the oilcloth. She had scoured the surfaces only half an hour earlier, but despite her annoyance with him for causing a mess, and for being so drunk, and for coming back without warning, she was alert to whatever he might ask of her. When he reached out an arm and said, 'Come and help me here, Winnie,' she stepped into his heavy embrace and waited, her palms flat to her apron, not knowing what she should do, while he continued to search through the bag with his free hand and their children warily watched him, this stinking soldier who had appeared in their kitchen.

His rifle slipped again and swung into her back, but Winnie dared not move, for it seemed she was required to help him stay upright, until at last he said, 'Got it,' and pressed a damp paper bag into her hands, from which she extracted a small, wizened orange – the first the children had seen – and a banana, squashed and mulchy and brown, and was grateful simply to have an excuse to slip out from under the weight of his arm. She placed them on the table.

'Oh, that's lovely, Eddie!' she said, surprising herself by sounding so pleased. Then, 'Let me see what I can do with them,' but as she bent to reach for her bowl he slumped as if shot and she had to grab hold of him before he collapsed to the floor, her cheek pressed against his sharp stubble and her arms tucked underneath his, the smell of him quite sickening.

Mabel helped her, of course. Together they manoeuvred him upright, and stood at the ready in case he should buckle again, watching as he braced himself with both filthy hands on the table, for a moment seeming as if he might vomit, his complexion quite ghostly. Then he nodded, and heaved a long breath, and cautiously they backed away from him.

'So, who would like a bit of fruit?' Winnie asked brightly, and passed the orange to Mabel to peel, then mashed the banana in her bowl with a little milk and her last sprinkling of sugar, showing the mixture first to Elsie, since she was standing the closest, but Elsie wrinkled her face, more distrustful, it seemed, than revolted.

'I'll have it,' volunteered Arthur, with a glance to his father, and made a decent show of enjoying it, then offered a taste to each of his siblings, including, finally, Elsie, who accepted, uncertain, after which they sucked the dry, pithy segments of orange that Mabel had peeled for them, and Eddie's now uncomprehending expression became something approaching a smile, his mouth a pitiful sight, his gums almost as black as his teeth. He gestured at the door to the stairs.

'I'm going up,' he said, suppressing a belch, and not one of them moved to assist him, since that was something he would never previously have tolerated, but silently watched as he leaned his rifle on the wall, holding the barrel with both hands and carefully positioning the butt on the floor. Slowly he unfurled his grip – first his left hand, splaying his fingers, then the right – and backed away from it with exaggerated concern, as though fearful it might fall and start shooting. He patted his kitbag, and worked the strap of his helmet from under his chin and passed it to Harold. Determinedly squinting, he lifted one foot in the direction of the stairs but found himself tilting backwards and stretched out his arms for support, grabbing hold of Dot, clutching her shoulder. His left leg was wobbling, his narrow gaze fixed upon the door, and with a growl he lurched forwards and in three rapid strides he was there.

James was grinning, Winnie noticed, and glared at him warningly. But there was no need to worry, for Eddie's attention was now concentrated entirely on the latch and the curious business of making it lift, which eventually he managed, though still there remained the problem of the door, which confused him by opening outwards, and then at last he was through, his bayonet and bottle clattering on the stairs as he clambered up on all fours.

Slowly the door swung shut behind him, and Dot allowed herself to rub the top of her arm.

'I'll make him some gravy,' Winnie said. 'Stay away from that gun.' But the children, for now, were more interested in the helmet that Harold had placed on his head and the kitbag that remained on the table, and when finally Eddie had ceased blundering about in the bedroom above them, and her cup of gravy was mixed, Winnie lit a candle and said, 'Please, don't touch that rifle, do you hear me?' She glanced quickly at Mabel, who held open the door for her, then followed her husband upstairs.

The room was curtained, dark and foul-smelling, and Winnie placed her candle and cup on the chest beside the bed and went straight to the window, clearing a passage with her foot through Eddie's clothes on the floor, stepping on the mud that had dropped from his boots. She dragged back the drapes on their cord, but the hinges were stiff and the window would open only a fraction – another concern she would need to take to Joe Orford, as soon as her husband had left them. Deeply she inhaled the night air through the slim gap, the faint familiar stench of the river, and turned and looked down on him, lying as pale as a corpse in the candlelight, his mouth gaping open. Already he was snoring, fast asleep on his back with his arms thrown out to each side, his right leg crooked at the knee, and he was naked entirely, his flesh shockingly white below the line of his neck but covered all over in boils, dark livid mounds with thick waxy heads.

Nauseated by the smell of him, and the sight and the fact of him, Winnie knelt on the mattress and dipped a finger in the warm gravy and dabbed it onto his whiskers – her evidence, should he wake in the night, that he had already eaten – and as she straightened she sighed, truly sorry: she had done enough for him now, cooked him enough meals, brewed him enough cups of tea, borne him enough children, taken enough of his blows, and she could not pretend to feel the least pity or affection or even pride in this man, her husband, who had been doing his duty for England after all, and was home for just a few days, and might never come back again.

There was a blanket. It had slipped to the end of the bed. Winnie gathered it up and flapped it across him – she made him decent – but still there was his face, his gaping mouth and the boils on his chest, and as she considered covering him over completely she wondered how much it might cost her to take the pillow from under his head and hitch up her skirt and straddle him, as she had straddled him in the past, and place the pillow softly over his face, and lie down upon it, for she was enough of a man now to do his work, and take his wages, and possibly she was enough of a man to take his life as well, since men were everywhere dying, everywhere killing each other, and if he should buck a little beneath her, that would be all, it wouldn't last long, for the strength was no longer in him – pugnacious fellow that he once was – and perhaps it would be as well for him to suffocate in his own bed beneath the warmth of his wife as to be blasted to bits in a field somewhere in France. It might be a mercy.

But though she did lift his head, and gently managed to tug the pillow from under him, she knew at once that she could go no further than that; she hadn't the courage, and sorrowfully she folded the pillow into a ball and cradled it to her stomach and looked at her reflection in the window – her once familiar profile, as plump as if she were pregnant – and accepted that tomorrow or the next day it would be she who lay on her back on this bed, and her husband who lay over her. He would expect it, and once again she would allow him.

Downstairs her children were becoming raucous, Amy and Elsie screaming with fear or excitement, and Winnie flung the pillow across to the wall, watched it flop to the floor, and took up her cup and blew out the candle and descended the stairs in the dark, leaving her husband to sleep.

24
Montague

the agony wagon

Miss Dobson says, 'It's very smart-looking, isn't it?'

Montague reaches around her to hold open the tarpaulin flap of the tent, and as they peer in through the gap he becomes aware of her warmth, and the faintly camphorous smell in her clothes and her hair, and wonders if perhaps he ought to have allowed her to leave so that he could have retired to his changing room with a jar of the pharmacist's ointment, since her proximity is so provoking to his condition, but much as he itches to scratch at his arms, his ribs, the back of his neck, he finds he also yearns to embrace her.

'Would you care to step inside, Miss Dobson?'

'Oh,' she says, as if alarmed by his nearness. 'I don't know, I'm not sure . . .'

'No, do take a look,' he insists, and guides her under the flap, then stands a few paces distant so that he may admire the prettiness of her profile and her dark heavy hair, with its white ribbon winding through the braid of her ponytail, and its neatly tied bow, and cannot help wondering if she might be posing for him, her posture as fixed as though she were modelling for a portrait, her hands daintily clasped and her head sadly tilted, and he recoils a little at the contrivance, if that is what it is; with women he can never be secure in his judgements. Above him the solitary black dot of a fly turns drowsily about in the pitch of the roof and as he looks up at it, obscurely annoyed, Miss Dobson begins a tentative tour of the beds, her heels starkly sounding on the bare boards.

'This would be for the better off to recuperate,' he says. 'The worst afflicted – the surgical cases, and so on – will be accommodated in the house.'

Miss Dobson glances at him, nods.

'That at least is my understanding, though it may also depend on whether, perhaps . . .' But Miss Dobson hardly appears to be interested, and he coughs into his hand and is silent.

'So many flowers,' she remarks then, approaching the table at the centre of the tent, on which is displayed a large vase of pink and white blooms. 'Aren't they lovely?'

'Donated by the patriotic public,' says Montague, 'though I rather think they lend everything the air of a funeral parlour. Wouldn't you agree?'

'Do they?' She frowns. 'I don't know, I haven't been into a funeral parlour.'

'Excuse me,' he says, 'no. That was in poor taste.' He folds one hand over another, and resumes, 'But the flowers do present a very charming sight, and the fragrance will be soothing. I'm sure the men will be most cheerful and comfortable here.'

'Yes,' she says, 'I think so,' and turns fully about to admire the preparations, the twelve metal-framed beds, perfectly spaced, with an identical cabinet next to each one and on top of each cabinet a glass beaker and a water carafe and a variety of other, smaller, vases containing yet more freshly cut flowers. Everything is spotless, oblivious to the filth and stench that is to come later this evening, and as he surveys the castors on the beds, all precisely aligned, Montague recalls his brief stay in the hospital in France and the boys – for they were no better than boys – screaming like the pigs on the market as they waited for the nurse to reach them with the agony wagon, the fresh dressings and medicines trolley, having woken to the shock of a limb or two missing, and the nurse, who seemed little older than Miss Dobson, crying because she was frightened, and perhaps unused to the swearing, the furious filthy language, but doing what she could for them, then afterwards – a couple of hours later – returning with the ward sister on her daily round of inspection and being reduced again to tears, this time because the castors on the beds were awry and there was a smear of dust on Sister's finger after she had run it along the top of a wardrobe.

'How *orderly* everything is,' Miss Dobson says then, indicating the mattress beside her, on which is arranged a pair of slippers, some striped pyjamas and a striped dressing-gown, all neatly folded, as crisp and clean as the bed linen. The display is replicated exactly on each of the other beds. 'But you must be used to it,' she says, 'from being in the Army. Everything's orderly in the Army, isn't it?'

'It is,' he confirms. 'Very orderly indeed.'

'I think your sisters will keep an orderly hospital, wherever they are.'

'I've no doubt they will,' agrees Montague, 'and the brave young Tommies will be very grateful to them.'

She nods. 'Yes.'

Montague holds out an arm. 'I wonder, shall we move on?' But Miss Dobson has now noticed the fly, and as she dreamily follows its gyrations beneath the canvas roof he thinks of the clouds that would descend on the men at the front, the incessant drone of them as they settled over the men's rations and the liquid shit in the latrine sap and the putrefying parts of the poor souls who had died and been abandoned to the battlefield, and seems to remember as well the smell of the soil, which was soured by the taint of human habitation, the boiled soup, the sweat and farts and the stinking breath of the men, and the seepage from the corpses as they turned rotten, and with some impatience he says, 'Miss Dobson, do come!'

'Oh!' She looks at him, startled.

'I mean, forgive me ... I think I heard somebody approaching.'

'Sorry, I see,' she says, and blushes and bows her head and hurries to follow him. 'We mustn't be caught, must we?'

'No, I think not,' he says.

a snap of her fine wrist

His mother, of course, disapproved of his sisters' adoption of so unrefined a young woman as their favourite, having insisted all through their childhood that they must be selective in their choice of companions, and though it was clear to Montague that their affection for Miss Dobson was sincere, to their mother it appeared a mere affectation, no more deserving of her approval than their insistence that they should be allowed to join in with the war, a theme on which they harped almost constantly, to the extent, early on, that Edwina even wrote to Lord Kitchener himself, proposing that it was the duty of anyone who was young and strong, patriotic and capable – whether female or male, without discrimination – to do the work that required to be done.

A reply arrived within the fortnight from Lord Kitchener's secretary, by which time Montague had received notification that he was to prepare to ship overseas, and he remembers descending that morning to breakfast in his uniform and finding Edwina and Emma standing in the light of the window, together holding the letter, and Edwina expelling a laugh so sudden and loud it resembled a shout, as triumphant as she was affronted.

'Edwina?' asked Mother.

'Lord Kitchener,' she said, with contempt, 'regrets to advise me that he does not approve on any consideration of women shouldering arms. It is the men's job to fight the war and to protect us, though he thanks me most kindly for my suggestion.'

She tossed the page with a snap of her fine wrist to the breakfast table, where it skidded elegantly, half turning, towards the coffee pot.

'On any consideration,' she repeated.

Her mother stared at her a moment, then sternly enquired, 'And your suggestion?'

'That we should be allowed to serve in the Home Guard, which would free some more men to join in the war. Women are replacing clerks and cashiers and lift operators and all sorts, so that the men may do battle. Father has even suggested they should be set to work in our factory. So why shouldn't we replace the Home Guardsmen, too? That is all I asked.'

'I see,' said Mrs Beckwith, standing up. Then quietly, with finality, as she went from the room, 'I think Lord Kitchener is very wise.'

But while Montague chose not to offer an opinion, since he rarely had the sense of debating with agile minds when he engaged with his sisters on matters of philosophy, politics or policy, their intelligence in those spheres being somewhat mechanical, though exceptionally well oiled – as when previously they had espoused the cause of universal suffrage, broadcasting the arguments of the Pankhursts second-hand, every answer predictable, every argument rehearsed by some previous thinker – he was nonetheless supportive, which his mother was not, when they threw themselves in with the national effort to recruit men for the war, since that at least would temper their political enthusiasms and provide an outlet for their frustrations, and there too, he recalls, they were able to recruit Miss Dobson to their cause, for she was a sweet, biddable girl, however lacking in breeding, and always glad to oblige them.

'no longer the ornaments they used to be'

'I'm sorry,' he says. 'You must find me very uncommunicative.'

Miss Dobson looks at him.

'I invited you to accompany me, and now I'm treating you to silence.'

'I don't mind.' She smiles. 'I'm enjoying the peacocks.'

'The peacocks?'

She gestures to the roof of a potting shed, where a nondescript female – a great lump of grey feathers – appears to be dozing.

Montague nods. 'I missed it,' he says.

'And there.' She points around him.

'Ah, yes.' Dutifully he looks. He has brought her down past the ice house, the old stables and the garage, the gardener's various sheds and seedbeds, and it seems to be here that most of the flies and midges have gathered and where most of the peacocks are now nesting, on the roofs and the walls, the most precarious places. 'They're becoming quite scrawny,' he remarks. 'They're no longer the ornaments they used to be.'

'The feathers in their tails are still lovely.'

'Yes. I suppose they are.'

'It would be nice to find one to take home for Mother.'

'I'm sure there will be some lying about,' he says, 'there are bound to be some,' though in fact he has no idea when he last saw one. 'Perhaps this way?' he suggests, and guides her through a gap in the wall and towards a long, unbroken lawn, a bank of dark trees behind it. The grass is grossly overgrown, seemingly more blue than green, and is scattered with flowers – scabious, betony, ragwort and trefoil. There are butterflies too, creamy-white, yellow-green.

'It's pretty here,' says Gertie.

'Yes,' he agrees, 'yes, it is,' but winces at the effort of lifting his knees, for the grass is too long and too dense for him to walk on, and he pauses, looking away from her. 'I wonder, Miss Dobson, would you mind if we skirted the perimeter? It's a longer way round, I'm afraid, but it does come out in the end by the lake.'

'No, I don't mind.'

'And it should be cooler down there,' he adds, ducking to take off his hat. Her hand leaves his arm. 'Excuse me,' he murmurs, and dabs at his brow with a handkerchief. 'It really shouldn't have been allowed to run to this length.'

'Mr Logan must be finding it difficult,' she says, 'now that he's on his own.'

'I dare say.'

'It must be an awful lot of work for him. Because the grounds are enormous, aren't they?'

Montague replaces his hat, and thinks of some of the estates on which he has weekended, and the stately homes to which certain of his university friends would return in the vacations – but Miss Dobson is plainly sincere, and he decides it would be ungentlemanly to attempt to correct her. 'Yes, they are quite vast,' he agrees, 'very large indeed.'

'And you're all on your own here.'

'I am,' he says. 'Quite abandoned.' He crooks his arm for her again, and as they begin to pick their way across to the path he glances at her, uncertain, and says, 'This is where the local children take their summer outings, their *gala days*. I don't suppose you . . . forgive me, were you ever among them? Did you ever come here as a child?'

'No!' she exclaims. 'Father wouldn't allow it. I would've needed to go to a Sunday School first, and he would never have let me.'

'Ah, good!' he says. Then, 'Good. I remember they were represented to us as fêtes for the crippled and poor – in all likelihood, they still are – so we could hardly refuse them, but I should hate to think of you as one of the crippled or poor, Miss Dobson.'

She laughs, and he is pleased. 'You're a bit like my father, I think. He doesn't like cripples or poor people either. Or stupid people. I think he's especially against *them*.'

Circumspectly Montague begins, 'That may be true, from what I understand of his views, but . . .'

'It is true,' she says simply. 'And the war is making a lot of new cripples, isn't it? And sending men mad, some of them – it's turning them into *imbeciles*, isn't it?' She glances at him. 'That's another of his words.'

202

Montague nods, and sombrely says, 'I don't know about imbeciles, but it can destroy more than a man's body, yes. There are a great many damaged men as a result of the war, not all of them obvious to the eye.'

Miss Dobson looks at him frankly. 'Are you damaged?' she asks then. 'Is that what causes this on your face, and your hands?'

Montague smiles at her directness, then attempts to correct his smile, registering something in her expression, the faintest recoil from what must appear to her as a leer or a grimace. 'It's not just my hands and my face,' he says. 'The worst is hidden from view, you'll be glad to know, but it is . . . *general*, whatever it is.'

She reddens, of course, since he has presented her with an image of his body as it must be beneath his clothing.

'Mainly it's on my arms and legs,' he continues, 'and my ribcage, but as to what causes it, or what its name might be, I'm afraid I don't know, and the doctors don't seem to know either.'

'That's awful,' she says, and lifts a hand to her neck, which is quite as flushed as her face.

'Well,' he says, guiding her down some stone steps, banks of rhododendron to either side of them, 'they've suggested various possibilities, but the symptoms are never quite consistent with the textbooks. One explanation is that it's some form of organic reaction to the conditions I experienced in France, the mud and so on. The damp.'

'Is the damp so terrible?'

'Only in what it might harbour – the germs, I suppose. I might have picked up an infection. The conditions weren't always hygienic.'

'You should talk to Father about hygiene.'

'Possibly, yes. That, anyway, is the physicians' approach, the medical doctors. But there are other kinds of doctor, as you'll know, who are more concerned with the psychology of the patient and the effect, as they put it, of emotional and intellectual processes on the organism – or of *sub*-intellectual processes, I should say.'

His words are clearly meaningless to her, but politely she nods.

'I'm sorry,' he says. 'How the mind affects matter, I mean.'

'Mind over matter, yes,' she says, and inwardly he smiles at the gameness of her response, her willingness at least to pretend to comprehend him.

'Mind over matter,' he confirms, 'though perhaps in a negative sense, not quite how we would normally use that expression.'

Miss Dobson is silent, her attitude thoughtful, and they walk for some way along a cinder track beside a brook, the water quite still, greened over with algae. He hears a small splash further upstream. A wood-pigeon clatters into the sky from the top of a beech tree.

'I'm not sure that I've explained it very well,' he says then, 'but my view is that I am the cause of my own complaint. It may be that I'm developing a thicker skin, as it were, to protect myself.'

'From what?'

'From the war.'

'From being shot at?'

'Well, that, yes. There is that. There is a great deal of shooting in a war.'

'But you're miles away now!'

'Geographically I am, undeniably. But there is still the memory of the shooting, Miss Dobson, how it plays on the mind.'

'I don't see why you should need a thicker skin for that. You probably just need to think of other things, don't you?'

'Other things. Indeed.'

'You need to start forgetting,' she says.

'Yes,' he agrees. 'I need to start forgetting, and to think of other things.' Her hand is now heavy on his arm, and Montague stands for a moment quite still, his eyes partially closed, and takes a long breath to disguise his annoyance, mentally excoriating himself for his foolishness in thinking to find companionship or understanding in this daughter of a chemist, whose bovine, stupid complacency cannot be expected to produce anything beyond such ignorant platitudes. He takes another breath. 'Can you smell that?' he asks at last.

Miss Dobson also closes her eyes. Her chest swells prettily in her white dress as she inhales, and he steals a glance too at the moist press of her lips, then looks quickly away, into the wood that encircles them, the air thick with thyme and the sweet scent of wild garlic. He hears the hum of insects, and a trickle of water from one of the several other brooks that feed into the lake. Miss Dobson exhales. 'Garlic,' she says.

'Yes.'

She stares at him a moment, then says, 'You're annoyed with me, aren't you?'

Surprised, he reaches again for his handkerchief and presses it to the back of his neck as they walk on. 'Am I?'

'You think I'm *glib*.'

He nods. 'Perhaps. A little. Your last remark perhaps, that I need to start forgetting.'

'I'm sorry,' she says. 'I expect you saw some gruesome, bloody things, and it must've been very upsetting for you. I think you must've had to do some gruesome things, too.'

'Quite so.'

'Because that's what it's like for a soldier, isn't it? You have to do your duty, even if it's awful.'

'Indeed.'

'And I expect afterwards it must make you feel very badly about yourself, if you're that kind of a person.'

'Yes,' Montague says, impatient now for her to stop talking, 'if one has that disposition.'

'Do you have that *disposition*? I think you do.'

'To a degree, I suspect so. But I wonder, Miss Dobson, have you ever been out on the lake with my sisters? In a boat, I mean. One of the rowing boats?'

'No,' she smiles.

'We're really very close,' he says, and gently he eases his arm from her grip and leads her along a narrow bend in the track, through a thicket of oak, alder and willow, the atmosphere dank, great brackets of fungus disfiguring the trees, clusters of mushrooms sprouting at their roots, and out to a profusion of willowherb and loosestrife, the lake suddenly before them and the sunlight glistening like gunmetal on its calm surface.

'But it's huge!' she exclaims.

'It is,' he agrees, and indicates the boathouse a few yards further along, a stone Gothic construction matted with moss, the roof tiles streaked with guano, and brambles obscuring the windows. The boats, he can see, are still worthy, though the water beneath them is stagnant. A dragonfly jinks in and out of the shelter.

'Would you like to take a turn on the lake? I believe I can still row.'

'Oh, yes,' she says. 'I would love to. If you don't mind. If you're sure?'

'Not at all,' Montague says, 'no, not at all,' and as he stands and contemplates the task before him he wonders at his wisdom in bringing Miss Dobson this far down from the house, and regrets that their conversation must after all continue, a prospect as troubling to him now as the darkening sky above the trees to the north, for a downpour is undoubtedly heading towards them and he would be a fool, he knows, to take her out on the lake in a storm, though that is what he is determined to do; he has offered and she has accepted, and they must now see it through.

25
Walter

another man recruited

The feather was dumbfounding. There was the soft impression of her fingers on his icy palm, and some sweet aroma from inside the house, and the imprint of her smile as she looked into his eyes, teasing him, admonishing. He felt such a queer stirring then in his guts and his balls, and closed his fist around the feather, gripped it so tightly that the quill pierced his palm, which brought him almost to tears, and perhaps he would have cried except that Cyril Greenland was waiting at the front of the house, and he supposed himself by then to be a man.

Walter heard the horse's hoofs on the stone setts, its snorting impatience, and when gently Gertie closed the door on him he turned and walked away with heavy legs, a heavier heart, and hauled himself onto the wagon with one hand, still gripping the feather, and said nothing to Greenland as they plodded up the drive, nor managed to look back at the house, where Gertie and the Misses Beckwith might have been standing at one of the windows, regarding him with some satisfaction, or pride – another man recruited, another scrimshanker called to account – though if he had looked he might have seen some approval and encouragement, too; he might have found Gertie waving him goodbye – *WOMEN OF BRITAIN SAY 'GO!'* – but Walter could not face them, and knew he was a coward for that, he hadn't the pluck, and sat hunched into himself all the way down Riverside Road, the ice creaking beneath its tarpaulin, the horse's voluptuous haunches pounding before them, and repeatedly sensed

Greenland glancing round at him, but in his mind he was already gone; he was already in khaki.

He slipped the feather into the pouch of his apron and resolved that this time he would not be turned away, and nor would he flee, and when at last they arrived at the top of Ice House Lane he said, 'That'll be me then, Mr Greenland. I won't be coming again. I'm going to join up, I've decided.'

Greenland glowered at him, and said, 'Don't be such a fucking fool. You're too young, boy!'

Walter shrugged. It was true, he was a fucking fool, and he was still too young, and yet he clung to his feather as he set off for St Saviour's Street Barracks, where the banner on the railings was beginning to sag, and the queue of men had become such a straggle. He shuffled inside with the others, and claimed again to be nineteen, and was taken at last at his word, before he submitted to a medical, raised his right hand for the oath, and finally received the King's shilling.

He became a soldier at his fourth attempt, many months too late to march behind the military band that once would parade down Balmoral Road with an escort of constables in capes and officers bearing arms, the company sergeant major up ahead with his stick, and the crowds urging them on with their gifts. There was to be no fanfare. Instead Walter and the other men were instructed to go out to the stables at the rear of the barracks to get their hair cut, where the barber that day was Ted Fordham from Riverside Road, wearing his best boater to dignify the occasion, a crisp white apron beneath his Sunday-best jacket, and the brick floor all fuzzy with hair, and it was that, Walter's short back and sides, which gave the game away to his mother the instant he stepped into her kitchen, his old cap no disguise. She whipped it from him and tossed it to the floor. 'Let me see you,' she said, and he thought she might strike him then, and stood his ground, quite prepared to be struck, until she slumped back to her seat and stared at him with such fury and sorrow he had to turn away. 'You'd better make me some tea,' she said to Doris, and would not look at him again; even when he came to say his last farewells, standing so straight and proud of himself in his khaki and cap, she would not look at him again, her eldest son, for she had warned him too – 'Don't be such a bloody fool' – and he had not listened to her.

nothing survived

In the years before he began his short-lived employment with the Beckwiths, and sometimes even after he was dismissed, Walter would trespass on this edge of their estate with his brothers and cousins and their cronies to gather flowers to take home to their mothers, such as the bluebells that grew near the old mill, a continuous carpet of blue that would astonish even them, as if their world had been inverted, the sky upturned beneath their feet. Then later, in another season, they would find such an abundance of fruit (blackberries, raspberries, apples, wild strawberries) they would be able to eat almost as much as they picked to take home, and occasionally too they would come here to catch fish, or simply to swim in the lake, and as Walter ambles down now from the road, kicking up stones from the narrow dirt track, he glimpses the grey stone mill through the trees, and recognises the boy from the market, the urchin he spoke to outside the Midden.

Walter smiles, and whistles, then lifting his boots, his heavy military footwear, he tramps through the tangled undergrowth to join him.

'Anything doing?' he says, and the boy gives a sad shake of his head, for the wheel is deadly still, and looks as though it has been still for many years. The wooden blades are bearded with weed, and where once there were so many fish you needed only to dip your hook in the swirl to come up with a catch – quick as you like, every time – now the water in the channel is stagnant, frothed over with scum and humming with insects. Further along, Walter knows, there are streams feeding into the lake that are wide and fast-flowing, clean enough to drink from, shallow enough to wade through, and when at last the boy shrugs and turns in that direction Walter turns too, happy to tag along in his wake, ducking beneath a straggle of branches as they enter a dense grove of hawthorn and hazel and birch, the sunlight streaking down in patches like rain.

The boy is shouldering a droving stick, at the end of which is a handkerchief, torn from a white sheet and knotted to make a pouch for his provisions, his chunk of bread and cheese, and the jam-jar that he will drink from – the water scooped from a stream and flavoured with sherbet – after which the hanky can be used like a net to catch fish (sticklebacks, stone gudgeons), the trick being to surprise them by spilling the rocks that they lurk beneath, then swiping them into the hanky as they attempt to dart free.

'But it's a shame, isn't it?' says Walter. 'We always used to forget them after we'd caught them. We tipped them in the jar and then we forgot all about them.'

The fish would die in their few inches of water, and the bluebells soon wilted, and sometimes too the boys would steal birds' eggs from their nests in the trees, and capture newts and mating frogs, and take home jars full of frog spawn, all of this a pointless waste – nothing survived; none of it was edible – though Walter did also come down here one evening with a catapult and his grandfather's Jack Russell terrier, his sole attempt to be a poacher of rabbits, aged perhaps twelve, and had to flee when a groundsman came after him.

'Do you remember that dog?' asks Walter. 'Jasper, he was called. Do you remember?'

Fleetingly the boy looks over his shoulder, his face grimed with dirt, his eyes a startling grey, and Walter stumbles on a dip in the ground, feels himself falling. He reaches out a hand, but the boy is already too far ahead of him, further ahead than he realised.

'He was on his last legs by then,' calls Walter, pushing himself up from his knees, brushing himself down, 'a proper fat old thing. Do you remember him? Jasper the Jack Russell?'

Somewhat older than Walter, the dog belonged to Grandad Barley, a trim little fellow with a permanently ruddy complexion, and whiskers that were whiter even than Jasper's, whose job it was for years to attend to the Corporation's streetlamps – cleaning the glass, cutting the wicks, replenishing the paraffin – and who had left school at just ten without being able to read or write, and never would learn, though he tried for a while at the First Day School in Paradise Place, and did manage at last to scratch out his own signature. As a boy Walter would sit with him sometimes in the tiny back room of his cottage by the football ground, sounding out the names and numbers in the racing pages of the newspaper, but Grandad Barley, always polite, refused to impose on Winnie and Eddie for anything, never once came to visit them in Mortuary Yard, just as Walter's father never would call on Grandad Barley, his own father, a widower living alone with his dog.

'Except for that one time, with the rat,' says Walter, 'Dad went along then, do you remember? A lot of the men went along then.' For besides his dog, Grandad Barley kept a few rabbits – bred them for eating, the furs to sell on – and one morning led Walter outside to wonder at a litter of babies all missing their heads, a rat having got into their hutch, the wood gnawed clean through underneath. 'We'll catch him, though,' said Grandad, 'don't you fear, we'll catch him,' and set about constructing a trap inside that same hutch, using some netting pilfered by a neighbour from Beckwith's Engineering, and a different litter of rabbits as bait, and within a few days they had him, a rat as big as any that Walter had ever seen, ginger and bloated and its tail as flat as if it had been stamped on.

'Now we'll have some sport with you,' said Grandad, and gave the trap a good shake, the rat turning a tight circle inside. 'Now we'll have some fun with you.' He laughed, and returned the rat in its trap to its hutch until later that evening, by which time the word had got out and a crowd had gathered around the long narrow strip of his garden, including Eddie Barley and his pals, a pair of old dears smoking their pipes, and several small boys perched on men's shoulders or sitting up on the walls. Bets were being taken, of course, since Grandad had recruited another man, called Bungo, and his own much younger terrier, named Jim, whose ears were pricked, eyes shining, the hackles risen all along his quivering spine.

It was to be Jim against Jasper, who was by then barrel-shaped and bulbous-eyed, but still snarling, as fierce as he had ever been. Bungo held both dogs by their collars as Grandad set the trap on the ground, and waited a moment or so, enraging the dogs, then finally punched down on the catch and stepped quickly away. The rat was sprung, and had nowhere to go but under the hutches, pursued by both dogs, then suddenly out, its tail slithering after it, seemingly making directly for Bungo, who hadn't the sense to step aside but gave it such a kick the animal flew three feet in the air, its back broken, as lifeless suddenly as any rabbit skin, and was caught the instant it landed by Jim, who had it at once by the neck, shaking and growling. Disappointed, a few of the men turned to go, then paused as Jasper sank his teeth into the rat's haunches and the two dogs, disputing the prize, ripped it apart, its guts slopping out: all bets were off, but there was a cheer for that, the messy end of the rodent.

'It was the end of Jasper too, really,' says Walter, his voice much quieter now, as if he were whispering into his own ear. 'That was his last hurrah. He didn't live too much longer. Or Grandad. It wasn't that long before he passed away, old Grandad Barley.'

But the boy will not hear him, for he has slipped too far ahead, following a track through the trees, heading deeper into the woods, and when at last he is gone, the gleam of his handkerchief the last that Walter will ever see of him, there comes a scent of thyme and wild garlic and the sound of a brook somewhere nearby, and as Walter turns in the direction of the lake he thinks how easily a thing will disappear, go missing, and pushes his hands into his greatcoat pockets and feels about in the fluff and tobacco strands and dirt that have gathered in the linings for the feather that the pharmacist's daughter once gave to him, and which he has managed to keep, in the hope that one day he might come back to her, a soldier in His Majesty's armed forces.

26
Gertie

a wrong thing to mention

The sky is the blue-black of bruises. The first drop of rain deto-
nates on the dark surface of the lake; another strikes further off.
But still it is warm, a late summer's afternoon, and Captain
Beckwith appears unconcerned as he angles the oars from the
water and allows their shallow craft to drift in the direction of
the peacock feathers that are floating a few yards away, not
merely one or two, but seemingly dozens of them, clumps of
green and grey and iridescent blue.

'How will I reach them?' she asks.

'You shan't,' he says. 'I will do it for you.'

'But you have your condition.'

'I think I shall manage, Miss Dobson.'

'What if you fall in?'

'Then I shall drown, most likely. And you will need to skipper
the ship.'

She grins, sitting facing him, in his boater and blazer, his
brown and cream brogues, and reflects on his affliction, the peeling away of his skin, which no longer seems so hideous to her,
now that she is used to it. 'All right,' she says, and shuffles along
on her bench to make room for the oars as he unclips first one
and then the other from its creaking lock, and lays them length-
wise inside the boat, the dripping red-painted paddles to the
stern, where Gertie is seated. She grips her bench with both
hands, alarmed by the sudden tilt of the boat. Montague is positioning himself to lean over.

'Is it deep?' she asks, squinting at the surface, which is placid and silky and green. Nearer to the boathouse she was able to see the fronds of underwater plants, but out here there is nothing, only the mirrored darkness of sky and the trees that encircle them.

'I don't believe it is, no,' he says, and takes off his hat, holds it by the brim. Carefully he stretches an arm over the side and Gertie watches him, the paler parts of his face flushing red, his neck taut with the effort. He selects a handful of the prettier ones, and comes up. The boat lurches and Gertie gives a small squeal.

'How about these?' he asks, and presents her with a dripping bouquet, his arm conspicuously shaking, but the boat is still rocking and she hardly dares let go of the bench.

'Yes,' she says, 'they're very nice.'

Sombrely he lays them at her feet, and says, 'Let's hope your mother appreciates them.'

'Yes,' she says.

Montague nods. He replaces his hat, the brim now shading his eyes, and shakes the wet from his hand, then sits for some moments quite still, looking away to the trees and the gingery fringe of reeds that surrounds them as slowly their boat turns about in the centre of the lake, the wide expanse of water intermittently pitting with rain. 'I should imagine,' he says then, 'that if one were to fall in – myself, I mean – if I were to fall in, and if I were able to keep my wits about me, not get into a funk, I should perhaps be able to stand on the bed with the water-level just about up to my shoulders.' He indicates the top of his arm with the flat of his hand. 'My head would remain above the water.'

'That means I would drown,' she says. 'Because I'm smaller.'

'Well, yes, perhaps, though I'm speaking hypothetically. I expect there's enough of an undercurrent down there that we'd both be swept away, actually, if we were to try to stand up. It would take some strength, which I haven't got, to resist it. But yes, a young woman of your build and stature would not be taller than the water is deep.'

He makes it sound like a riddle and this time Gertie does not blush, though he appears to be looking at her directly, assessing her stature, her build. A dark slash of rain appears on his sleeve. He takes up one of the oars, and casually says, as he relocates it in the lock, 'How tall are you, Miss Dobson? Might I ask that?'

'I think I'm five feet. Thereabouts. And I *think* you are six feet. Are you?'

'Somewhat less,' he admits. 'I'm rather less than most people assume.' Grimacing, he lifts the other oar. 'And do you swim?'

'Swim? No,' she admits, and thinks of that time at the seaside, and the gentleman on the beach, watching as she came ashore with her rescuers. 'I can't,' she says, and remembers that he too was wearing a boater; she pictures him clearly.

'Not that I would recommend it. Not in this water.'

'This water?' She looks over her shoulder and sees a line of ducks gliding out from the reeds.

'It flows in here from the river, Miss Dobson, and brings all the waste of the city with it. All the filth from the yards on Riverside Road. Not to mention the effluent from Beckwith's and the other factories. If one didn't drown, I imagine one would contract some terrible illness, some dread disease.'

'You're a Beckwith,' she says.

'I am.'

She frowns at him.

'I am, though I'm not an *industrial* man, unlike my father. I'm not industrially minded, but I suspect there's nowhere else for the waste to go, other than into the river. It's unfortunate, and I must say I balk at the prospect of visiting certain parts of the plant . . . I wonder, have you ever been in the galvanising shed, Miss Dobson?'

Gertie shakes her head. 'Only in my part,' she says. 'It's where they make the barbed wire'

Montague nods, and lowers the oars to the water, arrests the rotation of the boat. 'Or the cleansing shed?' he asks. 'Have you been there?'

'*No*,' she says, stifling a smile, 'only in my part,' and reaches down for the feathers because his face is so serious. She holds the bunch with both hands, tickles her nose with the tips.

'The galvanising shed is where the wire is passed through a bath of zinc, molten zinc,' he tells her. 'It spits black, which creates an appalling cloud of black fumes. And the cleansing shed is where the bought-in wire must go, every consignment of wire. It has to be dipped in a dilution of sulphuric acid – hot acid – then rinsed with water drawn from the river, and filtered, then dipped in vats of hot milk of lime. The walls in there are coated with rust – the walls and ceilings, everything – and I can't help wondering about the lungs of the poor chaps who must work in those places. I don't suppose hell can be much worse.'

'People say the war is like hell.'

Montague stares at her; he stares for a long time. 'Do they?' he asks.

'Some people,' she says, and now finds she is colouring, for clearly this was a wrong thing to mention. She shields her face with the feathers and turns to look at the boathouse, the peeling white paint of its exterior and the diamond-shaped panes of glass beneath the eaves, which are tinted amber and ruby and emerald, just like the jars in the pharmacy, then wonders if perhaps it is time she went home, for her father will be anxious about her, she is sure, and possibly angry that she has stayed out for so long. But when Montague begins again to row he takes them in the other direction, yet further away from the boathouse, the oarlocks creaking on every stroke, the paddles gently plashing to either side of them.

'Tell me, Miss Dobson,' he says after a while, his voice tightening as he draws on the oars, 'do you enjoy working in our factory?'

'Yes,' she smiles, surprised, 'yes, I do.'

'It suits you to be a factory hand?'

'I don't mind it.'

'And the pay is sufficient?'

Gertie nods. 'I think so,' she says, and tries to recall whether it is thruppence or fourpence an hour she receives, though the sum hardly matters since she gives all but a shilling and sixpence to her mother, the remainder going back to the factory, for she must buy ribbons to tie up her hair and black lisle stockings every fort-night, and give tuppence a week to the union, and a penny to the insurance, and spend a few pence every day in the canteen.

'Do you fit in, do you find? I am curious to know. Do you find you are at home among the other women?'

'Yes, everyone gets along,' she says, 'the rough with the smooth.'

'And you are the smooth?' he asks.

Gertie considers a moment. 'Yes,' she says, 'compared. But there's all sorts. Some of them are cousins and aunts, that sort of thing – but they're very friendly to me. Sometimes we have a sing-song.'

'A sing-song,' repeats Montague, as if the term is new to him.

'In the canteen,' she says, and thinks of the girls dancing, getting up a bit of a sweat, their tunics loosened, cheeks burning.

'I imagined you very differently,' he remarks, 'not like that at all,' and then he is silent, allowing the boat to drift along in the rain, which is coming heavier now, the threads of it everywhere prickling the surface of the lake. A heron flaps over them; she hears its wingbeats and glances up, seems to glimpse a flash of light beyond the trees.

'Oh,' she says. 'I think that was lightning.'

'Lightning,' he says mildly. 'Are you sure?'

'I think so, yes.'

Montague poises the oars an inch or so above the water.

'I wonder if we should go back now,' she says.

'You wouldn't like to see the channel that leads out to the river?'

'No, thank you. I'd rather not.'

'You wouldn't like to be conveyed to your home in a Beckwiths' boat, modest as it is? The river connects us, after all. It shouldn't demand too much of you in the way of navigation.'

'I think we're going to get wet.'

'Not very wet, I hope.'

'And my parents will be worrying about me.'

Montague sighs. 'Yes, of course,' he says, 'your parents will be concerned,' and working just one of the oars he slowly brings the boat around to face the other way, the treetops behind him appearing to dissolve in the damp of the sky, his jacket curiously luminous in the darkening air. Gertie hears a soft crackle of thunder. Montague looks at her steadily. 'I must confess,' he says then, raising his voice, 'I'm surprised by this notion of you as one of the girls, Miss Dobson.'

'Well, I'm not really one of them,' she answers, 'not exactly.'

'Not exactly?'

'No,' she insists, mindful of those few girls who do have an edge to them, a sharpness that inclines them to needling, though most will speak to her in the ordinary way, because she is young, and polite, and gets on with her work. She is content to listen to their conversation, and to watch their antics in the canteen, as if at a theatre, unselfconsciously smiling, and of course she would not think of mixing with them out of hours, just as they would not think to include her. Even Mabel Barley, who is a good sort, and much Gertie's age, will go her own way after work, and Gertie doesn't much mind that, for she enjoys being at home in the evening, secure in the company of her mother and father, and it is this that she ought to say to Montague Beckwith, as a spur to his conscience, a reminder of his duty towards her, but finds herself saying instead, 'Really, I think I only have one friend – Mabel, who used to work for you. She used to be one of your maids.'

For several long strokes Montague does not reply, then says, 'Did she? I don't remember her.'

'Eileen remembers her,' says Gertie.

'No doubt.'

'You should ask her.'

'Should I?'

'I mean, if you want to.'

'And you are friends, Miss Dobson? You and this Mabel, the maid?'

'At work, yes. Not out of work. But she's kind, and I feel sorry for her, because her brother went missing – in the war. They had a letter. Her mother did.'

'Missing,' repeats Montague, 'or killed?'

'Missing. Definitely missing.'

Montague laughs, a sudden loud bark, and Gertie flinches, surprised at him. 'I'm sorry,' he says, 'but there is no *definitely* about it, Miss Dobson. Taken prisoner, perhaps. In some way cut adrift from his regiment and wandering lost behind the lines, perhaps. There's a slim chance. But in my experience, missing very often means killed.'

Gertie observes a goose taking off from the lake, honking, its wings squeaking, a smudge of white in the rain against the dark of the trees, and bleakly she says, 'Why must it?'

'Why *must* it?'

'Yes, missing and killed? Why must they mean the same thing?'

'Because, Miss Dobson,' he says, 'nothing you think you understand about the war is to be trusted.' He lifts the oars from the water, angles them upwards. 'For example, as it happens, a good deal of my time was spent writing letters to the families of chaps who had died, and I'm afraid they were just so much dissembling – all of it balderdash, quite frankly – barely a word of truth in them anywhere.'

The sky flashes again; a sheet of sudden rain sweeps over them. Gertie cringes, and looks anxiously across to the boat-house, which hardly seems any nearer. She lays down her peacock feathers, holds tightly to the sides of the boat.

'Let me speak plainly,' says Montague then. 'Let me speak from first-hand experience. A chap might be blown to smithereens, Miss Dobson. His parts might be scattered to the breeze, and afterwards I would be required to compose a letter to the next of kin, some consoling nonsense about a single bullet to the brain, a clean strike through the heart – *an instantaneous end, no pain, he did not suffer*. Those were the phrases, Miss Dobson. And all of them lies. Absolutely every bloody word of them.'

He is angry, she realises, and softly she says, 'I'm sorry, you don't have to tell me if you don't want to.'

'I beg your pardon?'

She lifts her voice above the hissing rain: 'You don't need to tell me – I'm sorry – not if you don't want to.'

'But I will tell you, Miss Dobson, and you will have to forgive my language, because more often than not the chap would have been blown to buggery. Do you understand? The bits would have been buried where they landed. That's what *missing in action* very often means, I'm afraid. The chap is dead, all right, but we're buggered if we can find all the bloody bits of him to prove it!' He laughs. 'And you can tell that to your friend – tell that to Mabel the under-housemaid the next time you feel compelled to blow the sympathetic trumpet. Her brother – whatever his name is – will not be coming back, I can guarantee her that.'

'Walter,' she says. 'His name is Walter Barley.'

Montague stares at her, his eyes starkly red around the rims, and it is as if he were peering out through the holes in a mask. 'I'm sorry?'

'He's called Walter Barley,' she says again, and of course he does keep coming back, for Gertie has seen him, momentarily there in the crowds on Riverside Road, or reflected in shop windows, his expression unchanging, patiently watching her, seemingly waiting, and now as the thunder crackles above them she looks over her shoulder, scanning the trees that lead up to the house, half expecting to find him, curiously consoled to think he may be here too, and remembers the moment last summer when she looked out from the Guest Hall and saw him gripping the reins of the old ice-cart as it trundled down past the sunken Italianate garden – Mr Greenland puffing away on a pipe at his side – when she knew him at once as the boy she had petted in school, who sometimes came into the pharmacy, seeking a cure for his mother, and who had once appeared before her on Balmoral Road as she sat between the Misses Beckwith in their carriage, both of them wearing their furs.

On that cold October evening he was dressed in a bowler hat and his Sunday-best suit and he flinched as if stung when she smiled at him, but it was she who shrank away when he looked across from the ice-cart, turned his pale face towards her. As she retreated further into the Guest Hall she heard one of the Misses Beckwith remark that here was a young man who surely ought to have enlisted, and though Gertie knew he was too young – no older than she was – she did not correct them, but went out to the bowl in the small hallway, where the gardener had been instructed to leave any white feathers that he might find in the grounds, and selected a pretty one, as soft and white as the dress she has chosen to wear this afternoon, which Miss Emma once gave to her and which is now sodden, wet through to her skin – as Captain Montague can plainly see, for he is staring straight at her, exactly in the manner of poor Walter, who will be watching her still, of that she feels certain, for he has always been watching her; he keeps coming back to her.

27

Dobson

a want of mental equilibrium

As the clock begins to chime the hour, Dobson flips the sign on his door round to *CLOSED* and methodically reorientates the chairs that furnish his pharmacy and turns down the gas mantles, snuffs each of them out. He tidies away the paraphernalia of his trade, and closes the cupboards and drawers, then lights another cigarette, and stands and stares at his shelves, his many corked bottles of medicine, and feels a familar yearning for some relief from whatever it might be that is ailing him, though he cannot put a name to it, or identify its cure.

Wearily he sighs and lowers himself to a chair. He looks at the rain streaking his windows and wonders whether Gertie might already have left Beckwith House on her bicycle and will be forced to seek shelter somewhere on Riverside Road, or is perhaps taking tea with Captain Beckwith, which will require her to be driven home a little later in the motor-car – if the motor-car is available – and while this uncertainty about her whereabouts is unusual, and unsettling, he knows he cannot telephone the house to clarify or confirm the situation: it might be impertinent, and would mean revealing his dilemma to the stonemason Edwards, who is quite supercilious enough as it stands.

A flicker of lightning illuminates the Corporation men in their oilskins, who are sheltering at the top of the market, and Dobson gets to his feet and paces across to his counter. He stubs out his cigarette, lights another one, and paces back to the window, his shoe-leather creaking as he considers a third possibility, that the rain will persist into the evening and Montague will feel obliged to invite his daughter to remain overnight at the house, as she has done so often before as a guest of the Misses Beckwith, and though they are no longer there to lend respectability to such an arrangement, Dobson's sense of misgiving is less a matter of its propriety than of the deeper impression that Gertie might make on Montague Beckwith without his sisters to guide or disguise her, as must surely have been the case in the past.

His concern, indeed, is not that Montague will also find his daughter distracting, but that he will realise the extent of her shortcomings, and doubtless reflect upon their origin, the extent of Dobson's responsibility, though he has, he thinks, been a good father to her; he has offered her stability, authority, a regularity of behaviour. He has organised her schooling to her best advantage, and done all that can be done to protect her from harm, and while he would not deny his sense of gratification that the Misses Beckwith should have selected her as their personal dressmaker in preference to any other girl, her undoubted gifts as a seamstress could not account for their confidence in her, so he must assume that they took her into their home and treated her as their companion because they recognised certain qualities that were the outcome of her upbringing, since at bottom she is lacking not merely in intelligence but common sense, and it is her great silliness that most disquiets him, or perhaps her inability to see her own silliness, her blindness to the fact of it.

Her nature is simple, and he thinks it unlikely that the Misses Beckwith were unaware of this fact, so cannot allay the suspicion that their motives were also philanthropic and that Gertie represented yet another worthy cause for them to adopt, which is a possibility that causes him a degree of discomfort since he would not wish to be patronised, even vicariously, by the Misses Beckwith, who are to the masculine stock of their own family what Gertie is to hers: frivolous, somewhat excitable, an intellectually superficial firing of essentially feminine energy, which he would not take at all seriously except that in its more militant expression it can be so offensive to reason.

Their commitment to the patriotic cause is laudable, but any admiration on his part is tempered by the knowledge of their earlier, conspicuous enthusiasm for the suffragist cause, which he considered then and considers now to be a prime instance of the way in which a woman's psychology is dominated not by intellect but by sentiment, the root cause of which is a want of mental equilibrium and moral consistency that results from her enslavement to purely physiological urges.

In other words – as he argued in his last letter to Montague – so long as women of childbearing age are subject to recurring phases of irrationality and hypersensitivity, and women who are carrying children are as prone as they are to alterations of character, and women on the approach to the climacteric remain as vulnerable to mental disorder and the moral distortions that nervous pressure brings about – as long as women, in short, remain so susceptible to the symptoms of hysteria – then it is folly to trust them to exercise the vote or to participate in political life with the restraint and reasonableness that their fathers and husbands and, indeed, their brothers are able to demonstrate.

Montague Beckwith, being at that time engaged in the hostilities in France, was unable to reply to these arguments, and while the pharmacist is pleased to recall the correspondence they enjoyed prior to the outbreak of war, and is hopeful that they will re-establish this connection once the peace is restored, he does wonder whether it is quite sensible to continue committing his thoughts to the page when Montague's voice in their conversation has for the moment fallen silent.

all her vivacity gone

With a heavy sigh, Dobson thrusts his hands into his pockets and walks through to his workroom where he gazes down at the papers that are piled on his table, but the dimness of the light is unhelpful, and after some moments he strikes a match to the gasolier and picks up the top sheet of his letter, yet still the strain on his eyes is too much; at the close of any day's business he cannot read his own script without squinting.

He opens the door to the stairs. 'Dorothea!' he calls, and sits down. He rests his forehead on the heels of his hands, and as he waits he reflects on the time when it would have been Dorothea to whom he expounded his views, the opinions he had formed in his solitary reading concerning the Empire, the good that Great Britain could convey to the world, and how willing an audience she had once seemed to him.

This was before they were married, when she bore such a resemblance to his mother, who had died in his childhood, leaving a single posed photograph in which she sits in a dark dress beside his stout, bewhiskered father in a studio whose backdrop was a painted depiction of Greek columns and balusters. That photograph now hangs above his side of the marital bed, and while his mother has not aged, his wife unarguably has, all her vivacity gone – whatever zest she once possessed – as well as the easy affection she once showed to him in the days when she would visit town with her father, a poultry-keeper, to purchase seed and other supplies from the store in which Claude Dobson then worked for his own father.

It was Claude's job in fact to bag up the seed, and while the two older men smoked their pipes and conversed at the front of the shop, Dorothea would be sent through to help him, and perhaps it should have been clear to him then that she lacked the strength or independence of character that he thought he sought in a companion, and would always be his inferior, never the equal partner he imagined he most wanted. Yet her passivity was in some ways emboldening, and she has remained biddable, hard-working and largely dependable; she does as her domestic responsibilities require of her, however great the strain or discom-fort that might result from that, and sometimes indeed he will notice the wince, the tightening of her features, and become cognisant momentarily of the pain she endures as she becomes ever more frail. But for all that he may occasionally feel an affectionate sympathy for her, he must deal every day with the ailments of women and finds he has few reserves of concern to expend upon Dorothea. She keeps his home tidy, and cooks his meals, and attends to the fires, and assists in the pharmacy, but she does little more than occupy one half of their marital bed and has never borne him children and in this, as in other significant ways, she has not pleased him.

He sits up. She is not coming, and impatiently he tilts back his chair and again calls her name and hears the faintest of replies, after which there is silence, no suggestion of movement. It does not appear she is stirring, and infuriated he gets to his feet and shouts, 'Dorothea! Will you please come down here!'

Heavily he slumps forward and listens to the sounds of her, the creak of the bed on which she has been resting, her shuffling footsteps, the slow pad of her feet on the stairs.

'Yes? What is it?' she calls at last from the turn, her voice querulous, faintly echoing.

'Come down,' he replies. 'Please. If you would.'

She descends. She has removed her apron and, it would seem, her undergarments.

He holds out a page of his letter. 'I would like you to read this.'

Without remark, Dorothea stands at his shoulder, a little behind him, and angles the sheet for the light. 'I don't have the start of it, dear.'

'You don't need the start. Just' – wearily he gestures with one hand – 'proceed from what there is.'

'From what there is,' she repeats, 'yes,' and coughs, and begins: '*As to my own experience, I can confirm that the poor of this city, whom we might take to be representative of the poor of Great Britain as a whole, show little inclination towards deliberate regulation of the marriage state. Such volitional regulation, with the object of limitation of the family, has been documented among all social grades except . . .'*

'The residuum,' he says.

'. . . *the residuum . . . and is particularly prevalent among the professional classes.'*

Dobson turns to watch her and smells the alcoholic sweetness on her breath, notes the palsy in her hands.

'*And our concern remains,*' she continues, frowning to concentrate, '*that the birth-rate of the professional classes, which has shown a consistent decline over the last thirty-five years, will continue after the war, unless those officers who return can be persuaded that their patriotic self-sacrifice, the very foundation of our idea of what is noblest and most civilised in human conduct, should remain central to the character of the nation and influence the choices they make with regard to posterity. No one should be immune to the counsel of informed and educated opinion or neglectful of their responsibilities to others. The path of self-sacrifice is the path to racial progress, as has been—*'

She stops. He stares at her. 'It's the end of the page,' she explains.

'Here.' He wets his thumb, passes her the next sheet.

'*The path of self-sacrifice,*' she repeats, '*is the path to racial progress, as has been demonstrated—*'

'To yourself,' he interrupts her. 'Read it to yourself now. I don't need to hear it, I just . . . Please, to yourself.'

She stifles a yawn, and says, 'Yes, dear,' and obliges him then to endure the sound of her mouthing his words under her breath, from which he hears *margins of the race* and *sexually segregated*, and *procreate* and *proliferate*, after which she is silent, for he has written no further.

'So. What are your thoughts?' he asks, and holds out his hand for his pages.

'My thoughts?'

'Yes. Your thoughts.'

Dorothea hesitates, and Dobson replaces his spectacles, tugs at his beard. 'I think it is good,' she says.

'In what way?'

'In what way? I think it is exactly like you. He will be impressed, I'm sure.'

'I don't need him to be *impressed*,' Dobson says, clenching his hands. 'I would like to know what you think of my argument.'

'Your argument?'

Curtly he nods.

'I'm sorry. It's hard for me to follow, written in that way.'

'And yet it sounds exactly like me!'

'Yes.'

'Hard to follow!'

'I'm sorry, dear,' she says then, 'but I have a headache and you're confusing me. You'll have to excuse me.'

'A headache,' he says, and feels the pressure in his own skull, and his soreness of spirit. He lets his pages slip to the floor and gets abruptly to his feet as his wife turns for the stairs. 'Go then!' he shouts at her, so loudly she cringes. 'Go then. But you do not honour me!'

'I'm sorry, dear,' she says, placing one foot on the bottom step, reaching for the handrail, and he hears himself grunt as he strikes her.

Dorothea staggers. She attempts to lift her other foot, and Dobson hits her again, this time causing her to fall, such a tiny, bird-like thing, on the stairs. He steps away from her and is appalled at what he has done. He sits down in his chair. He chokes back a sob and sinks his beard to his chest and waits with tightly clasped hands for his wife to get up, for she ought to get up; it is inconceivable that she should not.

28
Montague

Beckwith's Barbican

The lightning crackles and he pictures his dugout, his dank-smelling cavern in the side of the trench, and the maps, the candles, the boxes of tea and biscuits and other treats and provisions, his gas-mask and holster, his helmet, and the rickety desk where he would compose the letters he was required to write, perched on the end of his bunk, and although it is raining and her dress is soaked through – her pretty white dress – it is only rain, which is harmless, and so he talks on, and sweetly she listens, for she is a sweet girl, and no doubt it was for the sake of such sweetness that England proceeded to war, to defend the sweetness and virtue of the likes of Miss Dobson, this daughter of a pharmacist, his sisters' companion.

She listens, and Montague's mouth rattles on in the rain as he attempts to describe to her the letter he was unable to finish, concerning Private Barley, since he hardly knew what to leave out, there being so many thoughts pressing in on his mind, and so much solid fact to commit to the page, including the history of his family's firm, which seemed to have some bearing then on what had occurred, beginning with the weatherboard construction that still stands on the southern bank of the river, the first of the factories to be established by his great-grandfather, Jeremiah, who was in 1834 no more than an ironmonger on City Parade specialising in the fabrication of hand-woven netting for the hutching of rabbits and keeping of hens, but who succeeded, after many years of experimentation, in the invention of a machine – a modified carpet loom – that would weave his netting into continuous rolls that could be sold throughout the region for the purpose of excluding rabbits from farms and private estates, a business that grew and allowed his premises and workforce to grow until he was able in 1857 to purchase some land on the northern bank of the river, where his son, the second Jeremiah, commissioned the construction of a watermill to power the machines, and had railway lines laid, and gradually saw to the diversification of the operation, not merely in terms of the products they made but the processes they handled on site – establishing sheds for acid-dip cleansing, annealing, and galvanising, for instance – such that the company prospered and came, by the end of the century, to be exporting tens of thousands of rolls of hexagon mesh to the colonies – advertised variously as sheep, rabbit or kangaroo netting – and not only that, but the angle-iron standards for supporting the mesh, and the staples that would fix it to wooden posts, and numerous other products besides – including insect screens, and sieves for domestic and industrial use, and a half-inch mesh for aviaries and cages that won medals at exhibitions in Paris and Philadelphia – but of course the product for which the company has become most widely known is barbed wire, of which it has manufactured thousands upon thousands of yards, amounting to miles, enough to enclose half the new world, and while this was used initially for the demarcation of agricultural land and the protection of colonial railways, now it is the scourge of no man's land in the war – as Montague found at close quarters – the entanglements laid in belts ten and twenty yards deep, sometimes three and four belts in succession, the most impenetrable being 'Beckwith's Barbican', a two-ply wire with four-point barbs, the barbs more numerous and more 'obvious' (as Beckwith's catalogue describes it, meaning longer and sharper) so that there can be no advance or retreat unless the wire is first cleared or broken through, which requires artillery bombardment or teams of men in pitch darkness, and in either case eventuates in corpses, the men blown to bits or picked off by snipers. And the tiresome irony, for himself as well as his men, was that these palisades, which were supposedly there to protect them, and which might have been manufactured by their mothers, wives, sweethearts, even daughters, also served to imprison them, and sometimes to impale them, such was the fate in the end of poor Private Barley.

It was this that Montague was determined to describe in his last letter, but that he was advised by the medical orderlies to lay down his pen and come out from what remained of his bolt-hole, for there was a war raging outside, the line had collapsed, his men were all dead, and very soon they would be overrun, captured or killed by the Bosch. 'Sir,' he heard one of them shouting, 'if you wouldn't mind, please, sir.'

Barley was a good soldier

Without doubt, weeks before, the battleplan would have seemed entirely rational and tidy to his superiors in the regimental head-quarters, every target and objective measured and named, the lines of attack plainly described, the men organised into their units, so many mortal men to each numbered sector and stage, and as the plan was passed down the chain of command it would have appeared to everyone who studied it, including Montague himself, to be sensible and achievable (assuming the necessary ordnance and reserves to respond in case of any setbacks). And yet as he waited at the head of his company for the word to go forward – a solid ceiling of noise seemingly inches above them, the ground vibrating beneath them, and nothing to do but hold fast to one's weapon, one's courage, and be patient – he lost sight of the plan and saw only confusion, for they were being joined ahead of schedule by yet more reinforcements to their rear, and impeded in their progress – should they ever be instructed to go on – by the remnants of the force that had been holding the line the previous several days, who were too blasted by the din and their fatigue to evacuate the area but thronged instead into the assembly trenches and collapsed at the feet of the men who were waiting – such filthy, stinking heaps of mud and fabric and limbs – while the communication trench that was to take Montague's men up to the front was itself clogged in either direction with stumbling messengers and munitions carriers, ration parties, engineers, medics and stretcher-bearers frantic to get the wounded away from the fray.

It was bedlam, and somewhere in the commotion he glimpsed Private Barley, several yards out from their shelter and attempting to make headway in the direction of the support lines, apparently intent on desertion.

Montague shouted futilely after him, then haltingly followed, quite prepared in his anger to shoot him, summarily to execute him for cowardice, but realised the instant he caught up with him, no further along than the next traverse in the trench, that Barley had gone as far as he was prepared to and was already about to return. Called to account for himself – the shells pealing over them, explosions illuminating their faces – Barley claimed to have seen his own father, who belonged to a different battalion and must surely have lost his bearings in the confusion of battle, and was concerned to protect him from any accusation of running away by helping him return to his company. And in truth Montague had scant cause to distrust him, since Barley was a good soldier, despite his youth and lack of physique, who had several times proven himself in combat and would set to at once, without a moment's pause, between the issuing of an order and his obedience to it, with never a hint of reluctance.

He did as he was told, and yet always his gaze held something Montague was unable to assess or identify, always some judgement being passed upon him, as though he held some secret knowledge about him, which was again the case as they confronted each other in the midst of that shambolic, cacophonous scene – the muzzle of Montague's pistol pressed to Barley's chest, a constant traffic of men shouldering past them – and why, those several days later, when the crisis of battle seemed to have settled once more to a situation of stalemate, that it was Private Barley and not some other poor blighter that Montague selected for the task of going out with him in darkness to reconnoitre the ravaged expanse of no man's land, the last significant skirmish having killed the scouts he might normally have chosen.

a terrible strain on the nerves

On many other occasions Montague had volunteered himself for such missions – to satisfy his own mind, to lead by example – since certain of the craters blasted out of the ground by the shells would be broad and deep enough to conceal several men, whether British or German, often in forward positions from which they might spy on the enemy, or snipe at him, and it was the purpose of Montague and his scouts to creep out in the calm succeeding an engagement to determine which of the existing holes had been destroyed, which were now occupied by sentries, and whether and where any new holes might have appeared, and of course it was a terrible strain on the nerves since the Germans too would be out on patrol, crawling in the opposing direction, such that one might at any moment find oneself face to face with old Fritz, though it was rare that either party would dare to open fire since that would broadcast one's position to the enemy's sentries – his *Kameraden*, his comrades – and draw down a retaliatory battery, or attract a sniper's attention, so each observed the other, said nothing, kept watching, and withdrew.

Yet still Fritz might be lurking elsewhere; the danger of him remained. Every mound in that darkness would take on human form, become the enemy calmly observing one's progress through the sights of his rifle, until the mound revealed itself to be a clod of earth, the outspill from a crater, or a corpse. Every twitching of loose wire – or a tin can, a lost helmet, a fragment of shell – might be the cocking of a pistol, and often as one made one's

234

way in the dark there would sound the crack of a rifle, or the flat, steady *cack-cack-cack* of a machine-gun, and for an instant one would tense for the impact of the bullet, every fibre alert, alarmed, then realise it was merely the random, round-the-clock exchange of puzzling, unsettling ordnance that was the background to every day spent in the trenches, though the fright to one's nerves would persist, and even sometimes become permanent.

But if the darkness was concealing of Fritz, it was Tommy's best disguise too, and that evening there was a solid ceiling of cloud, no moon, and Montague took only Barley, inching ever so cautiously onwards, stopping, listening, inching on. Their aim was to make for a gap in the wire, then head out into no man's land, but the shells were unending in that stretch of the line, a desultory but continuing bombardment; the guns would not be silenced, and that night they progressed only as far as the second belt of barbed wire when a shell landed near enough to them that it was not only deafening but as forceful as being charged over at rugger by the biggest chap in the school.

The impact of the blast knocked the wind clean out of Montague, and no doubt out of young Barley too, then all at once came a second explosion, so close it propelled both of them into the air. Montague heard the ghoulish wail of the shell's cap flying off; he heard Barley screaming, but there were no other sounds, not even from himself – though he was sure he cried out – and neither did he hear the mud that showered down on him as he landed on his back in a pit no deeper than a bathtub, his mouth full of soil that tasted of excrement, and other filth; he dared not think what.

How long he lay there, his legs and arms out-splayed as if he were soaking in the tub, his head pounding, consciousness drifting and returning, he cannot now calculate, but all through that queer stretch of time he remained aware of Private Barley, whose moans were unceasing: he heard them quite plainly. By the light of the blasts reflecting back from the clouds, Montague saw him quite plainly too, barely fifteen yards away: he was snagged on the barbs, almost upright, his arms outstretched on the coil, his head lolling, his chest and face blackened with lyddite, and there was a dark patch in his breeches that Montague mistook at first for a seepage of blood, then realised was something far worse, a gaping hole at his crotch.

He would not survive, that much was certain, but neither could his end come quickly enough, and yet Montague was unable to help him, for it seemed he had lost the use of his limbs and had no choice but to lie there and listen to Barley, whose moans continued for hours, through most of that night, and became almost like words, as though he were calmly conversing with Montague, patiently explaining why it would be reasonable to shoot him and so put an end to his agony and thus relieve the strain on the nerves and morale of the other men too, who would surely be able to hear him. And indeed Montague was still clutching his revolver, and had been known in the Officer Training Corps as a crack shot; he might have obliged him, but even when he managed at last to raise the revolver and aim it at Barley, much as one might take a gun to a suffering horse, he could not pull the trigger, and neither could he maintain his aim, or his grip on the pistol, which fell at last from his trembling hand to the mud, where it remained for several hours more as he lay and listened to Barley's moaning and feared he might become deranged with the sound of him and the bomb-illuminated flashes of his suffering on that coil of barbed wire.

the imbecile woman

'And the irony of it all,' he shouts through the rain, 'is that another shell buried him utterly. The bombardment began again in the morning and smothered him, though it gave me the spur I needed – I began to crawl back the way I had come, on my belly, on my own, and I'm afraid I saw the next shell that landed, the one that killed the last of my men. Every last witness to my cowardice. How about that, Miss Dobson? I was spared, crawling about there in no man's land!'

But Miss Dobson is no longer listening. She is cowering, he realises, for the rain is becoming a deluge and the surface of the lake is molten with it, tumultuous, as if it were boiling, the sky obliterated and the trees shrouded in sheets of grey rain, and though she is sodden – her dark heavy hair flat to her skull, her pretty white dress transparent to the next layer – absurdly it seems she is determined to keep her feet clear of the water that is pooling inside their boat, where her pretty blue feathers are now floating, and as she twists round, holding tight to her bench, Montague rests the oars in their locks and takes off his hat, which is ruined, the straw destroyed by the force of the downpour, and tosses it over the side and closes his eyes as the next crack of thunder and sudden shimmer of lightning causes Miss Dobson to squeal, a noise he cannot abide.

Grimacing, he lifts his face to the rain and unfastens his collar and the top of his shirt, and waits then for the return of some sensation of life to those parts of him that are the worst afflicted by his condition, and though he suspects he ought not to make a display of himself in this way to Miss Dobson, ought indeed to return her to solid ground and to safety, when he opens his eyes he finds himself looking not at her but towards a vision of Barley, who appears to be standing next to the boathouse, his face deathly white in the deluge, his wound hideously visible.

Montague shouts through the roar of the rain, 'Miss Dobson, I believe we have a visitor!' but she cringes, uncomprehending, and fixes her wide wounded eyes upon him, and despite the fact that she is so filthy wet, so unappetisingly soaking, he decides he really ought to embrace her – he ought to offer that comfort, and perhaps take some comfort himself – but when he makes to get to his feet he finds his clothing is sodden, horribly heavy now on his limbs, and he lurches. He stumbles towards Miss Dobson, who screams with alarm and attempts to scramble away from

237

him, then lifts her feet to repel him, kicks out at him wildly, which sets their small vessel to rocking and will surely tip them both over if she is not careful, the imbecile woman, but though he attempts to subdue her – 'Miss Dobson, please! I only wish you to see Private Barley!' – he finds he hasn't the voice to make himself heard, nor the strength to make her desist, and then feels the force of her heel in his midriff and knows in that instant, as the water slants up towards him and his vision of Barley is lost, that he hasn't the strength to save himself either.

29
Winnie

a man of Joe's standing

Winnie wakes with a start, sweating cold, and senses a flash at the edge of her vision, a ricochet of light, after which comes the thunder, an explosion so loud the window reverberates in its frame, the curtain trembles. Lying curled up on her side she gazes at the shimmering shadow of rain on the bare distempered wall and tentatively presses her belly, probes for some sign that Dobson's pills might be working, but there is nothing – the cramps have subsided – and she stretches, lowers her feet to the floor. The bed creaks as she stands. She needs to go down to the privy.

She has lost other babies of course, and if she must be relieved of this one she prays it might happen without obliging the pharmacist to employ any instruments, for which he will charge as much as two guineas, though Joe will help with the money, she feels sure, since he said he would look out for her and he does do, even now, despite the shortages brought on by the war and the strain it must place on his livelihood. He is a good man, and has always been kind to her. Should she go into his shop for a half – pound of brisket he will weigh her nine ounces; a pound of tripe and he might add in a pig's cheek; half a dozen trotters and he will wrap her one more. And she will accept whatever he gives to her, for Winnie never has been able to say no to Joe Orford, though in truth she hardly needs any extra, for even with the prices so high and her breadwinners gone, the Barleys have a better table now than they are used to, and more money to spare, since she and Mabel are earning, and she receives her allowance from the government, and there are two fewer mouths to feed than before.

Her poor Walter.

At the top of the stairs in the dark Winnie closes her eyes and listens to the rain on the roof and fancies for a moment that she can hear the train in the distance; she strains to hear it, and when she feels herself tilting she touches the wall to steady herself, leans against it, and remembers once being called up to this spot by her poor Walter, who was then so very young and standing with one ear cupped to the plaster, listening to Joe at work in his slaughterhouse, wrangling with the animals, killing them, his cursing as bad as any labourer's. She remembers how curiously tender she felt towards her little boy then, for not minding those noises, and how ashamed she became of herself afterwards, since she could not help but listen out for them, drawn less by the sounds than by the pictures that would flare in her mind of Joe red-faced and sweating, his shirt unbuttoned, his sleeves rolled past his elbows, blood streaking his arms and chest and darkening his trouser legs.

Such images would come to her as he wrestled some poor beast to its death and she would feel such an odd sort of tenderness for him too, so different from the gentleman he would appear to be in his shop, all waxed and brilliantined – immaculate, in fact, considering it was his job even there to hack into the corpses of animals – and so much the shop-keeper, with a word for everyone (and everyone's children), humorous on occasions, but always ready to hear a person's concerns, listening so attentively, as if he might be able to put this or that thing right for them, if only he were to listen closely enough.

Winnie would watch how he went on in his shop, and smile to herself, thinking of the slaughterman she heard through her wall, and possibly it was this that first attracted him to her, the appearance she must have given of possessing some private understanding about him, but while he continues to extend the same deference and courtesy to all the 'good ladies' who step onto his premises, lately he has begun to assume an ease and familiarity of tone with his 'dear Mrs Barley' that marks her out from her neighbours and is becoming conspicuous, she fears, and bound to provoke them to gossip, and envy, since any woman round here would be flattered to be favoured by a man of Joe's standing and suspicious of the solicitousness he shows towards any particular person (especially if her husband should be serving his country, gone from his home for months at a time).

She suspects he should be more careful, though she wonders besides whether this need always be their situation, whether the war in that sense might oblige her, whether it might bring her some relief as well as such pain.

some other muscular, shovel-chinned men

James has now left for the railway station – his shrimp and matchbox abandoned, the door left open to the rain – and Winnie's kitchen is heavy with the smell of the market-day animals, and soured by rot, the stench from her scraps bucket. Heavy-limbed, she gathers the newspapers from the hearth, and lifts the bucket from under the bench, and as she stares out at the downpour and the slick of rainwater sluicing their yard, a sudden sharp pain lances her midriff and she realises she cannot wait for the rain to subside.

Holding the papers over her head, and clutching her pail, she lurches out to the midden, swings open the hatch, a surge of fat bluebottles rising to meet her, and attempts to heave the bucket onto the rim, but it's too heavy for her to tip with one hand and she loses her grip. The mulch of peelings and slops spills over her feet and she groans and kneels down and sees that there are maggots as well, and retching on the smell of it, she rips away the outer page of one of the newspapers – *Kitchener's boys: New Armies push on* – and uses this to scrunch up what she can of the mess. With two hands she heaves the parcel into the midden and gets to her feet, slams shut the door, fastens the latch, and hurries across to the privy.

The narrow closet, usually so calm, is furious with the noise of the rain. Winnie feels for the wire hook, forces it into the loop, and turns and hitches up her skirt, pulls down her drawers, and as she sits and waits for the contractions in her belly that will signal the start of it – the end of it – she cradles the newspapers to her breast and remembers when it was Joe's practice to call on each of his properties in person to ask for his rent, however inclement the weather, and if the arrears were truly becoming a test of his patience he might seek out the husband in whatever pub he frequented, quite prepared to take it to fisticuffs if that was required, though usually his reputation was enough to settle the matter, since he was a boxer, as everyone knew, the only man besides old Patty the poacher to have gone the distance with Roughhouse Roberts, who used to travel with the fair and would set himself up in a tent at the top of the market, ready to take on all comers, and never once losing a bout, not even to Joe, though it was said to be close, neither man going down but both of them taking a battering.

A tie was declared, and while Winnie knew this only by hear-say she was all too aware of the feat it had been since she had seen for herself the damage that Roberts could inflict on another man, having witnessed the blow that had flattened her husband one gala day in the early years of her marriage, when Eddie had insisted on taking Winnie and their small children into the tent so they could watch the fabled fighter slug it out with some other muscular, shovel-chinned men – such as were shown on all the bill postings – except that they found him toying with a scrawny young country boy whose senses were clearly addled by drink, first backing him into a corner, sparring with him a little, then appearing to lose interest and turning away, inviting a clout round the ear, at which point Roberts swung his left hook, one hundred and eighty degrees of momentum behind it, and laid the boy flat.

Which was sheer wickedness, really; everyone afterwards said so. Roberts didn't need to put the boy down, but that was what he had done, and this so incensed Eddie Barley that he spun his hat into the ring, his sweat-stained old cap, and clambered up, five feet two inches of broad-shouldered, hard-headed fury.

Leaving his jacket with Winnie, who implored him not to be such a fool, he went after Roberts, growling and swinging his fists, and failed to land a single blow but ducked several in turn and managed for a couple of short rounds to make a monkey of the boxer, everyone cheering, including his children – Walter, Mabel and Dot – but then he took one square in the jaw and went down like the country boy. Silence fell, too. And after all the excitement of the fight, and of the parade in the morning – the white-feathered horses drawing the floats down Riverside Road, the acrobats cartwheeling, clowns tumbling, and a mock military band, all in red and gold tunics – Winnie looked at her husband, laid out on the canvas, and quietly folded his jacket over the ropes and led her children away, leaving one of the cornermen to try to revive him, sponging cold water onto his face.

Other indignities would follow, both for Eddie and for his wife, but no such humiliation would ever come to Joe Orford, who was a man of a different calibre, and neither would Joe ever bring any shame upon Winnie, for no matter how often she found she must apologise for not having his rent – her husband having drunk it all away – she never once met with anything other than kindness and sympathy. Joe would not press her, and neither would he go after her husband, no matter how many weeks they might be in arrears: 'You come on up when you have it, Mrs Barley,' he would say, 'and never mind the shop. Bring it along by my back door whenever you're ready.'

Wednesday was his half-day closing. Winnie began to pay her rent then, though in common with most other wives on Riverside Road she would sometimes have no choice but to pawn her husband's only suit in exchange for five shillings to tide her over until he received his wage at the end of the week, and sometimes not only his suit but her own few bits of finery, including her wedding ring (which she wouldn't have troubled to redeem, if only that would have released her from such scrimping), and so it was from time to time that she would go directly from Lincoln's pawnshop on Cattle Market Street to Joe's quarters in Bird in Hand Yard, where his back door was concealed up the narrowest of passages to the rear of his shop and the yard was as dark in mid-afternoon as on any mid-winter evening, hemmed about by the windowless backs of two other buildings and scratchy with the shuffling of rabbits, several dozen of them stacked in their hutches beside his privy and the bins that took the waste from his butchery.

It was a dismal, rank-smelling place, and in fact at the start it wasn't often Joe who received her money, but his old mother, who lived with him all the years of her widowhood and always required Winnie to remain at the door while she sat in the kitchen and marked the sum first of all in her ledger, then in the rent book, and signed both with a mean little mark, never once suggesting to Winnie that she might step inside and take a seat, let alone a cup of tea, both of which would be offered by Joe – his collar removed, expandable bracelets fixing his sleeves – whenever the old lady was 'indisposed' (as he termed it, as she increasingly became), and though Winnie was initially too proud, and too nervous, to accept his hospitality, soon enough she got used to it.

His mother, like her own, had a cancer of the stomach, and as she declined, slowly wasted away upstairs in her bed, Winnie came to know him quite well, shorn of his bluster, his butcher's heartiness and show, as well as the oil that glossed and flattened his hair, his stiff collar and tie, and the 'steel' that would hang from his belt whenever he was aproned for work. At first in his kitchen, then later upstairs in the parlour – where every item of furniture, including the overmantel and lights, had been covered or fringed about by his mother in muslin or lace – she would sit with him sometimes for an hour or more, neglectful of her children, her responsibilities at home, and allow him to sink a little into himself, becoming somewhat lachrymose, a more sentimental man than she would ever have supposed, and though in everyone's eyes Joe Orford was a natural bachelor, self-sufficient, a fellow with little need of a woman to love, cherish and obey him, he did at last confide in Winnie his great regret that he had never enjoyed the daily companionship of anyone other than his mother, whose passing he didn't expect he would mourn. 'No, I'll be glad when she's gone,' he confessed, and though he remained shy of admitting any more than that – on the matter, for instance, of his hopes for the future – he placed his heavy hand on the table next to Winnie's and looked for a brief moment into her eyes, and said, 'You're not a gossip, are you, Mrs Barley?' Then, 'No, you're not a gossip,' and warmly patted her hand before they both rose from their chairs to clear away their teapot and cups – it was time for her to go home – after which day he took to calling her Winnie, and she to calling him Joe.

They became affectionate, but however often he laid his hand over hers, and left it there, his big brutal hand that was so surprisingly deft with a knife and so accustomed to the bodies of animals – whether the beasts were alive and terrified in his abattoir, or skinned and quartered in his butchery – and however frequently she had visions of him placing that hand with its callouses gently over her mouth to stop her from making those cries that she could not help and which would shame her sometimes with Eddie (however often, in fact, she pictured Joe Orford's face purpling as he pressed into her, his jaw clenched, sweat breaking out on his brow and the veins in his temples engorging), it seemed he was determined to treat her as someone superior, someone so much better than her circumstances, someone in fact quite like his old mother.

He would lay his hand over hers, nothing more, and Winnie could not complain; she could not deny him the person he wished her to be, since he had favoured her above all the other women in the vicinity, and had allowed her, for just that hour or so on her rent day, to resemble the person she had always hoped she might one day become.

30
Walter

gala day

His perambulations, which are constant, take him back out through the woods and away from the promise of Gertie and the memory of what happened to Beckwith towards the last of the houses on Riverside Road, where a few ragged pieces of washing hang heavy with wet from the upper windows and the scene on the street resembles a Saturday – a gala day – before the start of the war, when City were riding so high in the league, going great guns, and hundreds of men and their sons would come in from the country and hurry along to the ground on a damp afternoon, then stream back up to the station at tea-time (the league now suspended of course and the football ground empty, abandoned, the terraces sprouting buddleia bushes and the pitch so over-grown it will require scythes to bring it to order), except that this evening there are so many wives and daughters as well, heading out to the station to welcome the first of the wounded – two hundred brave Tommies brought home from the fighting in France, or such at least is the rumour – and the road is already busy with the last of the auctioned-off animals that have been penned up for so many hours on the market, the clatter of their splayed hoofs on the cobbles dampened by the deafening noise of the rain, which is tipping down now as if all the moisture in the air, held there for days, has been suddenly let go, as if the sky has collapsed.

In parts the road resembles a river, its surface bubbling, and Walter stands for a while in the shelter of a dripping sweet chestnut and watches as a couple of farmers' wives wade heavily through it, clutching goods in their aprons, holding their headscarves in place, followed by a man – an amputee – with a sheet of oilskin cowling his head, his face washed of expression, then a trio of bicyclists hunched over their handlebars, their wheels slicing through the water and whipping up a spray that falls just short of the children who are racing behind them, shrieking with fear and excitement at the continuing flashes of lightning, the crackle of thunder.

Walter fastens the top button of his greatcoat, adjusts his cap, and steps into the road as a lumbering herd of brown Guernseys looms out of the murk, their great bellied sides almost bumping against him, their breath steaming, hides slick with the wet. The drovers, two grim-faced men wielding sticks, harry them on – *hup! hup! hup!* – and once they have gone Walter stares at a fat splat of manure as it is obliterated by the downpour, shot to pieces, then steps smartly aside for a convoy of seed merchants' huts, portable offices on wheels, the second, third and fourth hut in the train hitched to the one in front and a heavy, blinkered old dray dragging them along.

A boy of Arthur's age is leading the horse, cringing into his collar, and furtively Walter follows a few paces behind him, out past the fancy wrought-iron gates to the Beckwith estate, and then on a further fifty yards or so to the old Station Bridge and the end of Riverside Road, where the wheels of the huts and wagons and dogcarts trundle loudly over the boards and he seems to recognise a small scraggy dog heading in the other direction – back into town – its eyes white and bulging, ears flat, its squat little body appearing to lengthen in its hurry to find its way home.

Walter turns and watches until the dog has vanished from view, then leans over the side of the bridge and stares into the swirling brown and frothing white torrent below and wonders how long this deluge need continue before the river breaches its banks, since already it is many inches higher than it was an hour earlier and the current far stronger than he has ever seen it.

A watering-can passes beneath him, a garden shrub, an old wicker chair, a length of timber, and doubtless the drains and runnels on Riverside Road will be sluicing all kinds of other refuse into the water, whose force in full spate will surely take down the rickety structures that are everywhere to be found in this area, the lean-tos and privies, sheds, kennels and hutches, as well as the rabbits, dogs and chickens they house, and the tools and sacks of seed and hay, and possibly even the pigs that are kept on the allotments: all of this will be carried away in the storm, and as the river rises it will overrun the closets and drains and wash back up the alleys and yards, seeping into the Barleys' kitchen and the cramped, dim-lit room where Mabel and Dot share a bed, both of them forced to take refuge upstairs with Mother and the younger children as the floodwater delivers yet more filth into their home, as into every other home in their neighbourhood, where there are people by the score and so much illness and misery you might almost wish for a flood to sweep it all away, if only their lives could be cleansed, if only this kind of catastrophe could be relied upon to save them.

terminus

The honey-coloured terminus building shimmers dimly through the sheeting rain and the great clock above the colonnaded entrance shows three minutes to seven as Walter crosses the wide, tree-lined forecourt, his hands thrust deep in his pockets and one fist closed around his white feather, his gift from Gertie Dobson, which of course he could not return to her, no more than he could ever make her aware of him, on this or any other day; he must concede that now, and when a number eight tram clatters by him, displaying advertisements for Callard's Imperial Label and Jos. Wilkinson's Builders, the windows fogged by the crush of bodies inside the saloon, the top deck abandoned, he opens his fist to the rain, allows the feather to wash from his hand, and then wearily, resignedly, he trudges after the tram, following the curve of the silvery tracks in the asphalt, past numerous standings for omnibuses and coaches and the other trams that will loop in from the direction of the Railway Inn, and comes towards the loud, crowded entrance as the passengers begin to step down from the number eight, a lady constable shouting, 'Indoors quickly now, please!' her voice shrill above the hubbub of voices and the unceasing hiss of the rain. 'Come quickly, don't dawdle! Make your way inside, don't obstruct the entry!'

Walter stands unnoticed beside her in the shelter of the echoing porch and thinks of those times in his childhood when he would come out here to porter the bags of the travellers who stepped down from the first-class carriages, including on several occasions his own uncle Ronnie, his mother's brother, who would alight from the country train on platform three and tip him a farthing or two to carry his briefcase and umbrella, for all the world as if he were unaware of their connection – and possibly he wasn't: he seemed so remote from reality.

Others were more generous, he recalls, and some more peculiar, including the stationmaster himself, who was made up like a military man of a previous era, all starchy display, gold braid and brass buttons, a figure of fun and some fear to the boys, and a nuisance to the farmers whose livestock would have to be led around the outside of the station and penned up in the numerous enclosures beyond platform six, where the troop train is soon to pull in, and often in those days Walter would feel as if he were entering a theatre or even a church as he came into the main foyer, which was so spacious and hushed with its floor of blue-tinted stone and its glass-fronted timetables and the twin archways that led into the dusty light of the high-ceilinged concourse where there were mahogany shopping kiosks and teashops and turreted ticket booths, though very little of this can now be seen through the throng of rain-soaked civilians who are waiting to welcome the soldiers, much as they gathered in this place to cheer them away, and indeed the scene resembles one of those heady occasions in the early months of the war when crowds would appear almost everywhere to applaud the latest recruits to the cause, except that the mood this evening is so apprehensive, for who knows whether the men who are about to arrive will be local, and what sort of state they will be in?

As the next tram rattles over the forecourt, Walter drifts deeper into the building and surveys the many familiar faces among the assembly of well-wishers gathered behind the outstretched arms of the police cadets and lady constables – among them any number of youths who might otherwise have ventured along to the Chicken Run – and locates each of his siblings, whose eyes are fixed upon the far end of platform six and the curtain of rainfall through which the train is about emerge, for despite the incessant thrum of the rain on the roof Walter can now hear the locomotive, panting as it comes closer, which provokes a murmur of anticipation in the crowd, then some yelps of surprise as the immense doors to the freight depot beside platform one are pulled clatteringly open to reveal a cluster of miscellaneous vehicles – some of them horse-drawn, including a bread van, including a hearse, and all of them bearing the emblem of the British Red Cross – and then a small army of nurses and orderlies, who march self-consciously out past the buffers at the ends of the lines and turn right through the gates to platform six, the nurses dressed as though for chapel in their capes and dainty hats and chin straps, the orderlies pristine in black uniforms, their boots all polished up and their puttees tightly wound, stretchers held rigidly down by their sides.

Curious, Walter wanders across to look at the ambulances and meets no resistance as he approaches the first of the horses, which is blinkered and stands perfectly still, doesn't shy, as he reaches up to stroke its thick neck and shoulder. A ripple runs down its flank and he closes his eyes, presses his nose to its warmth, sleepily breathes in the scent of its sweat, and finds himself surprised by a memory as strange as any dream of boarding the boat that would take him to France, whose principal cargo was not men or munitions but mules – replacements from America, it was said, for the horses already destroyed at the front – who were kicking out wildly in their enclosures below deck, and as the vessel embarked for the continent after days of delay the hammering of their hoofs only worsened, as did the weather, the entire sickening journey undertaken to the constant pounding of those terrified animals, for which even more distress was in store: their crossing took them to Le Havre, he recalls, where it snowed and snowed and they were cut off, stranded for days without rations, the exhausted animals eating the ropes that tethered them, some dying of pneumonia, others of starvation, their war already over, and Walter's own war yet to begin.

'Lovely big beast, that one. Smashing.'

'Oh, hello,' laughs Walter, relieved to find Charlie Champion standing beside him. He rubs the corner of one eye with his knuckle. 'I thought you'd gone again.'

'No, no, not yet. Still here.'

'Keeping busy.'

'That's it,' says Charlie, and tilts his chin at the horse. 'It'd be a shame to waste this one. I hope they don't send it away.'

'No,' agrees Walter. Then after a few moments: 'But tell me, Charlie, did they have an Empire Day at the school this year? I missed it this time. I used to enjoy that.'

'Did they . . . ? I couldn't say, I don't think so. I must've missed it as well,' says Charlie, his mouth yakking the words like a ventriloquist's puppet in the Hippodrome, his face as white as if made up for the stage. 'It passed me by, I'm afraid.'

'That's a shame,' says Walter. 'They'll have missed you too, I think.'

'I expect so,' agrees Charlie. 'Oh, yes, they'll have missed me not being there.'

On Empire Day, Walter recalls, frowning now to remember it clearly, even the poorest of the children would attend school in their Sunday-best clothes, some of the boys blacked up with soot from the fire-grate as little Indians or Africans, and all of them waving their Union flags to greet the arrival of the Lord Mayor or Sheriff – the Big King Dick in his chains – who was to declare the half-day holiday, which explained the excitement; never mind the flags and the rest, the boys cheered like the blazes simply to have the time off, and as they dashed from the school gates they would pass Charlie Champion again, all puffed up and saluting, just as he is saluting beside Walter now, for the troop train is finally coming into the station, each of its grey carriages displaying the red cross and its engine still chuffing, the brakes straining, metal screeching on metal.

Softly it collides with the buffers and heavily sighs, and as it settles at last to a halt a cloud of steam tumbles upwards and descends from the wrought-iron rafters, and then there are doors banging open, and whistles, and shouts, and the gasps and cries of the onlookers, men distantly moaning.

Walter leaves Charlie Champion behind him; he pats him farewell on the shoulder and walks along to the end of the platform, where he stands to attention and watches as the medics begin the sombre business of preparing the worst of the wounded for the short passage back to the ambulances, while certain of the nurses circulate with enamel cups and bottles of water and the other men submit to the usual bull, the requirement even now to fall into something resembling a line, as filthy and ragged and weak as they are – every one of them in need of a shave and a wash and a change of footwear, clothing and dressings – and then at last they do come, these wood-turners and gardeners, publicans, bank clerks and butlers, greengrocers, shit-shovellers and schoolteachers, signwriters and farriers, who have never before in their lives ventured any further than the resort on the coast, and are now encrusted with the mud of Belgium and France, which they have brought back with them to spoil the spick and spanness of England, the lucky ones sporting mere Blighty wounds, many others on crutches or stretchers, and they stink; they are thick with the stench of the living, Walter realises, which carries the taint of the dead, but even more than the smell it is their silence that strikes him, as if this is a dream that no one dare disturb, since to wake might be worse.

Those who can walk shuffle slowly along, some with arms draped around the shoulders of their comrades, others blind-folded by bandages, their hands clasping the shoulders of the men in front of them, and it is a pitiful, shambolic procession, their dressings so dirty, puttees uncoiling, their faces gaunt, eyes blank, revealing nothing, no appearance of sadness or fright or relief; they have as much animation about them as the carcasses that Walter once handled in Joe Orford's abattoir, and besides the sighing of the engine as it cools and the beating of the rain on the roof and the shuffling of the men's feet as they make their sorry way across the concourse, and the murmurs and stifled sobs of the spectators, and the clip of the boots of the stretcher-bearers as they hasten back to the train for the others, besides all of these sounds, Walter is aware of the constant plaintive noise of the livestock that are penned outside in the rain, in the stand-ings beyond the platforms, where the ornamented stansions and beams give way to a sheet of drear grey, the continuing down-pour through which the vaguest impression of the faces of cattle and sheep can be seen along the trackside.

departure

Walter takes off his cap and wipes the sweat from his forehead with the inside of his wrist, and he would now like to press on – out along the length of the platform and into the countryside, perhaps, or back the way he has come – but finds he is snagged by a momentary uncertainty, his sense of direction or chronol-ogy confused, his wakefulness slipping, and is jolted back to himself by an elbow jabbing his arm, for he is now standing shoulder to shoulder with Eddie, his father, who grimly observes the passage of another poor soul on a stretcher and says, 'It's a poor fucking showing this, isn't it?'

'I suppose so,' says Walter, replacing his cap. He rubs his arm through his thick sleeve, and irritably adds, 'Though I see you managed to come out of it all right.'

'I did, yes,' says his father, with a twitch of a smile, as he searches for his tobacco, patting each of his pockets and taking his papers from one, his pouch from another. 'Yes, I did all right,' he confirms and appears to laugh to himself as he begins to roll a cigarette, his rifle awkwardly propped on his hip, his fingers stained amber with nicotine. There is a rusty patch of dried blood on the cuff of his tunic.

Walter looks at him steadily. He examines the grizzled side of his face – the grey hairs in his beard and the wiry tangle of his moustache, which is ginger and black, and the fleshy bulb of his earlobe, and the pores and pockmarks on his nose, which is crushed down at the bridge, broken in one of those brawls he always used to incite – and concentrates to recall the last time he observed his father this closely, which was, he decides, a warm spring afternoon in his childhood, ten or twelve years before, when he and Mabel came in from their Sunday School to find him smoking his pipe by the fireside, his cheeks flushed from the hours he had spent in the Crown and his eyes glinting as he whispered to them that their mother had spotted some grey hairs in his moustache and he would reward them with a farthing for each one that they found.

He closed his eyes while they searched him, his breath becoming even and slow, and not only did they find no grey hairs at all but the pipe slipped from his hand to the hearth and broke in three pieces, which might on another occasion have provoked him to shouting, but instead he continued to drowse, slack-mouthed, moist-lipped, his breathing sour with tobacco and drink, as Walter carefully picked up the browned bits of clay – seasoned by use, a sweet pipe to smoke – and placed them in his father's lap, then retreated to wait, and still, when Eddie woke, there was no anger, but a slow, puzzled frown as he fumbled in his pockets for some change and found a ha'penny for Walter to go and buy a replacement, the clay as white as bone, and the smoke a good deal harsher because of it.

And, of course, there were many other such moments, which also ought to be remembered, before their time in this place should be over, and with an effort to strike a friendlier tone, Walter asks him, 'So, how was your journey, Dad?'

'The journey?' repeats Eddie, and finally succeeds in getting one of his damp matches to light. He touches the flame to his cigarette and deeply inhales, then allows with a shrug, 'Not bad, I suppose.'

'Long?'

'Oh, ages.' A rueful smile, a nod. 'Long enough, I'd say.'

Walter waits, but his father offers nothing more, and for several minutes then they stand side by side, watching the slow evacuation of the casualties on their stretchers, and the flowers that are being thrown to them – the heads becoming detached from the stalks and the petals scattering over the concourse – until gradually he becomes conscious of the fierceness of his father's inhalations, his desperation to take in enough smoke, and says, 'Did you get shot then, Dad?'

'Did I—?'

'Get shot.'

'Yes, I did, but not too terrible. A direct hit. It opened me up a bit.'

His father tilts around to show him the wound, which is gleaming and magnified, a gaping mess on the right side of his chest where his lung has been ruined by a bullet, his tunic burned by the impact, ripped apart, the fibres stuck to the flesh.

'Not a pretty sight, is it?' says Walter.

'I expect not.'

'I thought you'd run away.'

His father laughs. 'No, no. I got lost, put it that way. Got separated from my lot and teamed up with another lot.' He drops the stub of his cigarette under his heels, treads down on it and Walter notices the sorry state of his boots, which have disintegrated, revealing the holes in his socks, the blackened stubs of his toes. 'My lot were wiped out,' he adds then, 'and the new lot weren't too sure about me. Couldn't blame them. I thought they'd have me up for desertion, but I stuck it out, I did all right. And I was lucky for a while, before I got hit. Old Jerry got me in the end, eh?'

'Yes, he did,' says Walter. 'You got what was coming to you, I think.'

'And you didn't?'

'Oh, I got mine, don't worry,' says Walter, with sudden conviction. 'He got us both in the end.'

'Let me see,' says his father, and leans forward, using his rifle to steady himself, the veins at his temples engorging. Walter suffers his scrutiny. 'Nasty,' says his father, and cheerfully winces. He straightens, and looks Walter in the eye, the first time he has done so, the first time in a long while, and finally offers a small smile of commiseration, perhaps of apology. 'That is a nasty one,' he says, 'that will have been the end of you, I shouldn't wonder.'

Walter nods, and thinks again of the boat that took him over to Le Havre, and the men consoling themselves with tales of the mademoiselles they would soon be meeting, including Walter, the youngest and smallest among them, who would shortly be getting his end away – getting no end of his oats – since the pretty French fillies would hardly be able to resist him, though of course Walter wanted nothing more than to find himself a sweetheart; he had no greater desire than to return from the war and walk out with the pharmacist's daughter, and to be able to kiss her, which the painted-up girl in the only whorehouse he visited was tetchily reluctant to allow him to do, while all too ready to plunge her hand inside his trousers, and when in desperation he tried to force his mouth onto hers he provoked such a barrage of French invective, all of it incomprehensible, that he grabbed his cap and blundered straight from her room into the next, where an older woman was washing herself from her previous customer and gestured drearily to her bed, and the dinginess of everything was so dispiriting he thought he might cry and closed the door on her too and went back down the stairs and into the street, bone-weary, and riddled with lice, and wishing only to sleep, as he wishes only to be allowed to sleep now, except that the regimental band has struck up a bright, brassy tune in the late-evening sunshine and the rain has receded – that cacophony silenced at least – and Captain Beckwith is once again striding into the terminus building, about to take charge of his men. He is heading directly towards them.

'I'd better make myself scarce,' says his father, and Walter nods as he goes, leaves him for good, then straightens his shoulders, pulls himself up to his full height, a bantam, a short-arse, a soldier after all; he stands to attention as best as he can manage in full marching order, with his knapsack and haversack bulked out with equipment and clothing – all packed as per the template, as per the drill – his steel hat affixed to his knapsack, his mess tin and bottle attached to his haversack, entrenching tools and bayonet slung from his belt, his boots and straps and pouches all polished and gleaming, his tunic and trousers uncreased. He hoists his rifle onto his shoulder and smiling, unable to stop himself smiling, he salutes the return of Captain Beckwith – chin up, chest out – and receives in reply the merest glance at his cap, which is a fraction too large around the crown and will not sit right, though Walter hardly cares whether Montague Beckwith should approve of him: after so many weeks of route marches and regular meals, exercise and fresh air and the cameraderie of the other men, Walter is better off than he has ever been, if only Mother were able to see him; if only Gertie Dobson should be here above all, but when he looks around the station he cannot find either of them among the spectators, or any of his siblings, for the living have now receded, gone from this scene, and the time has come again for him to make his departure since the sergeant major is barking at his men to quick march – *hup, one, two, three* – and off they proceed to platform six and the train

258

that will convey them from home, the engine already chugging in anticipation, gusting soft clouds of steam to the ceiling, and though Walter suspects his task now is to forget, and perhaps to be forgotten – a worthless man, the end of his line – still he cannot help but look over his shoulder as he prepares to step up to his carriage, half hoping even now to find the pharmacist's daughter waving him farewell, and is satisfied at the last that she cannot be here, that she at least has survived, and will endure, though of course it is the image of her face that remains in his mind as he takes his leave of this place; it is Gertie who illuminates his thoughts as he feels his eyes again losing their focus, rolling upwards, finally displaying their whites.

Acknowledgements

The origins of this novel lie in some interviews I conducted in my mid-twenties while setting up an oral history archive in Norwich, and I'm especially grateful for the privilege of having been welcomed into the lives of Joe Aldous, Norman Armes, Ben Burgess, Archie Campbell, Agnes Davey, Fred Fincham, Snowy Fulcher, Edna and James Gosling, Gertie Hall, Emma Lambert, James Mumford, Harry Thompson, Mabel Winter, and Edward and Jeanetta Wyer. All were generous with their time and their memories, but Agnes and Harry in particular adopted me as a worthy cause, and I hope this book repays their trust in me.

I have additionally drawn upon a number of histories of the Great War and the years to either side of it, several of which are themselves indebted to first-hand accounts. Among these I would like to acknowledge *Forgotten Voices of the Great War* by Max Arthur, *Eye-Deep in Hell* by John Ellis, *Somme* and *The Roses of No Man's Land* by Lyn Macdonald, *The Deluge* by Arthur Marwick, *Documents from Edwardian England* by Donald Read, *Kitchener's Army* by Peter Simkins, *The Edwardians* by Paul Thompson, and *Working-Class Wives* by Margery Spring Rice.

I owe my title to Gerard Oram's monograph, *Worthless Men: Race, Eugenics and the Death Penalty in the British Army During the First World War*, which is published by Francis Boutle Publishers.

Among the many other reasons I have for being grateful to

them, I'd like to thank my agent Georgia Garrett and my editor Carole Welch for their patience. This novel took a long time to write, and would have taken longer still were it not for Lynne Bryan, my first and most essential reader.

An earlier version of chapters one and two appeared as 'Walter Barley' in issue three of *Short Fiction*, published by the University of Plymouth, and I'm grateful to the editor Anthony Caleshu for his support.

Finally, belatedly, I'd like to thank Jemal Ahmet, whose help and encouragement resulted in my first published story and led to the writing of my first novel, and who gave me the spur to crack on with this one.